**A LITT**

Elizabeth awoke to the aroma of freshly made coffee. She could swear she smelled biscuits, but Chris was not in the kitchen. She looked out the window; he was on the front porch.

He sat on a twig chair, tilted back on two legs, his booted feet resting on the porch rail. A huge bouquet of wild grasses and the last of the golden aspen leaves lay at his feet.

He turned his face to her; he was glossed all over by the lemon-yellow of sunrise. Elizabeth felt a rush of desire run through her at the thought of his strong and tender hands touching her in love. His lips parted to speak, and she actually felt their pressure on hers, as they had felt last night.

"Good morning, beautiful lady," he said. He smiled at her, a lopsided puppyish grin. She smiled back, and his face glowed with her reflected love.

"Good morning, dear man." She went to his side, bent to kiss him. He tasted of green grass and sweet love; he smelled of soap and outdoors and pines and wood smoke. For a moment, she was paralyzed by the perfection of it.

# *A BRAND NEW LIFE*

## *KATHY THURLOW*

ZEBRA BOOKS
KENSINGTON PUBLISHING CORP.

ZEBRA BOOKS are published by

Kensington Publishing Corp.
475 Park Avenue South
New York, NY 10016



First Printing: March, 1994

Printed in the United States of America

# One

"Mrs. March? Mrs. March? Can you hear me?"

Elizabeth shook her head, not in answer but to clear it, and it didn't work. She opened her eyes to see the doctor, very tanned but fuzzy. She focused harder. He wasn't fuzzy. He was breathlessly handsome. Sun-bleached brown hair, dark lashes, lion's golden eyes. He got fuzzy again. She moaned.

"I'm dying," she said.

He reached out his hand to help her up and if she'd felt better she would have noticed how gently he touched her. She did notice the muscles in his palm and fingers moving against her skin like a liquid ice pack.

"Oh," she said, "your hand is so cool."

"I bet you say that to all the doctors." She opened her eyes to see his smile and his perfect teeth and perfectly shaped mouth. She tried to focus on his mouth. She lost it.

"I'm sick," she said and tried to focus again.

"Yes, you are. I'm Dr. Hanford–"

"Yes, you are . . ." she echoed.

He laughed and she thought of an actor friend of hers in New York who was often hired for his great hearty laugh. This doctor, who looked as if he were just out of medical school, had a laugh like that.

"You are either suffering from altitude sickness or–"

She interrupted him. "I've been in Colorado for three weeks. I was raised here."

"Well, it could be flu."

"I fainted in the grocery store." She thought she would blush from the embarrassment, but she felt too weak to even do that.

"Or, you are pregnant." He said that as if that were the only thing it could be.

"You *are* kidding," she said and tried to focus on him again.

"No."

"No, I'm not pregnant? No, you're not kidding? No what?"

"No," he smiled at her and then looked down at her belly, "I'm not kidding."

She struggled up from the table and when he tried to help she shrugged him off. "I can't be."

"Before you get too upset, let's take a quick test and be sure."

She attempted to get off the table, needing to escape. "No . . . nononono! You don't understand. I'm forty-four years old." She didn't add, "My husband just left me for some bimbo filing clerk in his office that he got pregnant." Her knees felt like rubber.

"I can't be pregnant!" She was nearly screaming.

"Let's just take the test to be sure. From everything you told the nurse and what I see, I'd say you are." Then he backed out of the room quickly.

*Coward!* Elizabeth screamed at him in her mind.

*A handsome coward. What am I thinking?* Elizabeth had been back in Vail for three weeks. Six weeks to the day from the morning her husband climbed out of their bed in which he'd just made love to her and told her he was leaving her because Jennifer, the file clerk on the second floor, was pregnant and he was going to "do the right thing" and be with her while she had his child.

The Wicked Witch of Wall Street, as Elizabeth Templeton Avery March was known, wished she really were a witch then; she'd have turned Elliot into a worm and Jennifer into . . . she thought at the time that just being pregnant with Elliot's child was punishment enough.

"Oh God!" she moaned out loud.

The nurse, who looked as if she were still in high school and had just been cheerleading for the home team, came in and with bubbling assurance told Elizabeth how to proceed. "And Dr. Hanford says to go down to the cafeteria and he'll meet you there."

Forty minutes later he strolled into the cafeteria and sat down at her table.

"Well?" she demanded as he sat.

"Well, I think you should call your husband and tell him you're going to have a baby."

*How could such a handsome man be such an idiot?* she thought.

"I'd have to call him on his honeymoon with the bimbo to tell him that," she said.

At the confused look on his face, she added, "He left me. We are officially divorced."

He didn't skip a beat. "Good. Listen, what do you want to eat? I don't recommend much here. You see, it's awful."

She laughed.

"Good," he said again and beamed his radiant smile that somehow made her feel giddy. Or was that morning sickness?

"You are beautiful when you laugh," he said. He gave her no chance to respond because he stood and made his way to the cafeteria line and began filling up the tray with food.

While she ate a salad and some fruit and he ate something resembling stew, he talked comfortably about topics that meant nothing, required no thinking, and allowed chewing.

Elizabeth watched him between bites and pleasant talk. He was by far the handsomest man she had ever seen. She was probably old enough to be his mother. *Older sister,* she corrected herself. *What am I thinking? It must be the pregnancy.* At that thought she was back in her panic.

Although she loved the shape of his mouth as he talked, she interrupted him. "Are you sure?"

He put his fork down and wiped his mouth. *Stalling for time? Trying to find a way to say it?*

"I'm sure." He looked at her, and she felt him hold her there by the sheer will in his deep brown eyes. *Stay calm,* they urged her. *It will be all right.*

Tears welled up in her eyes then and spilled over. He stood immediately and led her gently but firmly from the crowded cafeteria. *It must be dinnertime,* she thought. *I've been here since noon.*

She was hardly aware that he put her into his car and got in on his side. He sat quietly, handing her tissues from his white jacket.

"Do you want to tell me about it?" he

said when she seemed to have stopped crying.

"What is there to tell? I'm forty-four; I'm divorced; I've quit my job as a stock analyst and come back home to find my-self . . . and I find myself pregnant."

She stopped to take a breath.

"I wanted a baby once, when Elliot and I were younger."

"You aren't old. You don't look over thirty."

She ignored the compliment, "But it just never happened. Now Elliot has two women pregnant."

"I'm going to be very practical now," he said. "I'm not an Ob/Gyn. I'll recommend a good one for you to talk to."

She thanked him.

"But I want you to know I think you will be a beautiful mother."

Elizabeth burst into tears.

Clean winter sun streamed into the hotel room and warmed Elizabeth's skin. She woke feeling as if she'd fallen asleep in front of a roaring fire. She'd only fallen asleep fully dressed. Looking at her watch she was surprised to see she'd slept at least fourteen hours. She hadn't slept that long in thirty years! She didn't know if she slept so long because she was pregnant or had exhausted herself from crying so much.

Her hand moved protectively, tentatively to her abdomen. She gingerly pressed the firm area. Could she feel it? She held her breath, then realized she could and shook her head and took a deep breath.

She decided on a shower and some food. On second thought, she vetoed the food. But then to the cabin. Her home. She was raised there. Twenty-six years since she'd seen it. She bought it back from the latest owners sight unseen while she was still in New York, with money Elliot couldn't touch. He'd had nerve asking for support.

Elizabeth took her shower in a rage. *Damn the man!* She had made more money than he, she'd made more money than a lot of men at Holmquist DeBarge Investments. When he realized she'd fight him if he asked for money, he took off with the bimbo, divorced Elizabeth in

Puerto Rico, and married again before Elizabeth knew it.

She dried herself and dressed quickly in jeans, a flannel shirt, a sweater, and her parka. She'd packed very little for her move to Colorado. She left everything for her attorney to sell: the town house, the furniture, the artwork.

"Get rid of it all," she'd told him. "I don't want anything that worm has touched, breathed on, or looked at."

Three weeks in Denver to buy clothes for her new life, a Bronco four-wheel drive, simple rustic furniture, and kitchen things all to be delivered today.

Six weeks and one day. Six weeks and one day since her life had gone from knowing exactly what the day would bring and how she would handle it all, who she would see and talk to, who and what and where; what time she went to sleep . . . and with whom.

Six weeks and one day pregnant.

A wave of nausea overcame her as she drove. Unfortunately she was on a winding road with absolutely nowhere to pull over and let the sickness pass.

She made her mind go back to her

first time on this road. Forty-one years ago. The social worker drove the road so cautiously. Fearfully. The cabin in the pines with its golden lights in the windows. The social worker saying "Here" and handing over Elizabeth like a sack of unwanted laundry. One moment she'd been in her arms and the next the woman was gone.

Elizabeth felt sick again. *Better think about other things.*

But what? Why? Elliot had left her. She didn't want him back. But why did he leave? Why did he hurt her like that? Why had everyone left her? Everyone she'd ever loved.

*No. Those thoughts weren't going to help either.*

Back to the first time she'd seen the cabin. The first people who ever loved her. . . .

*"Why, George Templeton! The child doesn't have anything!" The small birdlike woman held out a brown paper bag to the huge man. He refused to take it, just shook his head. The little woman put the bag on a pine table*

*so big it looked to Elizabeth, from her vantage point beside it, like a small room just for her, with a ceiling just the right size. She was barely three. Just a shade over two feet tall, as skinny as the proverbial rail. She had been asleep most of the trip up here but even though she had no idea where she was, she was calm and quiet.*

*"She has no clothes; she has no underthings!" the little woman almost whispered the last word. "I thought there would be clothes in here," she pointed to the bag, "but it's nothing but an empty cookie bag and a pop bottle."*

*The big man looked down on the tiny form standing beside the massive four-by-four-inch pine table leg; she was not as big around as the table leg. "We knew Avery was no good," he said. He couldn't bring himself to use the blackguard's first name. "We tried to tell Ellen." He shook his head, then swooped down to Elizabeth's level. Her big brown eyes opened wide.*

*"Well, at last, some response. I thought you weren't real. I thought you were maybe a cigar store Indian." He winked at her and she smiled. They knew instinctively that they would understand each other. Of course at*

*three Elizabeth had no idea what a cigar store Indian was, she just knew it made that big man smile.*

*"She needs a bath," the little woman said. "Probably some real food, too."*

*"Well, there's two things we can do right now." He stood up to his full height again. Elizabeth, afraid he might be going away, reached out her tiny hand to him and grabbed hold of his baggy overalls.*

*"No," she said.*

*"What's that?" He acted shocked and swooped down to her level again. "A cigar store Indian who won't take a bath?"*

*"Don't be ridiculous, George." The little woman tried to look put-out but failed. She took Elizabeth's hand and led her to the sideboard by the big black wood burning stove. Picked her up under her scrawny arms and placed her on the scrubbed pine wood. Elizabeth squirmed. "Now don't you move a muscle, Lissy. Your grandpa is going to bring in some water and we'll heat it on the stove and have a bath. Then I'll make you some stew and maybe gingerbread. Would you like that?"*

*"Grandpa," Elizabeth called out and pointed her finger at him as he went out the*

*door. The scent of pine and impending snow and wood burning wafted through the one-room cabin. It was a smell that would stay with Elizabeth for a lifetime.*

Elizabeth caught a quick view of herself in the rearview mirror. The rose-white skin she'd inherited from her grandmother, the big brown eyes and sense of humor from her grandfather; the sense of purpose from her grandmother, the sense of self-possession from her grandfather.

The sense of abandonment from her mother and father. And now Elliot.

By noon she was cresting the mountain and on the last curve to her cabin in the pines. She was breathless with excitement. Then she was there. The perfect valley on a perfect mountain with the perfect little log cabin were right in front of her.

The cabin was just visible, all the pine trees had grown so big, a few leaned over and touched each other over the roof. The garden area was full of trash and an old washing machine and ratty sofa sat outside. *Small problems,* Elizabeth thought.

She pulled up in front of the cabin door, grabbed the ancient skeleton key from her purse. She rushed to the cabin door, skipping over the rotten wood on the porch and porch step. *Minor problems,* Elizabeth thought.

She had to struggle to make the key fit, then she couldn't get the door to open immediately. Elizabeth was tiny, but she pushed with all her strength. The door gave way, crashed to the floor and the resulting noise set off the raccoon and other animals that had taken up residence in the house.

It was a moment before Elizabeth fully took in what she was seeing. Breaking down the front door had been unnecessary; the back door was open wide, all the windows in the back were broken; the outdoors had actually begun to move indoors. Red-leaved vines grew in the back door and were twining around the kitchen cabinets. A tiny pine tree had begun its life, now six inches tall, in the middle of the living-room floor. Spiderwebs, birds' nests, rotten food and other things she didn't want to think about were strewn over the rest of the place.

If she hadn't been afraid of what she'd fall in, she'd have fainted. At the steep staircase to the loft, Elizabeth peeked cautiously up, only to see an owl asleep in the rafters. She brushed off a spot on the stairs and sat down. Putting her face in her hands she thought of crying, but no tears came.

*Strange,* she thought, *I've been crying incessantly for weeks, and now I can't.* She slapped her dry hands on her new jeans and pressed her lips together as her grandmother had done before every hard task. Elizabeth began to pick up the larger pieces of litter and tossed them outside.

With the new broom and mop she worked for several hours trying to get some space cleared for the delivery of her rustic—but not rustic enough for *this* place—furniture.

It felt like days, but it was really only four hours until the delivery van showed up. Two burly young men got out and emptied the truck. Elizabeth didn't worry about placement. She had them dump everything in the middle of the room, thanked them, tipped them (which surprised them), and shooed them out.

She then began to clean in earnest. Scrubbing and cleaning and scrubbing again. She carried water from the outside pump, heated it on the wooden stove, poured in gallons of antiseptic cleaner and scrubbed more. Pine Sol combated pine scent, and dust motes fought for space. By the time she collapsed on the cushions of the sofa, she was so exhausted she couldn't have undressed if she wanted to.

Again the sun woke her. Not in the luxurious surroundings of the hotel, but in what appeared to be a warehouse full of boxes and furniture. Elizabeth sat up and immediately began scratching her arms.

Twenty minutes later she was driving down the mountain to the hospital in Vail, heading for the emergency room.

Huge welts and fierce itching, burning fever and nausea were just the beginning.

*Same handsome doctor.* "Thank god!" she cried out.

"Let's wait and see," he answered.

"No! I mean it! If I had to explain to anybody else . . . I'm dying. I'm dying!"

"You'll live," he said, his beautiful mouth turned up in a grin that, if she hadn't been feeling like hell, would have captivated her.

"No, nonono, I'm sicker than that. I've tick fever. I know it."

He laughed and took hold of her vivid red arm and gently touched the welts. "Dry skin combined with strong cleaners," he said but continued to hold her arm.

"How do you know?" She didn't believe him, and her imperious Wicked Witch voice came up out of nowhere.

"You caught me." He dropped her arm and snapped his fingers. He shook his head and clicked his tongue, "Yep, you got me on that one. I don't *know* it's strong cleaners. I didn't do any scientific tests or anything. I'm really a scam artist . . . no . . . I'm a quack. . . . No, wait I'm a ski bum who just walked in here and picked up your chart just to get a chance to put my hand on your arm. I'm a pervert . . . that's it . . . I'm a pervert."

Elizabeth was mulling over whether or not to laugh, and decided a small one would be enough. "Okay, okay. You're the doctor, but how did you come to that conclusion?"

"I'm not telling," he said as he wrote a prescription for a salve.

"I'm too sick to care," she said.

"You'll be all right in a day or two. And I guess I'm going to have to feed you again."

"Oh, no. Really."

"Hey," he tapped the prescription paper he'd just handed to her. "Doctor's orders." And he left the room.

Elizabeth looked down at the paper. In surprisingly readable handwriting he'd written, "Twenty minutes . . . in the cafeteria . . . dress casual."

His head popped back in. "I'm actually giving you a break. I'd rather eat right now, but in twenty minutes I figure you can get the spider webs out of your hair and the dirt off your face and the grease out from under your broken fingernails and maybe you could smell like hand soap instead of pine disinfectant." The head disappeared again.

Elizabeth shut her mouth, which was hanging open in shock. No one had ever talked to her like that. No one but Grandpa.

She was in the cafeteria in fifteen minutes.

He was waiting for her, the white jacket removed. He did look like a ski bum, dressed in gold sweater, blue jeans, and cowboy boots. All he needed was a cowboy hat and mirrored sunglasses to look ready for a rodeo or a ski cap and skis to look ready for the slopes.

He held out a glass of orange juice before she sat down. "Drink," he insisted.

She did, then sat across from him. He pushed half a Reuben sandwich and a big bowl of homemade vegetable soup in front of her. He ate twice the amount she did and was holding out a slice of three-layer chocolate cake when she begged, "Enough!"

"Eat it anyway." He put it down in front of her. His cake had a side helping of frozen yogurt.

"No." The Wicked Witch once again.

"Feeling good enough to go a round

or two, are we?" he said in a funny old man kind of voice. Elizabeth raised her chin in defiance.

"Headache gone? HMMMM?" he egged on. "Dizziness subsided? HMMMM? Looks like we thought we were something special maybe? Didn't have to eat like normal people? Think we were better than everybody else maybe?" He was creating attention, people were looking at them and smiling. Elizabeth was not.

"Thank you very much, Dr. Hanford. Send me your bill." She stood up, too quickly. The next thing she knew she was opening her eyes to a bright pinpoint of light flickering from one eye to the other. She brushed it away. "Leave me alone." She tried to move away but she was on an examining table and nearly fell off. He caught her and held her firmly.

"You know, just once you ought to stop and think before you go off half-cocked."

"You talk like a book of clichés," she said and immediately regretted it; he let go of her. She missed the sensation of his strength. "Just leave me alone, and I'll go home . . ."

"Wagging your tail behind you."

"I'm beginning to not like you." She sat up then. All weakness replaced by pride.

He leaned back against the sink and crossed his arms. He stared at her, a long, lingering, daring stare. It would have made her squirm if she hadn't put the Wicked Witch persona back on. As it was, it made her tingle and feel hot. Or was that the rash?

All tone of humor was gone from his voice. "Where are you staying?"

"I just bought a cabin about an hour's drive from here," she answered. She didn't add, "if it's any of your business!"

"Where?" he demanded.

"Templeton Meadows."

"You bought the old Templeton place?" His voice was all soft and melodious again. "You can't go back," he said with absolute assurance.

*"What!"* she yelled. He'd gone too far. One more thing and the Wicked Witch became the Wicked something else.

"Cool off," he said. "You can't drive

that road half conscious and ready to pass out at any moment. Besides it's dark."

*"SO WHAT!"*

He looked at her in utter disbelief. "I said you can't drive back and I mean it. Call a friend and stay with them or go to a hotel."

Elizabeth jumped from the table and reached the door before he could stop her. He followed her out as she said over her shoulder, "I am going home. No kid doctor is going to tell me what . . ." She felt his hand grab her arm at the elbow, he pulled her back and as she was spun around to face him, she was immediately dizzy and nauseous. "You win," she said. "Damn you, you win."

"Of course," he said as if there were no question of it ending any other way.

"I don't have any friends here," she said quietly once he'd helped her back on the table.

He called for the nurse. "Amy, get Mrs. March a hotel room."

The little cheerleader shook her head. "No can do . . . the symphony, the ex-president, the ballet, and the balloon races. Vail is full."

"Try," he said.

Elizabeth smiled, "You sounded just like me then."

"Hah!" his short sarcastic laugh cut through her. "How could anybody sound like you? I mean how do *you* even sound like you? This beautiful face and figure and then *POW!* The Wicked Witch of the West!!"

"Wicked Witch of Wall Street, actually," she corrected him.

He looked thoughtful, slapped his hand against his forehead, "Of course! Elizabeth March! Well, those drawings in *The Wall Street Journal* don't exactly do you justice." She had the grace to look pleased. "I should have put two and two together."

"Do you always talk in clichés?" she smiled when she said it.

"Day in, day out," he said.

Amy returned. "No place. I'd take you in myself but I've got six kids and my in-laws visiting. . . ."

He shook his head in unison with Elizabeth's.

"I'll drive you back. We'll get your car to you somehow."

"No, please—"

"Hey!" he stopped her. "Enough already! I'll drive you back." He slapped her chart down on the table. "Give me ten minutes." He looked at her then, daring her to argue. She shrugged.

"Whoa!" Amy said. "He doesn't do that for just any patient."

"Just the ones who can't drive." He said it as if it were an everyday occurrence.

"Thank you," Elizabeth said. Then she closed her eyes and lay back on the table. *What am I doing?* she thought.

*What am I doing?* he thought. *Why is it I don't want to leave this woman? She's asleep in my car and I'm taking her home when I should be . . . what? I can't imagine anything I'd rather do.*

She'd fallen asleep, her face against the window. She was so beautiful. Black lashes arched against cream colored cheeks, dark brown hair almost blue-black in that silvered moonlight.

*What kind of man could have left her? She was beautiful, intelligent, a woman to be proud of. A woman to love and care for, to talk to, eat with, make love to. . . . Where did that come from?* He grasped the steering wheel tighter and squeezed it hard, trying to force the physical need for her into his hands where he could do something about it.

He didn't dare touch her. First, because he wouldn't stop. He knew that, he wanted her. The second reason was ethical, not physical: He was her doctor. She was his patient. No touching. No kissing. No making love all night and every night.

Squeezing the steering wheel hadn't helped. He looked at her once again. She stirred, making a childlike sound and settled again. The great Wicked Witch of Wall Street looked no more than a child asleep. A beautiful, sexual, haunting desirable woman/child.

He thought of kissing her, then thought of his live-in girlfriend. He stopped thinking of Elizabeth. *Christian Hanford, M.D. shape up! God! I should have had Amy do this, or at least brought her along!*

Chris looked at Elizabeth again. The moon went behind a cloud and without the silvery light he could see her skin still had a glow to it, something magical, ethereal. Was she a witch? She looked more like an angel.

*Concentrate on the road.* He forced himself to stop looking at her. *Just drop her off, don't go inside.* He hit the steering wheel in utter frustration. *Damn! The woman could accuse me of anything! Anything at all!* Why hadn't he brought along Amy?

A sharp turn jarred Elizabeth awake. She looked, for just a moment, like a child awakened in the middle of the night in a strange place, then quickly her features hardened into a protective mask.

"I must have fallen asleep. Are we almost there?" she asked curtly as if he were a taxi cab driver.

He looked at her for a moment, wishing he could will her back to sleep. "We're on our way down." Then he concentrated on the drive.

The moon was reflected in the mirror

of the mountain lake. It was a picture of eerie beauty. Either side of the valley ringed by the mountains. The stream, like a silvery ribbon, tracing down one side of the mountain, disappearing behind the ghostly log cabin. The lake, with everything reflected in it, perfectly still. A fish jumped, the silver flicker of its scales flashed, and the ripples made the scene more eerie than before. It was no longer a picture or painting, but a moving, living place.

"And ghosts," Elizabeth thought aloud.

"What?" Chris said.

"Nothing," Elizabeth answered. "I must have been talking to myself."

As they drove up to the cabin, Elizabeth's hand was already on the door handle. She jumped from the Jeep before he had it fully slowed and ran to the cabin door.

Chris didn't know whether to stop the car or just pull her door shut and go on. A scream decided for him.

Putting the car in park, he jumped out the door without shutting it, the annoying buzzer adding a jarring note to the crazy silence after her one scream. He leaped up the steps in one move and was inside in seconds. She was past him and *out* the door before he could ask what was wrong. But then he saw. A raccoon, as big as a poodle, was atop the refrigerator. He didn't move. Chris didn't either. Then Chris began to laugh. This insulted the raccoon, who took his head of lettuce in his mouth and slowly lumbered down to the countertop, then to the window, and with a backward glance at Chris, took his regal leave of what was obviously his own private grocery.

"Hey!" Chris called out. "Come on back!"

"I will not!" Elizabeth called back.

"I wasn't talking to you," Chris answered.

He heard her stomp as heavily as her one hundred and fifteen pounds could stomp across the porch. The door squeaked open and then slammed so hard he felt the vibration. Without turning around he said, "Now look what you did, you scared the little guy off."

"This is *my* place!"

"Then take possession," Chris dared

her. "You could begin by shutting the window." He gestured in the direction of the recent raccoon escape.

Elizabeth crossed her arms in front of her chest, put her feet in fourth position, tilted her head to one side and said, "It is."

Chris turned, pushed on what looked like the sill, but it swung open; the frame was empty of glass.

"Ah-hah. Then turn on the lights. You won't have any wild visitors if you turn on the lights."

"I'd love to turn on the lights, but there aren't any." The chilly tone of her voice surprised even her. "There are no light bulbs. There are no oil lamps. I can't find the candles—"

"Then what the hell are you doing here?" he said. The lights from the Jeep were shining on her from behind so he couldn't see her face as she allowed herself to crumble, for just a moment. Then the Wicked Witch took charge.

"It is my home." Her steely calm voice, each word spoken in precise bitten-off syllables. "I own it. I am going to stay. No one can make me leave. Not even wildlife." And then, for just a moment, she laughed. Then she cut it off as quickly as it had bubbled up and began to cry.

He was at her side in seconds. She could have died of humiliation, but he felt too good, smelled too clean, held her too closely. She was too tired and sick and miserable to push him away.

"It's okay." Chris felt an uncontrollable urge to hold this sobbing woman like a child. He cradled her head against his chest, and rubbed his cheek in her baby-fine hair. It didn't smell even remotely like a child's clean head—it smelled of dust and mold and sweat. She was tired and sick and miserable. He'd never felt so protective of an adult in his life.

"Let's go back down to town. I'll find someplace for you to stay. You can't stay here. Not yet." He felt her try to push away from him. All her strength went into the effort. She couldn't do it. He gently held her away from him. His long slender hands wiped tears from her face.

"I'm not usually like this, you know," she said between huge gasping sobs.

"I know, I know. It's okay." For a moment he wanted desperately to kiss her. There was never a woman so much in need of a kiss. But something held him back. Guilt? Fear? He didn't want to look at that just now.

She moved well out of his reach, wrapping her arms around herself tightly. She suddenly felt as if she wanted this man to hold her forever. *No, never again!* "I'll be all right," she said. "I am just tired. I didn't really plan this very well." She laughed again, a tightly controlled laugh this time, not one likely to break into sobs as before.

"And this wasn't planned very well, either." She waved her arms around and spun herself in a giddy circle. "All my blankets and clothes and even my toothbrush are still in my car."

She was now in control of her voice and her body. Yet she still felt his arms around her, and his warm breath in her hair. She wanted to push back into his arms and cry out for him never to let her go. *And for heaven's sake protect me! . . . I must be out of my mind,* she thought to herself.

"You're not crazy," he said, and for a

moment she thought he must have been reading her mind. "This place will be a wonderful home," he said as a matter of fact, not conjecture. "But we'd both better get back to town." He tilted his watch so he could read the face of it in the car lights. "It is nearly midnight, and I've been up since six."

"I'm so sorry. I guess neither one of us thought this out."

"I'm not sorry," he said as he took her arm and firmly led her out of the cabin. "I'm glad I got up here. I'm glad I met you. And I'm glad you can't stay here."

"Why are you glad of that?" she said while he helped her into the passenger's side.

"Because," he went to the driver's side and buckled his seat belt and then hers before he finished his sentence. "I wouldn't have a chance to talk to you more, and it's one more hour until we get back down."

The car started easily, and they were back on the winding road. She turned to look back at the silvered scene. "It is the most beautiful place on earth," she said. "It's my home."

* * *

Chris pulled the Jeep into a carport and parked. Elizabeth continued talking. He listened to her with more attention than the many journalists and reporters who had interviewed her on her prognostication for the financial future. She suddenly realized they had parked.

"Why have we stopped?"

"We're home. My home, that is." He got out and stretched, a big yawn and another stretch. "Come on."

Elizabeth hesitated only a moment. She opened her car door and waited for him to lead the way.

The house was modern/rustic. Big airy rooms and big glass walls. The more she looked around the more she thought rustic was perhaps the wrong word. A love seat in rough nubby blue tweed sat in the center of a huge main room that could have held three full-size sofas. She spied a twig chair with no pillow padding. A lamp, a telephone and telephone book sat on the floor, while a trash can, dragged in from the kitchen, brimmed with garbage beside those items. A note seemed to be taped to the trash can.

Chris took the note, looked at it for only a moment, then ran up the curved staircase to the second level. She could hear him go from room to room.

Elizabeth looked around the deserted house. The raised dining area held nothing but two plates and a glass on the floor. No table, no chairs, no picture on the wall. She took a second look around the living room: no pictures, nothing, not even drapes.

Chris came down the stairs. It seemed as if every bone in his body was threatening to melt and he would not be able to hold up his muscled body. He sank down on the bottom step.

"Well, looks as if we both got quite a welcome home," he said quietly. He looked up at her and grinned. "I came home late one too many times."

She looked so horror-stricken he stood up and went to her side. "That was unfair of me. It has absolutely nothing to do with you." She didn't know what to say to that, so she merely said, "I'm sorry."

He walked to the love seat and slumped down on it, draping one long leg over the arm. "Nothing for you to be sorry about. My girlfriend has been threatening to leave me since the day we got together. She chose tonight, or maybe it was last night. I really don't know. Or care." His voice was raw and scratchy. He cleared his throat and looked at her.

Elizabeth started to say something but closed her mouth and shrugged. What could she say other than the trivialities her friends had said to her when Elliot left?

"There is a bed upstairs, turn right at the top, last door. A bathroom . . . she may have left towels. . . ." His voice faded. His eyes followed her as she went up the stairs. He closed them when he heard the door shut.

"Thank you, Casey. Thank you for everything," he whispered. Casey Merritt of the hotel Merritts. He'd met her on the ski slopes while he was still in undergraduate school. She had followed him like a puppy, refused to go home with her parents when the spring break vacation was over. She'd gone back to Denver with him and moved in. Her family disowned her. His family shook their heads in disbelief, anted up more living expense money, and he got a job that had longer hours. Casey stayed home in their two-room apartment to learn how to cook, how to make a bed, how to do laundry, how to budget. She never had been inside a grocery store. She had no idea how to cook even with a microwave. It was a disaster from the beginning. But they believed in each other. At least so it seemed.

And the wild nights of sex in every possible way, in every possible place they could think of. Casey loved sex with him. She always said she loved him, then. Only then . . . during sex.

*Love—no, sex—no! It was love! I had loved her! It was love! I am capable of love!* He ran his hand through his hair, pushing back the strand that always found its way over his forehead. *Not just sex! I loved!*

The sound of the running shower brought him back to reality. He looked about the huge room. She'd taken everything. The other rooms, except for the extra bed in the guest room, were stripped bare. She'd left nothing. A rustling of fabric brought him back once again. He looked up to the top of the staircase where Elizabeth stood. She was wrapped in a white sheet, her washed hair coal black against the whiteness. Her skin scrubbed to a rose-white hue.

She stood for a long moment looking down at him. She felt her breath come in shallow little pants. She took one long deep breath to try to clear her mind, but what was on her mind would not go away. She wanted to hold him. She wanted to put her arms around him and caress him. She wanted to kiss his eyes and cheeks and lips.

He stood and took long strides to the staircase and was beside her in a moment, before she could run or turn away or prove to him she was just a dream, not flesh and blood. He pulled her to him roughly, and she eagerly clung to him as a vine clings to an arbor. She wanted to shape her body to his, she wanted to feel his chest against hers, his flat stomach hard against hers, his thighs, and the maleness of him. She wanted him.

He ran his hands over her body, searching her as if he'd find some treasure there. He kissed her with a hard and unknowing passion, her lips opened for him with no resistance. He kissed her until she gasped for breath and pulled away.

"Don't!" he cried out. He took her face between his hands and pulled her back for another kiss that left them both breathless. She wrapped her arms around him and the sheet began to fall. Still kissing her, his hands pulled the sheet off and then he lifted her into his arms and carried her to the bedroom.

Placing her gently on the mussed bed he began to kiss her neck and then each round breast, making her gasp in pleasure. He licked and sucked each nipple to exquisite torture and she urged him on, her hands in his hair leading him farther and farther down her body. Before he reached the dark triangle above her thighs, he stood and began to remove his clothes.

Naked, his lust making him shake like

aspen leaves, he fell on her and she responded with all the passion she'd held inside her for a lifetime. All the passion she'd kept in some deep dark recess of her soul. If she'd been able to think then she would have been surprised at the feelings and love she was pouring out on this stranger.

She wasn't thinking. She was responding to sheer, raw, lusting emotion. Primitive and animalistic, she moaned and made low sounds in her throat. They both cried out as their passion spent itself and left them, for the moment, unable to separate themselves from the glorious end.

She'd no idea how long she lay there, still connected to him, still a part of him. That connection seemed to be the only real thing in her life at this moment. When she felt him slipping away, she began to cry. He held her closer to him. "Shhh," he whispered. "It's all right, everything is all right." He pulled the blanket and quilt from the floor and covered them, tucking them in tightly, then held her tightly in his arms. "It's all right," he said again.

"It isn't." Her head was resting on his chest, just under his throat, and she could feel his heart beat. "I don't even know your first name." For some reason that seemed to be the epitome of the whole thing. She had just given herself to a man she didn't know, and she was too tired and confused to think about why it had happened.

"Christian," he said quietly. She felt him relax and fall asleep. She couldn't move from his arms if she'd wanted. The release of their lovemaking combined with her exhaustion made her feel as if she'd lost all control of her own body. She fell into a deep sleep with only one thought on her mind: Christian.

There would be time to think about it another day. Time to worry about things later. Right now she was in the arms of the most passionate and tender man she'd ever known. Right now, she was safe and secure and if there were things she should worry about they seemed not to matter when he held her this way. When she felt his heart beat and the strength in his arms, when she could hear him breathing and enjoyed the firmness of his thighs against hers, she could only think of him. Christian.

Tomorrow, she'd think differently. Right now, nothing mattered.

Elizabeth awoke from a profound sleep. She stretched and was startled for a moment when her toes touched other toes and her fingertips touched a masculine chin with stubbly growth. She quickly remembered where she was and who she was with. She watched his face for a moment, listened to his even breathing and decided he was more soundly asleep than she had been. She smiled at the memory of his enfolding arms, but she resisted the thought of waking him.

She rose without disturbing him, picked up her clothes, and ran naked down the stairs where she dressed. She looked out the window when she heard a car drive up in time to see her four-wheel drive and another arrive. Before she could get out the door, the two men had left.

Inside she searched for a piece of paper and pen, found both in the trash can by the telephone and hastily wrote a note to Christian: "*Thank you for everything. I'll never be able to repay you. Elizabeth.*"

She went out to her car, started the engine and began to back out when she saw him, standing naked in the front door.

She stopped the car and opened the door and stood outside the car with one leg still inside, to make it clear she was leaving.

"Go back inside! You're naked!" She tried to sound like a scolding parent, but her voice caught. *God, he was so perfectly made. Strong and long and golden in the sunlight.*

"I don't need to worry about it," he said and waved his arm in a wide arc. "There isn't a soul around for miles."

Elizabeth felt uneasy, the way he just stood there, a slight smile on his face, his eyes never leaving hers.

"I don't think you've thought this through," he said.

"What's to think through? You helped me, I'm better, I'm going home."

"That makes perfect sense." He folded

his arms across his chest and took a deep breath before he went on. "But . . . you haven't the faintest idea where you are or how to get out of here. You don't think things through, do you?"

Elizabeth got fully out of the car and slammed the door. He was right. She hated it when the obvious was presented to her and she had not seen it to begin with. She hated it more when she was told this by a naked man standing like some Greek godlike statue. She walked around to the front of the car and leaned against the hood, and she stood in imitation of him.

"All right. How do I get out of here?"

"Hold your horses and I'll lead you out." He started to go inside but she yelled at him and he stopped, his bare backside to her.

"Just tell me. Contrary to what has been happening in my life recently, I can take directions and I can follow them."

"Take my word for it, ma'am, you'll need me to lead you out," he said without turning around. He slammed the door, and Elizabeth thought of getting into her car and peeling out like a frustrated teenager, but she didn't. She waited.

He came out in a few minutes, dressed in tight jeans and a purple T-shirt. Cowboy boots and his car keys dangled in his hands.

"Just let me get my boots on," he said.

# Two

All the way to the cabin, Elizabeth raged inside. She fumed and sputtered and yelled in silence. She made up names never heard in this world to call him, and she relied on a few time-tested names as well. She compared him to animals, reptiles, and her ex-husband. She thought of running him off the road and other forms of revenge. All silently.

In the lead, Chris thought of all the crazy women he'd known in his life and decided Elizabeth was the craziest. He had never wanted to shake a woman to her senses before, but this was one woman who needed it. He compared her to several animals from kitten to tiger to cow and then he compared her to Casey. All silently. He looked into his rearview mirror to see her following a little too closely, both hands firmly on the wheel, lips firmly compressed. God, how he wanted to kiss those lips.

If Elizabeth could have passed him, she would have.

If Chris could have turned off the road, he would have.

Once they reached the cabin, Elizabeth was out of the car and at his car door before he could turn the motor off.

"Thank you. Now get off my property," she said and pointed just to make sure he knew the way.

"Gladly. But first I'm going to leave you the name of the Ob/Gyn—"

She interrupted him. "I'll pick my own doctors, thank you. Now go."

He sat in the car and didn't move. Elizabeth spun around and walked to the back of the cabin. *Let him sit like an idiot.* She had work to do.

She ignored the scurrying sounds as she entered, banged a few things around to scare the creatures off, and began to put things away in the cupboards with as much slamming of doors and crashing of pans as she could muster without breaking anything. She didn't hear him come in.

"About last night . . ." he began. She dropped a can of fruit and it rolled to his feet. He bent over to retrieve it and said, "I just want to say—"

"Don't you dare say you're sorry." She had spun around to face him, huge tears welling up in her eyes. *When will this unending faucet of tears quit?* she thought. "The last thing I want to hear is that!"

He came toward her with the can held out to her. He looked as if he were trying to get close to a wild horse. "I wasn't going to say that. I was going to say it was wonderful."

She grabbed the can from his hands and turned her back on him. She didn't say anything else. She wanted him to leave. Or make love to her again.

He left.

When she heard his car start and realized he was leaving, she threw the can with all her might. Fortunately it went out an already broken window.

The hard drive and determination and concentration that turned Elizabeth Templeton Avery March into a financial wonder came to the forefront. She focused on the work to be done on her house. She drove all other thought from her mind. *All* other thoughts.

By the end of July the cabin was fit for human habitation. She still had no indoor plumbing hooked up, nor had she the electricity or telephone connected, but all the work was done and just waiting. She'd arranged for builders to add another room and a bathroom, she'd re-roofed, put in all new windows and cleaned the yard area. She had appliances installed, although she still had the big black wood stove in the kitchen area.

She learned how to make curtains when she bought a sewing machine, and she was thinking of taking lessons in how to crochet. She'd read the instruction book, but it was like a strange foreign language.

In three months she'd turned the derelict log cabin into a home. She'd bought new furniture, as close to the furniture she'd grown up with as possible. She rose one morning from the big brass bed she'd piled with quilts and went downstairs for a cup of coffee. The sun was streaming in the sparkling windows and the golden wood floor was warm to her toes. She sat at the foot of the stairs and drank her coffee quietly, happily, absorbed in the pride she felt at her accomplishment. She felt a small flutter just below her rib cage.

Elizabeth had never been pregnant; she didn't even recall knowing anyone well enough to talk to about being pregnant. But she knew what that flutter was, no matter how hard she tried to put the thought back into a compartment, all neatly closed up.

Her baby was moving. She put her hand down to the minute swelling, rubbed it gently. Her baby wouldn't be put out of her mind. Her breasts were swelling and there was a slight difference in her sense of balance, almost unobservable things that only she would notice. Her baby. Growing.

She heard a car arriving; she was expecting a delivery of new wood for the deck and the hot tub she was putting in; they must be early.

She was shocked to see that it was Chris. He slammed his Jeep door and started calling out to her before she could get to the door.

"Where are you?" he demanded. "Elizabeth!"

She opened the door and poked her head out, keeping her body behind the door. She was wearing only a huge man's shirt.

"What do you want?"

"I want you," he said and was up the steps and reached around the door to grab her arm and pull her out on the porch.

"You haven't gone to the Ob/Gyn," he said. He had her by both arms now, he held her tightly, his fingers digging in to her flesh. "For someone as intelligent as you are supposed to be, that is a very stupid thing to do."

She struggled a moment, then just stood, glaring at him. "It is none of your business," she said, her voice just above a whisper.

"If you are going to have this baby, you need to take care of yourself. If you are not going to keep it—"

"Not keep it! You mean *abortion?"* She went white. "I'm keeping this baby! It's none of your business, but I'm keeping this baby!"

He loosened his grip, but still held her, looking at her as if he'd not seen her before.

"Then why haven't you been to the doctor?"

She eased away from him and rubbed her arms where he'd held her. She looked confused. "I didn't know that I had to go yet." She added, "How would I know? I don't even know anyone who has had a baby!"

"Women in business have babies all the time," he said.

"That doesn't mean I had anything to do with them."

"That is the . . . how could you. . . ." He ran his hands through his hair and put them on his hips. "Listen, lady. Go to a doctor. You don't have to go to the one I said, just go." He shook his head and left the porch in two long-legged steps.

"Hey!" she called out to him. "How do you know I haven't been?"

He stopped in front of his car and turned to face her. "I asked."

*He'd asked.* She couldn't help herself. She felt a warm tingle go through her just then. *He'd cared enough to ask.*

"Would you like a cup of coffee?" she invited. "It's made."

He said yes and followed her in. He gave a nod of approval to the work she'd done on the house.

"You like it?" she asked.

"It's great!" He looked around then took the coffee from her. He wondered for a moment if she realized her shirt didn't quite cover her derriere, but decided not to say anything. He enjoyed the view. "Actually I thought burning it to the ground was the only way to make it better, but you've proved me wrong."

She laughed. "I thought it might be better to burn it myself. But then I thought, no, it couldn't be rebuilt for anywhere near the cost of simple things I'm having done to make it better. Plus . . ." she paused.

"Plus what?"

"Plus my grandfather built it originally in the 1930's." She looked into her coffee cup; just the thought of the man who raised her brought back waves of emotions.

"Your grandfather?" he said. "George Templeton? He's your grandfather!"

Elizabeth saw the look on this face; you'd have thought he'd found a long-lost friend.

"You're Lissy!" he cried out.

Elizabeth couldn't believe her ears. No one had called her Lissy in twenty-six years.

"How do you know about Lissy?" she said.

He stood up and slapped his hands against his thighs, then he shook his head and then he laughed that beautiful laugh. "You're Lissy!" he said again.

"All right, I'm Lissy. What about it?" She was irritated now. *Why was he acting like this?* "How do you know he called me that?"

"Hey! *I* called you that!" He stood in front of her and made an exaggerated bow. "Little Jack Horner."

She shook her head in confusion.

"You spanked me." He was laughing so hard he could hardly get the words out. "The Christmas play! God! How old was I?" He paced in front of her, back and forth, his hand to his brow. "Six? I had to be six."

And she was sixteen. And she didn't like being reminded.

"I bit you." He sat down then. "I bit you on the leg and you grabbed me and spanked me." He looked at her, expecting her to laugh with him about the event. The look on her face was anything but happy.

His enthusiasm waned, but he tried again. "Nobody had ever spanked me." A little laugh, then total silence. "Nobody has spanked me since." He looked at her stone face.

Absolute silence.

He cleared his throat.

She cleared the coffee cups and stayed at the sink. Unfortunately that showed her barely covered derriere.

"Uh, Elizabeth?" he said. "I didn't mean to upset you."

"You didn't."

"I see you've still got the scar," he said.

Then she did laugh, hastily pulling

down the back of the shirt. When she turned to face him she was blushing.

*Incredible,* he thought. *She blushes. The Wicked Witch can blush.*

She walked over to the flight of stairs and ran quickly up. When she came back down, she had on gray sweats and was smiling.

"I'm glad you're smiling," he said. "It helps the baby."

"I'll take your word for it."

"It's true. A happy mother makes a happy baby."

"Sounds like another cliché." She smiled when she said it.

"They are only clichés because they are true," he said, then looked at his watch. "I hate to throw a temper tantrum and run, but I do have to be in ER soon." He stood up and took a card from his pocket and put it on the table in front of her. "It's the doctor I'd like you to see. She's really good."

"For older women who are having mid-life babies?" she said with a slight edge in her voice.

"For beautiful women who are having beautiful babies and don't know a thing about it which I find hard to believe in this day and age . . ." He rattled on in unintelligible words as he left. She picked up the card. She looked at it thoughtfully. He was so kind. So silly. So handsome.

*I made love to someone I spanked when he was a baby,* she thought. *And, damn, if I wouldn't love to make love to him again.*

# Three

Chris was exhausted after a full day of emergencies from a multi-car accident to an earache. It didn't seem to matter. He found himself going up the winding road to Lissy's cabin just as the sun was setting. He wanted to see her again. He had a feeling that every day, every hour wouldn't be enough.

Lissy heard the car and saw him come up the drive. She was on the porch when he got there.

"What are you doing here?" she asked then added in a put-out voice, "I haven't made an appointment, I don't have a phone in, yet."

"It's not that," he said, "although I could make it for you . . ."

"I'll handle it."

He looked at her standing on the porch, her arms akimbo, looking like a puppy ready to tear a rag doll to pieces. "I wanted to know if you'd come in to town with me and let's eat out at a nice place. Nicer than the cafeteria." He smiled.

She smiled back, "Give me a break. I have no plumbing, no way to iron clothes, no way to get ready for that kind of evening."

"I thought of that. I made reservations at an exclusive little place I know of, a small inn. I got a room for us, you."

She cocked her head to one side. Presumptuous of him. But a real bath . . . hot water she didn't have to heat on the wood burning stove first. Someone else cooking when she didn't have to get wood first.

"I'll be right out," she called and was inside grabbing shampoo, clothes, and her blow dryer.

Two hours later she luxuriated in a steaming tub and thought of how much she missed the little things that seemed so ordinary in New York.

By nine she was in the small dining

room, filled with people. If she noticed how people turned their heads to follow the beauty in rose silk, she didn't let on. Chris noticed. She was incredibly beautiful.

He'd ordered for them both and although she thought once again of the presumption of it, she liked the fresh trout and the vegetables and dessert of cheesecake with raspberries.

He couldn't take his eyes off her. He was surprised he hadn't spilled food in his lap for all the times he'd stared at her instead of at his fork. She was no child despite her small size. She was a woman, ripe and full. There was no promise of beauty or sensuality to come, it was already there. The only way he could take his mind off loving her was to think of odd trivia, minute facts to make his mind scramble all its chambers and find an answer, but then his eyes would wander from his plate and fork again and her beautiful eyes would draw him in. He could see her body outlined beneath the thin silk dress. He could see she wasn't wearing a bra. At one point she caught his eyes looking at her with such lust that she blushed. "I ran out so quickly I forgot a few essentials."

His breath was held for a moment. "Tell me more," he said.

"No underclothes. No panty hose."

"Don't tell me any more . . . I can barely keep from carrying you out of here and making love to you."

She looked at her plate for a moment, a short moment. She carefully placed her fork on the edge of her plate and slowly reached her hand across the table to take his hand. "I can't even taste the food." Her voice was ragged, "I want you." She pressed his hand so tightly, as if he were her lifeline in a raging sea of emotions, then let go of his hand. She felt as if she would have to hold her breath or stop her heart to survive the loss of contact. She slowly stood, walked to the hall and staircase that led from the public dining room to the rooms above. *Rescue me,* her soul cried out in silent desire.

He followed her, racing up the stairs two at a time to take her hand and pull her closer to him. The pulsing flood of desire flowed between them as they continued up the stairs and down the hall to her room. He had his arm around her waist and swung her into his arms for a bone-crushing kiss at the door. She felt her knees go weak and leaned back against the door frame.

He ran his hands down the silk of her dress to touch every part of her, to arouse every nerve in her body with the heat of his hands through the slick fabric. He had given up any semblance of gentleness or tenderness in his kisses, and she gave back with a lust that was heavy and palpable.

He could smell the essence of her, the hot aroma of her passion. It drove him on. He began to suck on her nipples through the silk and he cupped her buttocks in his hand, dragging the silk up her thighs. At any moment someone could have come up the stairs to one of the dozen rooms on this floor, but the two of them were oblivious to the danger.

She wrapped her arms around his neck and grabbed two handfuls of hair, her nails sending shivers down his scalp and into his spine. He moaned, but she pulled his lower lip with her teeth until he kissed her again. She raised her leg and wrapped it around his hip and thigh, molding herself against him. With one hand he lowered his zipper, then he placed his hand behind her head and holding her up with the other he lifted her from the tips of her toes. She let one shoe drop and wrapped her other leg around him as he positioned her. "Look at me," he demanded. "Look at me!" She opened her eyes and leaned her head against the door as they moved together toward total ecstasy.

Ignoring where they were, forgetting they could at any moment be discovered, not caring about the past or the future, they existed in just the moment, the now. In what seemed an eternity, but which was only a few extraordinary moments, she recovered her key and her shoes and opened the door. The loving in her room was slow and tender and sweet but as deeply intense. The covers stayed in place, the tempo moved like a waltz, not some wild tropical beat. Three more gratifying, gentle times they made love, sleeping for only minutes before their desire woke them. Dawn was just turning the antique-filled room pale shades of pink and gold when they finally fell asleep in each other's arms.

Hours later Elizabeth woke. The fluttering beneath her rib cage brought the reality of her life back to her in a flood. Carefully removing Chris's hand from across her belly, quietly leaving the bed, she stood beside the bed frame with a quilt wrapped around her shoulders. He looked so young in sleep. The face so calm and handsome. He slept as if she were still there, his body curved to hold her close to him.

She felt a tugging deep inside, a pull almost painful, deep and burning. She loved this man. She knew she loved him. But she was pregnant with another man's child. A man she didn't love, but the unborn child was there. She knew it was unfair of him, unfair of her. They had no right to be doing this. His longtime girlfriend had left him. She had just been divorced, and the trauma of the unexpected pregnancy did not make for sane or sensible thoughts. They had used each other, and dangerously unprotected at that. "I'd do it all again," she whispered.

He stirred and reached for her in his sleep, a look of confusion came over his face, then almost helplessness. She hurried back into the bed and gathered him to her. He nestled to her and without opening his eyes began the slow deliberate movement of love. She took him into her. This time they slept until the sun set.

They bathed together that evening, made love again, stayed in bed the rest of the night finding new ways to pleasure each other. He took her home in the morning. She had cried a few times during their lovemaking, but when he left her she felt less like crying than she had in months. She felt whole and wanted and capable. Almost like the woman from Wall Street who could make powerful men do what she said. That woman, or that version of her, was long gone. Elizabeth liked the new woman better. She felt more comfortable with her. The new Elizabeth.

He'd said he'd be back as soon as his shift was over at the hospital. The sun had shone on his hair and gleamed in his golden eyes. His every movement sent shivers of desire up her spine. She could wait for him, but not for long.

That night she heard the car on the drive, heard the engine shut off, the door slam. Each sound bringing him closer to her. She ran to the door happier than she had ever been.

"Darling!" she cried out as she flung open the door.

"I'm surprised by the welcome," came the answer. But it wasn't Chris.

"Elliot."

"Yes. Sorry it isn't who you expected."

She stood very still, didn't move to open the door farther or to step aside to let him in. She said nothing.

He looked around her to the glowing interior of the cabin. "You've finally done it," he said with a nod to the inside. She remained silent. "Finally made your little paradise away from it all." She still made no response. The sound of another car on its way down the drive and the glare of headlights still did not make her move or respond.

Chris came up to the porch, moved to place himself between Elliot and Elizabeth. He said nothing and Elizabeth, frozen, said nothing. Elliot finally said. "I'm Elliot March. Her husband."

Neither held out a hand to the other. Chris finally said, "I'm Chris Hanford, and you're her ex-husband."

At that Elliot uttered a sarcastic biting laugh. He pushed his way between Elizabeth and the door, shoving Elizabeth into Chris's arms. "Well, technically, I'm still her husband." He spun around the room, hands out to balance him like a whirling dervish. "Great place, great place!" he repeated, then finally stopped in the dead center of the room. He pointed a finger at Elizabeth and winked. "You've told lover boy everything, huh?"

Elizabeth stepped from Chris's protective arms and stood in front of him. "Leave, Elliot. You have no right here."

"I have every right to be here. Community property, husbandly rights . . ."

"You aren't my husband anymore. You divorced me. You married Tiffany or Jessica whoever."

He pointed his finger skyward. "Ah, little change here. You see, I really didn't marry Jennifer because I didn't really get divorced from you." He looked at Elizabeth and shrugged. "Jennifer wasn't pregnant after all, and the divorce and marriage were, shall we say, not strictly legal in the United States. So . . ." he turned around in a tight circle once again. "Honey, I'm home."

Chris took two steps around Elizabeth, his fists clenched. "Get out!" he said, his voice nearly a growl.

Elliot looked to Elizabeth and grinned then looked shocked. "Who is this guy? John Wayne's illegitimate son?" Elizabeth flung her small body in front of Chris then. "It's all right. Please." She put her small hands against his chest and her eyes pleaded with him. "Chris, please. I can handle this." She could feel his heart pounding. "Please," she said without a hint of pleading. This "please" was a command. The Wicked Witch emerged full-fledged.

Shocked at the change in her voice, so mad he believed if he touched the man he'd kill him, Chris turned and left the cabin. The slamming door echoed in the silvery night. His car finally started after throwing gravel and recklessly spinning his tires. For a moment, Elizabeth felt as if she might faint. Then Elliot spoke. "God, where do you pick up these people?"

Elizabeth pulled strength from the very toes of her feet and commanded herself to be the woman she knew she was. She turned to face Elliot. She looked at him from head to toe. "Sit down, Elliot," she said. "We've some negotiating to do."

# Four

Without a word Elliot's whole emotional position changed. He stopped being the obnoxious boor, stopped being aggressive and insulting, he even stopped being handsome. He shrunk into himself in a way Elizabeth recognized. He was in trouble again.

*What have you done this time?* she wondered. Not talking to Elliot usually brought out what he really wanted to say. The longer she kept silent the more he squirmed on the sofa.

"Do you have a phone?" he finally said. "I want to call my lawyer."

Elizabeth sat on the carved chair at the dining-room table purposely behind him so he'd have to move to see her. "No."

"How can you exist?" he queried but

immediately looked sheepish. "Actually you look like you exist very well." For a moment he looked like his old self, pale blond hair, thinning she noticed, blue eyes, pale skin, he'd not spent much time outdoors in his tropic hideaway with Tiffany or Jessica or whomever. He shifted around on the sofa to see her better. He had his "seduce me" smile on. *Not this time.* Elizabeth sat as still and quiet as stone. "Don't give me the silent treatment," he said.

"I'm not giving you anything," Elizabeth said, and immediately regretted it. He jumped on it like a starving tiger.

"We aren't divorced!" He jumped from the sofa and nearly cleared the back of it, but his trailing foot caught on the back of the couch. He balanced himself and was up in a moment like the character on TV who said "I meant to do that" after every failure.

"Not yet," Elizabeth said. "But I'm sure the fact that you signed everything months ago giving up your rights to anything of mine will hold up in court in my divorce proceedings."

"I don't want to divorce you." He

changed tactics again. Now he was at her side like a pleading puppy. The pleading puppy usually worked. Of course, he'd never done anything quite like this before. He bent his head and took her hand, expecting her to jerk it away. When she didn't, he continued, "I made a mistake, Elizabeth. I never loved Jennifer. She was just . . . I don't know, a middle-aged fling? I don't know." He looked up into her eyes. The coldness gave him a chill. He shivered in spite of himself. "I love you." He put her hand to his lips and turned the palm up, kissing it and the fingers and fingertips. Elizabeth pulled her hand away. "Don't, please!" He cried out, "Elizabeth, please forgive me! I love you!"

"You must think I'm a complete fool," Elizabeth said. She began to stand, but Elliot clung to her, wrapping his arms around her waist and burying his head in her abdomen. At that moment Elizabeth felt her baby move. She was paralyzed with it. She sat motionless. Elliot pleaded with her. She didn't hear the words, just the rapidly beating heartbeat that could not be hers. She couldn't help but think Elliot heard and felt it, too. Their baby. The child they had tried so hard to have for so many years. The fight went out of Elizabeth.

She knew him well enough to know that he'd not noticed anything but his own distress. She also knew him well enough to know that there was something other than forgiveness behind his pleading to take him back. She also knew what he did not know: She was pregnant with his child and he was her husband. So she gave in. "Stay, Elliot," she said. Then she shook her head. It had sounded like a command to a puppy. *What the hell, he was acting like one.* "Just let me get some rest." She loosened herself from his hold and stood. She didn't notice the look of anger and hatred in his eyes. By the time he turned them to her, she could only see gratitude and relief.

"Yes, darling," he said. "Go rest. I'll be right there."

Elizabeth was on the steep stairs and said nothing to him, but seconds later he turned just as she threw down blankets, a quilt, and a pillow. "You can sleep on the sofa," she called down. Then she slammed the door to the stairs which became the floor in her bedroom. She pushed the latch to lock it.

Elliot picked up the carved wooden chair as if to hurl it through the ceiling. He thought better of it, put it down quietly, and sat in it himself.

Hours later, Elizabeth heard him settle down for the night. She stayed awake until her eyes could no longer peer up into the rafters. *What am I going to do?* was all she could think until she finally reached oblivion.

The next morning Elizabeth woke at sunrise, dressed and was downstairs making as much noise in the kitchen as she could. Nothing seemed to awaken Elliot. *Jet lag and his ability to never feel real guilt?* After all, anyone else would have awakened from the sound of a fifty-pound iron stove door being slammed shut, the aroma of coffee and gingerbread cooking, the smell of wood smoke and the crackling of flames.

Elliot was awake, but not about to let

her think she'd disturbed him. Better to hold his breath and not move a muscle, better to force his breathing to the slow shallow one of deep sleep than to let her know she had any control over him. At the moment Elizabeth took the fragrant pan of gingerbread from the oven, Elliot stretched and faked a yawn and slowly sat up. "Oh, you made me breakfast like the old days."

Elizabeth immediately walked to the back door with the steaming pan of bread and opened the door wide, surprising the raccoon sitting on the rim of the trash can. Using a spoon she picked up from the counter, she scooped out all the hot stuff into the trash can and slammed the door hard enough to make the panes rattle. "No. I didn't.

"I'm going into Vail, if you want to make a phone call you'd better move it."

Elliot slipped his sockless feet into the expensive leather loafers and grabbed his jacket. Even rumpled from sleeping in his clothes, he looked rich. Maybe not important, which is what he strived for, but he did look rich.

He pulled a small silver flask from his

pocket and took a long swig. He toasted her afterwards and said, "No toothbrush."

She wanted him to follow her in his rental car, but he climbed in beside her. She chose not to argue, but dropped him off at the grocery store nestled in a hillside shopping mall. "I'll be back in two hours." And she drove away. She did look into her rearview mirror. She couldn't help it. As far as she knew, Elliot had never been inside a grocery store. For a moment she wished she were a small bug on his shoulder so she could watch, but then she thought that he would probably go into his helpless male routine and some sweet young thing would do it all for him. Then she thought of the sweet young thing who apparently had done it all for him, and she was furious once more.

She drove to the hospital immediately. She used a phone in the main waiting area and called her attorney in New York.

"You've got to get me out of this" was her desperate plea after telling him everything, including her pregnancy. The rest of the conversation was only punctuated by her occasional "uh-huh" and "Oh God!"

She then called the Ob/Gyn on the card Chris had given her. They could see her now; it was one block from the hospital.

Chris saw her from a window in the doctors' lounge. He tried to get to her before she was out of the parking lot, but he didn't make it. The disappointment and then the longing showed on his face and in the slow way he returned to the hospital. Amy, the ER nurse, walked in step beside him on her way for her shift. "Cheer up, Doc," she said. "She just went over to Harriet Clough's office."

Chris stopped in his tracks, a big grin on his face. "Good! Great! Ha!" He ran to catch up with Amy, "How did you know?"

"I was there when she called in."

"So, does this make an even dozen kids for you?"

"You aren't funny," Amy said, but her smile and warmth couldn't agree with her words.

"How can you afford them?" he said seriously.

They were inside the hospital now, she stopped at the door to the nurses' changing room and turned to look at him with big moist eyes. "You know, I don't know how we afford them. David is in construction and it's good around here, but it isn't enough. We just . . . do." And before tears could drop she went into the dressing room.

Chris checked out and was soon on his way to the Medical Building where Harriet Clough and her partners had their practice. The staff knew him and he was in the examining rooms in seconds, looking for Elizabeth. She hadn't gotten that far yet. She was being weighed.

"What are you doing here?" she said.

"Holding up this wall." He leaned against the wall next to her, so close she could smell the medicated soap he'd washed his hands with and the crisp smell of the outdoors that seemed to be with him at all times.

"You allow very strange people in here," Elizabeth said to the nurse.

"He is one of the strangest." The

woman dressed in very un-nurselike blue jeans and T-shirt which read "SKI THE RADS." She smiled and pushed him out of the way. "Sit down here and I'll take your blood pressure."

Chris watched and tsk-tsked when her blood pressure was too high.

"Don't make that noise to me," she said. "Do you have any idea what I've been going through?" She apologized immediately. "Of course you do," she said quietly.

He went with her to the examining room and shut the door which the nurse left open.

"Tell me," he said. He was holding his arms across his chest, and she could see his muscles flex as if he were holding himself tightly to keep from exploding.

"I don't know everything, yet." She sighed and lay back on the table to look at the ceiling and wonder if it was true that counting every little hole in those damn panels and not missing one would make your dreams come true.

"I love you, Lissy," he said. She wondered if that was one of her dreams coming true. "I love you," he said again and came to her side. He took her hand and held it to his heart.

"Thank you," she said. She couldn't think of anything else to say.

His pager buzzed and he reluctantly let go of her hand to use the wall phone to call his service.

"I've got to go." He kissed her forehead and the tip of her nose, took a quick nip at her breast through her chambray shirt, and left the room.

*I hope they don't take my blood pressure now,* Elizabeth thought. *They'd put me in the hospital immediately.*

Harriet Clough was Elizabeth's age, straightforward but tender and helpful.

The ultrasound showed everything to be on track, although they couldn't tell the sex. "I don't want to know," Elizabeth said.

"Come back in a month. Call me if you feel any need to." No worries, no "My aren't you old."

Elizabeth felt better than she had in months when she walked out of the building and climbed into her car.

Elliot was standing outside a ski rental

shop with two big sacks in his arms. He looked put-out and frustrated.

Elizabeth did not help him get in or place the bags. She was off before he had the door shut.

"Do you have your credit card?" she said.

"Why?" He sounded angry.

"Because you are going to get a room here." She replied in the same tone he used on her.

"Well, I can't."

"You're going to whether you like it or not."

He turned to put his back against the door and stare at her. "I don't have a credit card because you shut me off. I don't have a job because you left the firm, and I don't have any money because I had to give a retainer to a securities attorney and fly out here."

She counted to ten, then spoke in her hardest, cruelest voice. "I shut you off because you left me for someone else. I left my job because I want to live here now. You lost your job because you are no good at it. You don't have any money because you ran off to . . . where was it,

Elliot? You ran off and spent your money—"

Elliot interrupted, "You and I are going to be indicted for insider trading."

Elizabeth felt her blood drain, then heard the pounding of her heart forcing blood into her system again.

"You son of a bitch," she said just above a whisper. "I never made an improper trade in my life."

"Well, it's their word against us." Elliot couldn't look at her. He looked out the big windshield, but really saw nothing but the reflection of Elizabeth's enraged face.

Elizabeth pulled off the road the first moment she could. She felt like she'd just been pushed in front of a subway car by Elliot.

"What did you do?" she asked.

"Nothing." Elliot still couldn't look at her.

"Don't do this, Elliot. What did you do this time?"

His head spun to meet her, his face livid, his eyes glaring at her with hate and contempt and just a little fear. "Oh, right! Blame me! Easy to do for the

Wicked Witch of Wall Street. The perfect example of a woman in the workplace! Blame me! You never helped me! What else was I supposed to do? What? You could do it all, better than anyone, better than any man! Let me take you back to our honeymoon . . . you predicted the bio-med upswing. I asked for twenty thousand to invest, you said no. Well, I got the money anyway through some information of my own and I invested it in our name. OURS."

"I never signed—" Elizabeth began but he interrupted her again.

"You never signed anything because I can sign your fabulously perfect handwriting. Hell, a moron could forge your signature."

"What else?" she demanded.

"Nothing else. It just grew and grew as I traded on your predictions. I did it out in the open, took them years to see what was going on under their noses."

"You are a moron," she said.

"And you are married to me."

"I won't get you out of this." She started the car and was about to pull out on the highway again when he answered.

"You don't have to worry about getting me out of it. You have to worry about getting yourself out of it." The smirk on his face was hideous.

The baby chose that moment to make itself known with a quick flutter.

Elizabeth woke that night thinking she heard her grandfather snoring. She sat straight up in bed, eyes wide open to the full moon shining through the small upstairs window directly onto her bed. Perhaps it was Elliot. She lay back down but sat up again. Elliot had many unnerving irritating habits, but he'd never snored one snort through that thin patrician nose of his. She heard it again and this time turned her head toward the sound. It came from a rocking chair she'd placed beside her bed. An exact copy of the pressed back rocker her grandfather sat in every night until he fell asleep, snoring soundly.

There was no one in the rocker, and the noise did not come back. Elizabeth settled back into her pillows and tried to go back to sleep. But all she could do was think of her grandfather.

*"George, you'll spoil her to death rocking her that way." Alice Templeton shook her head. "You never rocked your own daughter so much," she reminded him.*

*He continued the slow steady rocking with the musical creak of the rocker against the pine floor. "Maybe I should have."*

*Elizabeth pulled on the chain tucked into his bib overalls to pull out the big railroad watch he kept in his bib pocket.*

*"Time, Grandpa?"*

*"Your bedtime," Alice said.*

*Elizabeth laughed. "Grampa's bedtime!" She squealed when he tickled her.*

*Her bed was made in the corner next to the big black stove so she would be warm all night. The two older people kissed her goodnight. Her grandma's kiss light and birdlike, her grandpa's scratchy and bear-like. They made their way up the steep steps, the oil lamp light fading as they went up. In moments her grandpa was snoring. All was right with Elizabeth's world. She could sleep now.*

*She closed her eyes and didn't wake again*

*until the big black cast iron door of the stove slammed shut in the morning on homemade buttermilk biscuits. Life in heaven began again.*

Elizabeth awoke, smiling. She felt a wave of warmth and contentment go over her like a huge warm hand tucking in a quilt. "Grandpa?" she said aloud. Then she fell asleep.

The next morning Chris came by just at sunrise. Elizabeth was feeding her "pets," the raccoon and birds. She was in jeans and a jean jacket, standing on the front porch throwing the bread crumbs and seed. Her long brown hair fell across her shoulders like a hood.

"You have got to get a phone," he said in greeting.

Elizabeth opened her mouth for a Wicked Witch type retort, but found herself still smiling. She felt an almost childlike joy at seeing him. He looked the way he always did, jeans and a jacket, but the sun coming up made him glow with a rosy pink-gold beauty, his eyes sparkled, his hair gleamed. She had thought him handsome, but now she thought him beautiful and precious. The depth of the feeling amazed her. By the time he'd reached her side, she couldn't speak. Her emotions were too close to the surface.

He smiled at her. "You look like you've just found a long-lost prized toy," he said and kissed her forehead lightly.

She looked up, kissed his chin, then rubbed the top of her head into the space between his jaw and chest. She could hear his heartbeat, feel the need for her.

"You're no toy," she said muffled into his chest.

They stood like that for a long while. The sounds of the mountain waking and the fresh crisp scent of the air surrounded them. For a moment they were alone and apart from all the problems of their world. A huge rumbling noise, a truck coming over the dirt road, broke their moment of perfection.

Elizabeth looked toward the road and laughed "Ask and you shall receive," she said, and pointed to the telephone company truck just pulling up. Chris turned his back to the truck and began to whistle.

"What?" Elizabeth said.

"Just keep them out there for a few moments," Chris said, then he turned around and said, "What the hell, I love you and I don't care who knows it." He held his arms out wide like a magician revealing a trick. It took a moment for Elizabeth to understand what he was talking about, but when she did she began to laugh and she suddenly remembered she hadn't laughed in a very long time.

Elliot's timing to poke his head out of the door then didn't even dampen her happiness. She just laughed harder.

"Are you still here?" Chris said.

"I belong here." Elliot said. Chris looked at him with one eyebrow cocked.

"I don't think so," Chris said. He took one long stride and was off the porch steps and by Elizabeth's side in a moment. She was talking to the phone installer.

"It won't do much good," she said. "I still don't have power."

The phone man was young and jolly.

He smiled and said, "Don't worry, we co-ordinated. I passed him on the interstate." And at just that moment, the electric company truck, a massive eighteen-wheeler, rumbled down the road.

"Hooray! Phone, electricity, hot water, all in one day!" She ran to the porch, to the step in one leap and pushed Elliot out of the way of the door. She was going to make coffee and coffee cake. She found herself laughing again. The Wicked Witch of Wall Street whipping up a batch of homemade goodies. Unbelievable!

# Five

The telephone man was gone in a few minutes, but the electrical men stayed and stayed. They even helped prime her water pump. At dusk they left.

Chris and Elliot stayed far away from each other. In fact, Elizabeth didn't remember seeing Elliot outdoors at all, and she never saw Chris inside. *All the better,* she thought.

With the sun going down, though, something was going to happen. She went around each room of her house, finding Elliot asleep on the bed in the new room, and turned on all the lights. She then went outside and walked all the way to the end of her drive and turned to look back.

The sun had set, the stars were not

out, the lake looked like a flat piece of dull metal. Only the creek sparkled as it went past her lights. Her log cabin, lit up, looked like a music box she'd seen once. It came from the Black Forest, a small log cabin with a green roof and a red door and it played *"Edelweiss."*

She hugged her arms tightly around herself and spun on her heels in a circle. *Almost heaven. Almost.*

Chris came down the road and stood in front of her.

"I feel better now that you have a phone," he said. "You are safer."

"Thank you," she replied. She was so unused to someone caring about her. Chris had shown her over and over again that what she accepted from Elliot, his total self-absorption, was not what life had to be like.

She stood on tiptoes and quickly kissed him. Then she took his hand and began to walk back. Neither of them saw Elliot standing in the shadows on the porch.

"How cute," he said.

Elizabeth pulled her hand away from Chris's.

Chris pulled her closer to him.

"Now, kiddies," Elliot taunted, "none of that roughhousing."

"Oh, Elliot, shut up," Elizabeth said. Then she pulled away from Chris. "I'll call you," she said to him and went inside.

Neither man moved. Elliot broke the silence first. "She is my wife, and I think I'll keep her."

Chris stood in the dark, out of the light from the windows. Elliot couldn't see any expression on his face, just the solid blackness of his form.

Chris turned and went to his car. He got in, started the motor, and sped out of the drive.

Elliot waited until the red lights disappeared, then, shivering, he went inside, calling for Elizabeth. She didn't answer but he could hear the water flowing in the bathroom, so he walked in. Elizabeth was in the tub, the hot water steaming around her as she let her head loll on the rim. She sat up quickly and covered herself.

"Good God, Elizabeth, I've seen you naked, you know." Elliot said. Then, ignoring her anger, he sat on the side of the tub and trailed his hand in the water. "Don't use up all the hot water. Or did you intend for me to share the bath with you?" He gave her no time to say no. He got in, clothes and all, water spilling over the side.

"GET OUT!" Elizabeth screamed. He was on top of her or she would have gotten out herself. "GET. . . ." She didn't finish. Elliot was lifted like a mewling kitten from the tub, streaming hot water all over. He tried to hit at his attacker, but he slipped on the floor and landed on his seat.

"Better be careful," Chris said calmly. "But if you do break something, there's a doctor in the house." Then he bent over and helped Elliot up, pointed him in the direction of the door and gently shoved him out, closing the door behind him. "I'll wait while you round up your things and get into your car and go into town." He didn't sound angry, but that made it all the more menacing.

"Elizabeth!" Elliot called out.

"Just get out! she screamed from behind the door. The door opened, and she came out dressed with a towel wrapped around her head. "Go Elliot."

"I can't. I have no money."

Elizabeth went to her purse in the big main room, the two men following her. She got her credit card and held it out to Elliot. "I want you out. I will call and pre-approve hotel and food and a ticket."

"Ticket?" Elliot looked at her, bewildered. "What do you mean?"

"I mean go back to New York. I mean get away from me. I mean I'm once again going to rescue you, but I don't have to have you under my roof to do it."

Elliot looked at the card and appeared to be measuring his chances of staying. He then took it, grabbed his jacket, and was out the door, slamming it behind him. Elizabeth stood still until the sound of his car was long gone.

"Are you all right?" Chris asked.

"Oh for Pete's sake! Of course I'm not all right."

He tried to pull her to him to comfort her. "Lissy, please don't push me away."

"I need to be alone," she said, leaving no room for argument. "I said earlier I would call you and I will."

* * *

Again, she waited until she could no longer hear his car. She stood in the middle of her room, her hands in fists at her side. She was suddenly shivering. She wasn't cold. She wasn't afraid. Well, yes, she was afraid. She was afraid that as soon as Elliot had a moment to go over what just happened, he'd be back. He'd be back because there was no way he couldn't have seen she was pregnant.

She picked up the phone and called the credit card company and made the arrangements she'd told Elliot she'd make. There was no problem; he'd been on her card before.

She went to the kitchen and began to make a pot of decaf coffee. She had to laugh at herself; she was making it on the wood burning stove although she now had the electric stove top.

"It will taste better," she said aloud.

*Everything will be better,* she reminded herself. *Everything will be fine. Everything* is *fine.*

She stood by the oven and closed her eyes. It was the first of August. She had to get all this taken care of and Elliot out of her life before the baby was born. She had to be free. She went back to the phone and called her travel agent in New York. An hour later the agent called back. Elizabeth was booked on a flight leaving for New York tomorrow night.

She put the coffee back on the stove, refilled her mug with orange juice. She was not going to sleep tonight, and neither was her lawyer. She spent the rest of the night on the phone and drinking juice. The anxiety was enough to keep her wired and awake.

Chris pounded on the door the next morning. "Elizabeth! Lissy!" he cried out. Elizabeth opened the door just as he was about to open it himself. "What is going on? You get a phone, I can't reach you . . . what is going on?"

She stood aside to let him in, closed the door, and walked over to the phone. "Harry?" she said into the receiver. "I'll call you back." Then, she stacked up the notes she'd been making and sat down. She thought for a long time before she spoke. "I am not married to Elliot. I got a true divorce in the state of New York. It won't be final for a few more months, and Elliot can fight it, although so far he hasn't."

She stopped talking and looked at Chris. She couldn't help but smile at him, he looked so worried, so wonderfully caring and anxious. "I don't think he knows," she said. "He hasn't paid his attorney, so he won't take his calls."

Chris sat on the sofa and put his elbows on his knees and grasped his hands, leaned forward and said, "How can I help?" Elizabeth wanted to run to him and cry out thank you, but she stayed where she was. She knew if she were much closer to him she'd touch him, and he'd touch her and then they'd . . . better she sat where she was.

"Elliot has implicated . . ." Elizabeth stopped and shut her mouth tightly, pursing her lips as if to make the words not be real. Then she spoke again. "More than implicated, he has made it appear as if I did over three hundred illegal trades using my insider knowledge." Tears came suddenly to her eyes.

"It's as if he set out fifteen years ago to destroy me."

Chris was beside her in seconds. He stood by her, at first ready to hold her, but something held him back, some set of her shoulders or look in her eyes that said "don't!" He ran his hand a scant inch over her head as if caressing her, but not touching her. Elizabeth stood and walked to where he had been sitting, and sat in the manner he had sat. "What really destroys me is that he really makes me look like a complete fool."

"You didn't make those trades," Chris said.

"It's not that alone. It's the fact that every trade he made lost money. He sold too soon or too low or bought too high or the company folded . . . Pan Am . . . Tri R. . . ." She ran a hand through her hair. "Stupid things, he did. Ridiculous things. In my name he lost around $600,000.00!" She shook her head in disbelief. "Lost it! Options! He never understood options!"

"Where did he get that much?" Chris said.

"He made that much over those years

in salary." Elizabeth laughed at herself and added, "I should say, I paid him that much."

Chris came to the sofa and sat close to her but didn't touch her. "How are you? How's the baby doing?"

Elizabeth felt herself melting then, as if she were an ice cube dropped into hot tea. She melted against Chris, wanting to blend herself into his strong body. "Oh, Chris," she said in a whisper. "I have never felt so out of control, so wrong, so messed up in my whole life. I'll be forty-five in two weeks and my life is a mess." She ran her hand up his neck, turned her palm toward herself and ran her fingers along the line of his jaw, then felt with her fingertips along his lips. "Hold me, Chris."

He crushed her to him, his arms wrapped around her shoulders and he nuzzled his jaw into her hair.

"How can I help?" he said again.

"Just being here, I guess." Elizabeth let herself soak up all his strength, she felt as if she were a sponge sopping up all his power, doubling her size with his strength.

They sat quietly, his breath becoming more ragged, hers following, his heart beating a hard rhythm, hers following.

"I'm fine now," she said.

The sound of a car in the drive made them jump apart like high-school sweethearts caught by parents.

Chris looked at his watch. He kissed her quickly, hard and with an ownership she liked.

"I'll call you," she said just as Elliot opened the door and came in.

"You need a lock to keep the unwanted animals out," Chris said. He raised an imaginary cowboy hat at Elliot in greeting, then left.

Elliot did not acknowledge Chris in any way. He only looked at Elizabeth.

Once she heard Chris's car was gone, she spoke. "What do you want?" She crossed her arms across her chest, then lowered them across her midriff.

"Too late, Elizabeth," Elliot said. "Your secret is out."

Elizabeth was too good at negotiating to show he'd hit a nerve. She remained silent.

"You are pregnant." He ambled to the

wingback chair and sat down. "You are pregnant, and it's the cowboy's."

She remained standing and silent.

"I hate it when you don't answer." He spat the words out in sheer anger. "I hate it when you treat me like a child!"

"You think I treat you like a child?" Elizabeth said.

"Yes!"

"I had no idea."

"You never had any idea about anything that didn't have to do with stocks and financial statements and your career."

"Why did you ask me to marry you Elliot?"

"Why did you accept?" he shot back.

"I guess it's a good thing we are divorced," she countered. "I'm hungry." She went to the refrigerator for eggs and milk and cheese.

"We are?"

"*I* am."

Elliot stood and straightened his clothes. "No, you aren't going to do this to me. You aren't going to change the conversation. You are pregnant by that cowboy, you are going to be indicted, you are my wife—"

Elizabeth interrupted him. "I am not. I'm your mother, and you are a very naughty little boy."

"I've had it, Elizabeth." He was beginning to lose his temper. "I've had it. I'm going back to New York."

"You can't; you're grounded." She laughed again.

Elliot started to say something but stomped out of the main room and slammed the front door behind him.

When she was sure he was gone, she stopped beating the eggs, turned off the stove, and went upstairs to her bed. She lay down and curled up in a fetal position. She cried herself to sleep.

Chris woke her hours later. She heard him knock and call out and she met him at the foot of the stairs. He kissed her forehead then held her to him and said nothing. She held on, her arms wrapped around his waist. They sat down on the bottom step and she leaned her head against his shoulder.

"He's gone?" Chris asked.

"For now." She nestled in closer to him.

"I've got a surprise for you," he said.

"I don't know if I can take any more surprises."

"This one you can take. We're going on a picnic." He helped her up from the step. "Now go get dressed, bring a jacket."

Elizabeth didn't hesitate a moment. She was dressed in jeans she could just barely zip and a T-shirt that was beginning to stretch too tightly across her breasts. She caught sight of herself in the dresser mirror, was shocked and quickly changed into a drop-waisted corduroy dress from a designer. One she thought would always look too big on her. This time the waist was snug. She grabbed a bulky sweater in an Indian pattern and her short cowboy boots. On the spur of the moment, she grabbed one of the quilts off the foot of her bed.

"I'm ready," she said. Chris looked up at the staircase as she came down. He smiled. "What are you smiling at?" she demanded. "You can't see up my skirt."

"No, but I can imagine."

"If I remember which little monster you were, you were always trying to look up the girls' skirts."

Chris took the quilt from her and opened the front door. "Christmas and Easter were the best for that," he teased. "The girls wore those ruffly slips to make their skirts stand out and fancy underwear, too. I loved it."

"I didn't wear fancy slips and underwear."

"I know." Chris ducked as she threw her sweater at him. They both were laughing by the time they were in his car.

"You haven't asked where we're going," Chris said when they were out of her drive.

"I trust you," Elizabeth said. She put her hand on his.

He grasped her hand in his and squeezed it. They drove in silence, enjoying the closeness, the calm. Elizabeth had lived here all her young life. In moments she knew where he was taking her: the other side of her lake.

*I will get a boat and build a landing for it,* she thought. *I will make a boat house. I'll build a raft in the middle!* She shivered then; no matter how warm the air, the lake water, straight from the glaciers and snow, was always freezing. No swimming across this lake. It wasn't at all like the lakes in the East which warmed enough to swim in. The shallow parts along the edge got bearable at high noon, but never the middle. No, just a boat and dock. The car was stopped and Chris got out. He pulled the box of food from the back and then opened the door for Elizabeth. She was still lost in thought.

"Hello," he teased, "Earth to Lissy."

"I knew you'd bring me here," she said as she got out. "I just knew it."

Chris ran away from her like a child released from school early. She couldn't keep up, didn't try. She knew where he was going and she could get there without following him. He'd laid the quilt down, covered one corner with a small red tablecloth and laid out the lunch by the time she reached the spot directly across from her cabin. He was splayed out on the rest of the quilt, face to the sun singing "Achy Breaky Heart" in a good baritone.

"Murlow's Point," Elizabeth said.

"I'm not through with my singing," he said. He finished the last verse and chorus; Elizabeth's face ached from her ear-to-ear grin. "You call it Murlow's Point?" he said without taking a rest between singing and talking. "I called it Templeton's View."

"Looking out on the Templeton cabin, over the Templeton land and lake, real original, Hanford," she teased.

"So, I was twelve, what are you expecting?" he sat up and kissed her quickly. "Who's Murlow?"

"Grandpa's dog."

"This is named after a dog." He looked around and then said. "I'll bite, what's the story?"

Elizabeth took her time, arranging her skirt around her feet and putting her hand in an elegant pose on her lap.

"Once upon a time Grandpa had a dog of indeterminate species. I never knew this dog personally, just by reputation."

"Many times that is the best way to know anybody," Chris said.

"Are you going to let me tell this story?"

"Please, continue." Chris put his head in her lap and looked up at her, but she ignored him.

"Murlow was found here," she said.

"That's it?" Chris said and sat up. "That is the whole thing? A stray dog is found here, and it becomes Murlow's Point?"

"Grandpa was very sentimental."

"Let's eat," Chris said.

"Story not exciting enough?"

"I'm hungry," Chris said. "I'm always hungry."

"Eat!" Elizabeth said.

She picked up one of the paper wrapped packages and found beautifully made salads, chicken, and crusty bread. Chris held up a bottle of natural apple cider and poured it into real crystal goblets. They ate in silence, occasionally looking at the other and smiling. The food was good, the temperature was in the high seventies, the sun made the lake pure reflected blue. The cabin looked as if it were from a fairy tale, painted in soft water colors, all edges crisped by outlines.

Small tarts of kiwi and strawberries in

custard made the perfect finish to the picnic. Elizabeth put the trash in the box, and Chris sat out on the very edge of the point to watch the lake. Fish began to jump in their evening search for food.

Elizabeth tried to lie on her stomach, but was uncomfortable, so she sat with her legs drawn up and wrapped her arms around her knees. She was content, wanting nothing further. At ease with the now. All of it so new to her.

Shadows began to creep along and soon her back was in the shade and she put on her sweater. Chris sat still as he was. Elizabeth realized they hadn't said much to each other. Conversation hadn't been demanded or expected.

Chris sat a few minutes more, then came to her side. He hugged her with one arm and then lay back on the quilt, drawing her with him. They looked up into the clear sky, cloudless, clean. It looked as if you could see forever into the ether of the future.

"I want to say things to you," Chris began, "but I don't really know what words."

"You don't have to say anything."

"Having to isn't the issue. I want to. I want to ask all the corny things like where have you been all my life and how did you end up with a jerk like him—"

"Don't bring Elliot up, please."

"I'd like to never mention him, but he's there." Chris let go of her. Elizabeth felt the contentment drain from her as if a vein had been opened. Her heart began to beat rapidly.

"Please don't," she said.

"Lissy, I want you." Chris sat up and leaned over her. He scanned her entire body as if he must memorize it or lose it forever.

Elizabeth shivered. The shade was chilling her, or was it the words?

"Let's go back." She sat up and then got to her feet. Chris tried to pull her back, but she pulled her hand away. "Let's go back now."

He pulled her dress hem, "Please sit down. I won't say anything more. Just please sit down."

She pulled the hem from his hands and began to pull the quilt up from the ground, ignoring his being on it; she just tugged harder. When he didn't budge she tugged harder still until he stood up and helped put things away. The drive back to the cabin was in silence. Elizabeth felt as if she were trapped. She couldn't understand the feeling, the confinement the car and Chris made her feel. Claustrophobic. Panic. *Let me out!*

She was out of the car, practically running to her cabin. Chris followed her in and stood with his hands on his hips.

"What happened?" he demanded. "What did I do?"

"You are a cliché even when you're angry," Elizabeth said.

"I'm a very boring man. I don't think up flowery phrases or witty repartee: I say what I feel, without a lot of the lies attached. I think that is pretty good. I say I want you and I mean that. I say you are beautiful and I mean that. What did I say that made you want to run?"

Elizabeth choked back the panic she was feeling. She choked back the words that the Wicked Witch wanted her to scream out. She had never felt so split, so pummeled, so totally unable to deal with a situation in her life. Every day since Elliot left her she had been hit with one thing after another.

"Just go, Chris. Please, before we say things we don't want said."

"I *want* to say things!" Chris punched at his chest with his fist. "I want to say what I'm saying!"

Elizabeth turned from him to run to the stairs but he caught up with her and swung her around. "What is wrong?" He held her elbows tightly, but let go when he saw the look in her eyes. "I'm sorry," he said quietly. "Whatever I did or said that made you feel . . . I'm sorry."

"You didn't do anything."

"Must be hormones," he quipped.

"Don't make fun of me."

"I don't want to go away like this." He shrugged his shoulders when she said nothing in response. "Call me."

Elizabeth walked to the door and held it open for him. He left without another word or looking back.

Later that evening she called her attorney and told him to meet her in New York and when. She packed a small bag, called Chris at the hospital, knowing he wasn't there, and left a message. Hours later she was on a jet at Stapleton airport in Denver, waiting for takeoff.

*"George, they are making fun of her," Alice said.*

*"About what?" Grandpa asked Elizabeth.*

*"Everything," Elizabeth said. She was six, just barely tall enough to see over the massive wooden table. "They call me names."*

*"That hurts your feelings?*

*"More," Elizabeth said in a sad little voice. "They hit me."*

*"They hit you?"*

*"I'll be standing by myself, reading a book and they will come up and hit me on the arm, or hit the book out of my hand and then they run away." Elizabeth began to cry.*

*Alice handed her a bandanna handkerchief, faded from red to rose from years of use and washing. Elizabeth blew her nose noisily.*

*Grandpa tapped the newspaper he was reading and hemmed and hawed a bit as he brought the words he was going to say into order. "Well, Lissy, there are two things to think about here."*

*"What?" she said and sniffed extra loud for emphasis.*

*"No one should hit you. Ever."*

*"I don't think so too," she said.*

*"And then why are they hitting you and making fun of you?"*

*"I didn't do anything!" she cried out, about to begin sobbing again.*

*"No, but they think you did. You were reading a book, you say." She nodded yes. "And what were they doing?"*

*"Well, it was recess and they were playing four-square and tether ball and red-rover."*

*"But you were standing up reading a book."*

*"Yes."*

*"Well, you see, it's easy. They thought you didn't like them."*

*"I don't."*

*Alice said, "You must like everyone."*

*Grandpa snorted. "Not likely, Alice. No, she must learn to get along."*

*"Can I get along and read?"*

*"Of course." Grandpa picked up his newspaper and said, "Just do what I do. Tell them you are going to read now and you'll play with them later."*

*Alice looked at her husband. "George, have you been doing that to me all these years?"*

*"You just noticed?"*

*"I noticed you don't play with me later," she said in a knowing tone.*

*"I'll play with you," Elizabeth said.*

*Grandpa put his paper down and looked meaningfully at Elizabeth. "Now those are the exact words you must say to the children at school. I'll play with you. You say those words, and do it, and you'll be fine." He picked up his paper again and said, "Solitary people scare other people. You have to open up to them, you have a lot to share with them."*

# Six

She was met at the airport by her attorney, Harry Steinberg. He had his limo waiting for her and she sat in the corner of the gray interior. The smell of the city, the noise and the lights made her nauseous. She was not glad to be back. In fact she felt worse as the drive to his apartment on Central Park dragged on and on.

Suddenly, she cried out, "Driver!" She grabbed her attorney's coat sleeve and cried out, "Harry! Something is wrong!" She called again to the driver, "Get me to a hospital! Oh God, Harry! Something is wrong!"

The trip to the hospital was only marginally closer than the apartment would be. A nurse came out with a wheelchair, instructing the men to get the limo out of the ambulance driveway or the next ambulance on the scene would be taking a healthy bite out of its side.

Harry stayed by her side as long as they would let him. Then he left to call his wife. He'd never had to deal with his own wife in the hospital until after the blessed event. He wasn't about to start doing it now, not even for Elizabeth. DeDe Steinberg hailed a cab and arrived in a flash.

Flaming red hair in Las Vegas showgirl flamboyant twirls and curls, expertly made up to cover the latest plastic surgery bruises and scars, dressed to the teeth in capes and flowing garments, DeDe would never be lost in a crowd. "Elizabeth March," she said, "how could you go and get pregnant?"

"DeDe . . ." Elizabeth began, but a cramp, one of the hardest she ever felt, stopped her in mid sentence. When it passed she finished, "Just lucky, I guess."

"Where is the doctor?" DeDe asked, then didn't wait for an answer. She pulled out her portable phone and called her own Ob/Gyn. "Get over here right now."

Elizabeth said, "He probably has other patients."

"He'll get over here if he wants to keep them. I'll have you know every one of them is in some benefit committee or philanthropic group I belong to. He'll be here."

Elizabeth nodded her head. If DeDe Steinberg said it was so, then it was so.

"It's none of my business, but whose baby is it?"

"DeDe!" Elizabeth was shocked. "You know perfectly well it's my hus . . . Elliot's."

"Don't get upset, dear. I was just wondering. Too bad. He'll inherit that awful thin hair."

Elizabeth laughed. "Thank God you exist."

"Well, if I didn't, they'd have to invent me," DeDe said. Then she picked up Elizabeth's ice cold hand and patted it with her other hand. "Don't you worry. My doctor won't let anything happen. If he did I'd have his . . . well, Harry would have his ass in a sling in a minute."

In spite of another sharp pang, Elizabeth said quietly through clenched teeth, I'm not worrying any more."

"What am I going to do with you, kid?" DeDe said. Elizabeth didn't answer. It was one of the rhetorical questions DeDe was famous for. No answer expected, no answer desired.

DeDe's doctor was a middle-aged man. Although Elizabeth had been more comfortable with her female doctor, he was professional and quickly summed up her problems. He confined her to total bed rest, and admonished her for letting herself get worn out and stressed out.

She told him who her doctor was, and he said he'd place a phone call to her and tell her what was going on. He left before she was sent to a floor for her stay.

"But he didn't say how long!" Elizabeth was saying as DeDe saw him out. "How long?" she called.

DeDe waved her hand at her impatiently. Elizabeth lay back on the uncomfortable examining table. For someone who had never been sick in her life, she was certainly seeing more of these types of places than she liked. She sat up. "Elliot."

"Is a no good son of a . . ." DeDe

came back in, but didn't finish her sentence. "He's not worth the breath. Harry says we put you in, and we tell those people at the main desk that you don't exist." And so it was done.

Elizabeth would have liked something to help her sleep, but knew it was ridiculous to ask. She lay awake in the room. The lights from the city seemed to send a glow through her window.

She had come back to take control of her life, just like in the old days. She had come back to get Elliot out of trouble and out of her life. But this little life growing continuously inside her kept taking over, making decisions for her, moving her life this way and that.

Elizabeth sighed. *Well, better this little life than anyone else,* she thought, *except maybe Christian?*

She wondered if he knew where she was. If he'd gotten her message, all he knew was that she was in New York. She had meant to call once she'd settled at Harry's and DeDe's. At the moment she didn't even know where her address book was. The baby didn't like her position and kicked hard to let her know. Elizabeth rolled on her side and felt the baby settle. How wonderful. I move; she moves. Elizabeth caught her thought and held it. *She. A girl. A strong, willful girl.* Sleep came at last.

"Six weeks!" Elizabeth shrieked. "In bed!" She threw the business section of *The New York Times* across the room. The doctor easily stepped aside. Many women had violent reactions in his practice. Hormones, he had decided long ago.

"If you are very, very good I can shorten it, but probably six weeks of bed rest. You are not on complete bed rest. You can go to the bathroom and take showers. You can dress yourself."

"I don't believe it." Elizabeth was sitting up in bed in one of DeDe's less ornate nightgowns—no feathers or lace, but lots of ribbons which kept getting tangled in the sheets. She yanked a few more ribbons out from under her and sighed as she crossed her arms around her drawn-up knees.

"What am I supposed to do for six weeks in bed?"

The doctor looked at her as if she were a naughty child. "You are going to give your baby some time to grow and yourself some time to calm down."

"I can assure you that six weeks in bed will not calm me down."

"You never know until you try it," he said and patted her toes under the tented sheets and left the room with a quick wink. Elizabeth never realized how much she hated men who winked until then.

"Sexist!" Elizabeth yelled. "Chauvinist!"

"You called?" Elliot entered behind a huge bouquet of yellow roses and baby's breath.

"How did you know I was here?" Elizabeth asked, refusing to take the bouquet from him.

"Harry is notoriously cheap and the chauffeur needed to pay his bookie," Elliot said. "I got a cash advance on my quarterly from my grandmother's estate." Then he added, "Before you think I used your credit card for anything other than the amount you allowed me."

Just as Elliot tried to lean down and kiss her cheek, Elizabeth activated the bedside controls and sank out of reach. Elliot took the hint and began to search for a place to put the flowers. He decided to use the plastic water pitcher and defiantly crammed them into it and placed it on the windowsill. Equally defiantly and with great flourish, he pulled a chair beside Elizabeth's bed and sat down.

"Don't bother getting comfortable," Elizabeth began. "You are leaving."

"No, I'm not. I'm staying."

"I don't want you here."

"Elizabeth, I already know the baby is mine. And I know I was wrong to accuse you of anything with that cowboy."

Elizabeth felt an uncomfortable rush of blood and hoped he wouldn't notice. "You have always been the perfect wife. I am the one who . . . strayed, shall we say?"

"Go away."

"I'm begging you to take me back." He didn't sound as if he were begging.

"Go away."

"I'll get on my knees and beg if you want." He sounded as if he were cajoling a six-year-old.

Elizabeth looked at him in complete

awe at his ability to act as if nothing had happened and this were a minor event, easily handled by flowers and an apology. She said no more, just stared at him.

Elliot was soon squirming around in the chair, crossing and uncrossing his legs, shifting from one hip to the other, looking about the room for something to occupy his mind so he could ignore her continuous piercing stare.

"Damn it, Elizabeth!" he finally yelled out. "I hate it when you treat me this way." He ran his hands through his pale blond hair and then stood to pace the room. Elizabeth followed him with her eyes.

He stood at the foot of her bed and put his hands together in a plea. "I want you back, Elizabeth. I need you. I need you." She did not respond. "Please Elizabeth, I can't make it without you. I want our life back."

Elizabeth shook her head and the responded. "What life! What did we have together that was so wonderful you had to run off and leave me for someone else? What did we have?"

"I made a mistake, Elizabeth. Jennifer

was a mistake. I'm sorry, I will never do that again. We had a good life."

"That isn't what I'm talking about, Elliot," Elizabeth said. "I'm talking about you and me and what you want to insist we had together. Not your fling with what's-her-name."

Elliot shrugged his shoulders and slowly walked to the door. He stopped in front of it and turned back to Elizabeth. "I'll be back. I'm not willing to give up. I need you."

*"Lissy, for someone as smart and pretty and sweet, you help your grandma a great deal. But for someone who has all those wonderful character traits, for that someone to lie! Lissy, I can't believe you lied to your grandma."*

*Elizabeth was thirteen. Never tall, yet still giving the impression of being gangly, she stood shifting from one foot to the other and not looking her grandfather in the eye.*

*"I didn't mean to lie," she said.*

*"But you did."*

*"I didn't* try *to lie. It just came out and then I couldn't take it back."*

*Grandpa looked at Elizabeth and nodded in understanding. "Let me see you try to sit in that chair," he said, nodding his head at his rocking chair.*

*Elizabeth rolled her eyes in her head, "Grandpa~"*

*"Go ahead, just try."*

*Elizabeth sat in the rocker.*

*Grandpa shot up from his chair at the table and said, "I said try to sit. You just sat."*

*Elizabeth looked at him as only a teenager can.*

*"Do it again, Lissy."*

*"What?"*

*"TRY to sit in the rocker."*

*Elizabeth stood and began to sit again, but just as her seat was about to meet the rocker, Grandpa yelled out, "STOP!" But it was too late.*

*The startled Lissy plopped back onto the rocker with suck force the rocker tumbled back, and Elizabeth hit her head hard on the floor. Grandpa caught the rocker and replaced it. Then he took her from the rocker with one big hand and sat in the rocker himself. "I tried to warn you," he said.*

# Seven

Christian Hanford scratched at two days' stubble growth on his chin and tried to stretch out on the too short roll-away bed the hospital provided for the doctors in the ER.

"Rough night?" Harriet Clough said.

"Worse." Chris sat up and yawned. "A family reunion with food poisoning and a stabbing."

"At the same family reunion?"

"One of the brothers decided that one of the other loving family members was trying to poison them all, so he picked up a butcher knife and tried to kill his closest-in-proximity brother. Fortunately, food poisoning being what it is, he was too weak to do much damage. Twenty-three adults and thirty kids. They ought to outlaw family reunions."

Harriet laughed in spite of the horrible event and then patted him on the back. "Well, I guess on top of the other news, that was quite a twenty-four hours."

"What news?" Chris asked.

Harriet looked at him as if he ought to know. "Oh, you haven't gotten any messages?"

"I've got several, I was just too tired to hear them."

"Well, your favorite patient is in the hospital."

Chris looked confused. "My favorite who?"

"Elizabeth March."

Chris jumped up from the bed and took her arm, "Lissy is here? Where? What? Why?"

"Wait a minute. I'm sorry, I've got this out of order since you don't know anything." She took his hand from her arm and rubbed where he'd been holding her. "She went to New York and apparently began to have labor pains." At the look of fear on his face she added, "She's all right now, but she is on bed rest. A little bit of raised blood pressure, a little bit of tension, and a big amount of denial caused her problems."

Chris ran his hands through his mussed hair, his normally healthy pink skin looked drained white.

"She really is your favorite patient," Harriet said. She pointed to the bed and Chris sat down again. "Want to talk?"

"She opened her eyes—"

Harriet interrupted. "Opened her eyes?"

"In the emergency room," Chris explained. "She'd fainted at the grocery store. I did some tests. She was pregnant, her husband had left her, she looked at me and I fell flat on my face in love."

"Messy," Harriet said and shook her head. "Uh-uh, very messy indeed."

"Messy?"

Harriet nodded, "Falling in love, it gets all over you."

"Very funny."

"I thought so." Harriet had a big smile on her face. "What did Casey think of it all?"

"Casey left me—that very day, I think.

I'm not sure actually when she moved out but I found out that day."

"That is the first thing I've heard that doesn't surprise me." Harriet sat down next to him on the bed and slapped her hand on his thigh. "Well, big boy, I suggest you get your messages. And if you want to know anything else, ask her." She stood up and went to the door, then turned around to say quietly, "If you really love her, you'll help her deal with this denial. She refused an amniocentesis and didn't really want to talk about the baby's development. She didn't want a copy of the ultrasound, didn't even want to look. She is in major denial."

Chris put his head in his hands and shook his head. "I've met the father of this baby. I think I'd be in denial myself."

"It's her husband's?" Chris nodded yes. "You are too nice a man for all this crap," Harriet said. She didn't wait for an answer.

Alone in the lounge, Chris picked up the phone and called his service for all his messages.

* * *

"There's another chauffeur looking for a job in New York today!" DeDe said as she swept into the hospital room. "Now, we have arranged for your room to be changed and no visitors, except, of course, for *moi.*"

Hospital staff were right behind her and soon Elizabeth was on another floor and in another room, this one with a view of the river.

It did not help Elizabeth's mood. She enjoyed DeDe, loved to hear the chatter and gossip, but she couldn't stop thinking about spending six weeks in bed. She could read and she could write, but not for hours and hours each day, *every day.* Not without getting up and going out to walk around her land.

Her land. Her cabin. Her lake, her stream, her animals, her furniture, her food! "Oh, De!" she cried out and interrupted some endless tale of gossip from the Palm Beach season.

DeDe Steinberg looked like a selfish, self-centered lady of ease, but she loved "causes," and Elizabeth had become a cause. She was at her side and holding her to her chest in a hug that would suffocate Elizabeth soon if she didn't extricate herself quickly. "What, my darling girl? What? Just tell me and I'll do it. Shall I have Elliot murdered? I can do it, you know."

Elizabeth laughed and pushed her away, gently but firmly. "Not necessary. Thanks anyway." She tilted her head to look at DeDe. "You could not have Elliot murdered."

"Oh good heavens," DeDe said, "for enough money you can have anything done."

"I don't want him murdered."

"It was just an idea. I mean, think of the interesting people you'd meet. You know, some one who would kill your husband and make it look like an accident for the cost of, oh, a tummy tuck."

Elizabeth shook her head and began to roll her eyes back in disbelief, but suddenly an idea came to her. DeDe saw the expression on her face and said, "Giving it a second thought? I'll just make a few calls—"

Elizabeth called out, "NO! I mean yes you gave me an idea."

"But I can't get him accidentally run

over by a taxi or shoved in front of a subway?"

"Elliot doesn't take subways. That isn't the idea." Elizabeth smiled. "The idea was the one about with enough money you can have anything done."

"Absolutely," DeDe said.

"I've enough money to do what I want."

"You've plenty."

Elizabeth pulled back her covers and began to pace the room. "I want to go back to Colorado, back to my home. I can hire someone to stay with me. I don't have to stay here."

"Yes, you can. But why would you want to go to that place when you can be here?"

"I have the new room which is right next to the bathroom, the kitchen is maybe ten steps away . . ."

DeDe's doctor came into the room. He was a nice-looking man and had been very pleasant and helpful. But one look at his face and even the formidable DeDe edged her way out of the room without being asked to go. She closed the door quietly.

"Elizabeth, get into bed, please," he remarked. Although the words were polite, the meaning was do it or else.

Elizabeth was settled and about to say something when the doctor held up his hand to stop her. "Before you say one word, let me say what I came in to say." He sat on the extreme edge of the bed. "I talked to your doctor in Vail. She told me she had seen you once, you refused the procedures she recommended for a woman of your age having a baby . . ."

Elizabeth opened her mouth to speak, but he held up his hand again. "You are exhibiting some signs that I am very worried about. For instance, you were walking around the room. I stood at the door and saw you for quite some time. I told you bed rest. If you don't stay in bed except for bathroom and shower and dressing, I will make it complete bed rest and that means you will not get out of this bed for any reason *whatsoever.* Am I making myself clear about what bed rest means?"

Elizabeth nodded.

"If you intend to have this baby—"

Elizabeth interrupted this time. "Everyone says that to me."

"It could be because you do not act as if you care. You are about five months pregnant, you are showing, you aren't in comfortable clothing that doesn't restrict. You are ignoring advice from your physicians, you were up for well over forty-eight hours and then flew here without thinking of your health. You are showing no interest in the development of this child and your own health."

"That isn't true," Elizabeth said.

"Isn't it?"

"I can't help but think of this baby. It's there, isn't it? Moving, making me move because it isn't comfortable. It's there. How can I ignore it? If I hadn't wanted to keep it, I'd have aborted it. Abortion *is* still legal." Elizabeth's attitude was defensive and angry.

"Elizabeth, you aren't an ignorant woman unaware of the many options available to a pregnant woman today, nor are you poor and unable to get medical help and guidance, nor are you a combination of the two." He stood then and picked up her chart. "I'm putting you on two weeks of *complete* bed rest."

Elizabeth glared at him. "I am also not ignorant enough to know that I don't have to stay here."

He quit writing and put the chart back at the foot of the bed. "No, you don't, but you will be jeopardizing yourself and your unborn child if you try to leave." He went to the door and opened it, DeDe nearly fell into the room. He waited until De had gained her composure. "I'm sure your attorney can tell you that I can get a court order forcing you to take care of yourself, but why would that be necessary?" He softened his voice and his body seemed to melt, and he slumped as if the weight of the world was on his shoulders. "Why do you want to learn this lesson the hard way?"

*Grandpa sat still in his rocking chair and thought a long time before he spoke. "Why do you want to learn each lesson the hard way?"*

*"Grandpa!" sixteen-year-old Elizabeth whined.*

*"Your grandmother and I have only a few*

*rules, nothing complicated about them. Tell us where you are, be where you say you'll be, and come home when you say you'll be home. When you have the truck and you don't come back when you say you will, I have to walk to find you."*

*"You don't have to go looking for me. You embarrassed me to death when you showed up at Barry's place."*

*"I do have to look for you."*

*"Oh, you do not!" Elizabeth whined again. "You just want to rule my life! You just keep trying to make up for the way you treated my mother."*

*Alice Templeton gasped. "Lissy! We did nothing wrong to your mother!"*

*"You made her run away, didn't you! She hated it here and ran away!" Elizabeth was crying.*

*Grandpa began to rock. He thought again before he spoke; Elizabeth sobbing dramatically in the background. Alice clicking her knitting needles.*

*"I'm too old to go walking around at three in the morning to find out why you aren't home. Until you can keep your word and think of your safety and mine, you will not have use of the truck."*

*Elizabeth let her jaw drop in exaggerated shock. "How long?"*

*"Until the lesson is learned."*

"I don't seem to have learned," Elizabeth said.

"Learned what?" De asked. She'd been talking of lunch choices and Elizabeth was nodding and suddenly, this.

"What?" Elizabeth said. "I didn't hear you."

"I said *what.* Never mind, dear." De patted Elizabeth's hand. "Just tell me what you want."

*My grandmother and grandfather back.* Elizabeth smiled and said, "I'd like some clothes. I appreciate your nightgown, but I'd really be more comfortable in a sleep shirt or a long T-shirt. I brought one in my bag."

De clapped her hands and smiled a megawatt smile. "I know just what I'll do. I'll plan a fashion show to be held right here in your room. Beautiful clothes, fantastic clothes!"

She went on and describing the fashions. "I just wanted a T-shirt," Elizabeth said.

"You have a lot to learn, dear. Just a T-shirt! Well, all right, while you're in bed just a T-shirt, but *what* a T-shirt!" DeDe picked up her purse and coat. I'm so excited! Oh, this will be marvelous, splendiferous!" De created so much movement just putting on her coat, the room seemed filled with her. Quite out of character for De, she stood quietly for a moment and said in a small voice, "We all just need to be needed." Then she jumped into her old character like a child playing hopscotch and with exaggerated gestures kissed the air goodbye.

The room was quiet, and Elizabeth felt alone after DeDe left. She sighed, picked up a newspaper section from the bedside stand, read the same sentence three times, and put it down.

"I'm sorry, Grandpa," she said and put her head into her hands. "I didn't learn anything."

She heard a phone ringing in another room, and it made her wonder why Chris hadn't phoned. Then she remembered that the desk held all her phone calls.

She saw her address book across the room. She pushed back the covers and began to climb out of bed.

*You don't learn anything.*

Elizabeth heard her grandpa's voice. Or was it her own conscience? She pulled the covers up and buzzed the nurses' desk. After the aide left she looked up the number at the hospital in Vail and placed a call to Chris. He wasn't in, and she left another message. Then she slammed down the phone, picked up the TV remote and began to flip channels.

Chris had the clerks at the bookstore in Vail running from counter to aisle like well-trained retrievers.

"Not enough!" he said. "She needs more books. More of the ones on newborns and the one about breast-feeding . . . she really needs some on nutrition and maybe that one on baby names. No, give me all the baby name books and one of those books where you keep a history of the baby!"

He bought nearly every book on the child care shelf and then he bought four books from the business section and a few of the latest novels. He included a picture book of the Rockies. He had them packed in a shipping box and took them out to his car. In a few hours he was on his way to New York.

The hospital hadn't allowed him to talk to Elizabeth, hadn't even admitted she was there. Harriet arranged for Chris to talk with the doctor there. After hearing what had happened that day, Chris made arrangements to take off for a few days. Now he was on his way to Denver for the flight to New York.

"If Mohammed can't go to the mountains, the mountains must come to Mohammed," he said to himself like a mantra. He fell asleep on the long flight, dreaming of harem women, all with eyes and faces and bodies like Elizabeth Templeton Avery March.

# Eight

Early the next morning Elizabeth heard steps and the door to her room being shut. She thought it was the morning nurse come to take her temperature and blood pressure. She opened one eye and saw a body in blue jeans and a dress shirt holding a box on one hip with one hand and books held up fanned out to cover the face.

"I think you have the wrong room," she mumbled in a sleepy voice.

"I don't think so."

"Christian!" She held out her arms.

He dropped the books on the foot of the bed and sat down on the edge. He pulled her close to him, crushed her to him. He kissed the top of her head, her eyes and nose and cheeks. He crushed her to him again.

"God, I've missed you," he said.

"How did you get in?"

"I sneaked in."

Elizabeth laughed.

"Laugh some more." She sat back to see his face "You don't laugh nearly enough."

He started to pull away, to get the books, but she pulled him down. "Climb in," she whispered. "They'll never find you here."

"It's okay." He got up. "I flashed my 'I'm a doctor' badge, and here I am."

"I'm so glad." She looked as if she would cry.

"You don't look glad," he said. "But, I have brought you some presents. See?" He held up the first book, the picture book of the Rockies.

"It's beautiful. Thank you." She put it down without looking at it.

Chris began to pull out books, one after the other, piling them on top of her. Soon the bed was covered with books. Elizabeth was stunned. Not only with the amount of the books, at least fifty of them in all sizes and shapes, but with the generosity of it, the giving and care of it.

Chris shoved some books over, and a few clattered to the floor. He sat down and picked up a baby naming book. "Have you thought of a name?" he asked. Elizabeth shook her head. "Well, let's see here. Boy? Girl?"

"Girl," she said. He looked at her and smiled.

"You're sure?"

"Girl," she said again and nodded emphatically.

*All right!* he thought. *She's personalized it. This won't be so hard after all.*

"Annette? Ah, yes! Annette. Mickey Mouse Club, girl of my dreams, still a girl to dream of, beautiful, talented, built."

Elizabeth shook her head no.

"Arabella?"

"No."

"Belinda?"

"No."

"Grace, Gwendolyn, Lucy, Kathleen?"

"All of those names for one little baby? It needs a small name for a small thing."

Chris stood up from the bed. "Oh, no! She needs a big name for all the magnificent things she will do, a name that will show the world she is someone to contend with. Victoria, Eugenia, Catherine . . . the great!"

Elizabeth laughed again. "I'm so glad you're here," she said. "How did you get away?"

"If you remember I *can* get away for a few days occasionally." He raised his eyebrows at her in an exaggerated leer.

"I remember. Nothing has been right since then." All the humor was gone. She was as if he'd never made her laugh at all.

He sat down again on the edge of the bed and gathered her into his arms, books sliding to the floor in an avalanche.

She allowed the embrace, limp at first, not participating, just taking the strength. She slowly began to let her arms crawl around his neck, drawing his head down as she lay back in the hospital bed. He lay across her, his head nestled on her swollen breasts. They stayed that way until the nurse arrived.

"I think I'll get some breakfast," Chris said. Elizabeth was reluctant to let go of him, but he whispered, "I'll be back."

The nurse, a plump red-cheeked girl who looked as if she had just come in from the farm, giggled and said, "I just love it when the daddies come to visit! I hope my husband will be as sweet."

Elizabeth acknowledged the words with a smile, but didn't correct her. She did wonder if this nurse knew she wasn't supposed to have any visitors except De and Harry. But Chris was magic. She let the nurse bathe her and kept quiet, complaining as little as she could. Chris was here. He was here. That was what mattered.

Chris ate sparingly . . . for him. If possible, this hospital's food was worse than his own hospital's. In fact, it made his hospital food seem gourmet. He only ate three cinnamon rolls, two glasses of sour orange juice, and one glass of milk.

He waited the amount of time he thought it would take for all the morning duties. In the elevator he was crunched in behind a woman with flaming red hair, three women with racks of clothing, a man with a ponytail, and two giddy housekeepers chattering and giggling in some tropical language that sounded like music. He missed the mountains already.

He seemed to be following the redhead and her entourage. All of them arrived at the same door, and all of them tried to open it and go through. The redhead took charge. She went through first. She held open the door for the man with the ponytail, the three women with clothing racks, and slammed the door in Chris's face. He stood looking nonplussed a moment, then opened the door and wound his way through to Elizabeth's side.

"Who do you think you are?" De said.

Chris put on his best bedside manner and opened his mouth to tell her, but Elizabeth stopped him.

"This is Dr. Christian Hanford. My doctor in Vail."

Chris said, "I was going to say that."

Elizabeth patted his hand and said, "Of course you were."

"Oh my God, they get younger all the

time," De moaned. "A long way to come for a bedside visit."

"He's my friend," Elizabeth said. She blushed.

"Right," De sounded skeptical. "Do you want to watch the fashion show?" She asked in a tone that said she doubted it.

"I wouldn't miss it for the world," Chris said. He settled down on the bed, putting his cowboy boots up on the lightweight spread. "Hey, let's get this show on the road, strut your stuff, show your colors, get a move on." He folded his arms across his chest and nodded to the first rack.

Elizabeth giggled, stifled it, and said, "Please, De."

De looked put-out, but then she waved a hand dramatically. The woman at the first rack pulled a shirt from the hanger and laid it across the foot of the bed. The man with the ponytail began to describe the beaded T-shirt.

"This is called 'Hollywood.' Notice the beading to spell out Hollywood like the famous sign we all know and love. I was inspired by—"

Chris interrupted, "The Hollywood sign we all know and love."

The man with the ponytail pursed his lips and said, "Well, yes. Now the next one I call 'Flamingo.' " Another woman displayed a hot pink T-shirt with satin appliqués in shades of teal, turquoise, and orange in the shape of a palm tree. "I was inspired by—"

Chris interrupted again. "A flaming palm tree?" Elizabeth began to giggle.

"De, I won't go on if he keeps interrupting." The man with the ponytail went to the window and turned his back on the group.

"Emilio, dear!" De cried theatrically. Then in more New York street tones, she turned to Elizabeth and said, "Curb your animal."

Elizabeth lost all control over her giggles. She began to laugh and laugh, when she thought she could get in control she would say, "I'm sorry." But then she would begin to laugh harder. Tears were forming.

Emilio's feelings were hurt. He snapped his fingers, and the women pulled the racks out the door. De was right behind them, begging them to come back. Chris was laughing at Elizabeth's laughing.

When they were alone, Chris finally stopped laughing. Elizabeth, however, had reached the point where she could not stop. In seconds the laughter was hysterical. She sobbed. De came in and stood by helplessly as Elizabeth cried. She watched as Chris held Elizabeth and let her cry. It was over in a few minutes. "I guess I needed that," Elizabeth said as she dried her eyes.

"I'm sorry, dear," De said. "I was only trying to help."

"You did help," Chris said. "You helped her get rid of some held-in emotions. She was like a pot about to boil over."

"Does he always talk in clichés?" De asked.

"Day in and day out," Chris and Elizabeth said in unison. Then they both laughed.

DeDe looked at the two of them, nodded her head and smiled. "I'll get you some ordinary T-shirts if you like."

"Just don't get anything with writing

on it. Plain." Elizabeth was adamant. "No, 'BABY IN TOW' or anything else."

"I understand." De came to the bedside and kissed Elizabeth's cheek. "Once you are out of here, though, I'm taking you on a shopping binge, and you are going to like it." She shook Chris's hand, the one she could pry from around Elizabeth's shoulder. "You'd better pick up those books, young man, or you will be setting broken bones and cracked heads from people falling. Oh, and it's been a pleasure." De waved with her usual flourish and left.

Chris began immediately to pick up the books from the floor. He put them on the bed beside Elizabeth and on the bedside table. Elizabeth was far more interested in watching him pick them up, the love and hope flaming from her eyes like a beacon on a dark night. When Chris stayed out of sight for a while, she picked up a book and looked at its title, then another and another. The look on her face changed. She looked at each book then, everything from books on pregnancy to books on toddlers, books on breast-feeding to books on child development.

When Chris had rounded all the books up and began to put them in the box again, Elizabeth's demeanor was completely different. Her face was pale, set; her eyes showing not love, not hate or anger, something he couldn't read.

"I thought you'd like to read while you are here," he said.

"Thank you."

He looked at her intently, questions on his face, but no words. She had swung once again through the whole spectrum of emotions.

"I realize this is a hard time," he said.

"No," she insisted. "This isn't hard."

"All right." Chris looked about the room as if he expected to find properly worded cue cards. He found nothing to help. The uncomfortable chair at the bedside began to look more inviting than the edge of Elizabeth's bed. He sat down and stretched his full length, his cowboy boots making a noise on the tile floor. Elizabeth didn't react to the sound. Her demeanor remained stiff and cold. "It's been a long day," he said, and stretched again.

"Perhaps you should go to your hotel."

He sat for a moment, looking at the toes of his boots. Then he stood up and kissed her cheek, began to say something, and changed his mind. He left without another word.

Elizabeth didn't have time to think before a tall woman in an elegant suit covered with a white hospital jacket came in. "My name is Barbara Ennis. You're Elizabeth March."

Elizabeth nodded but offered nothing else.

"I'm a psychologist."

Elizabeth sighed.

Barbara picked up a book from the top of the box. It was a baby memory book. "Oh, how much fun! You know I kept one of these faithfully for my first child. Every little thing, every smile, every move. Sometimes I even drew little pictures of what she did!"

Elizabeth looked at the woman and said, "That's nice."

"By my third child I didn't even buy one myself. Poor thing, he is probably feeling very neglected." She laughed, a warm infectious chuckle. "Come to think of it, I don't think he even knows he doesn't have a baby book. All that guilt for nothing."

"What do you want?" The Wicked Witch was speaking, all defenses in place, attack imminent.

Barbara placed the book back in the box and looked Elizabeth straight on. "I'm here because people are concerned about you."

"So I've been told."

"I'm here because people who care about you want to help you."

"I don't need your help."

"Then I don't have to stay," Barbara said easily. "But I do want to tell you something."

"Do you have to?"

"Yes, or I wouldn't bother. Two years ago you saved my life."

"Oh, please!" Elizabeth's skepticism was palpable.

"It does sound farfetched. But you literally did. An article about you did, so I guess that makes if figuratively." Elizabeth folded her arms across her chest and looked at the ceiling.

Barbara went on, "I just lost my husband and the insurance and pension money was substantial. The phone calls from sales people were even more substantial. The day of the funeral I must have gotten ten calls from men and women who said they'd be glad to help me with Roger's money. Two of them even told me they were his brokers and they'd handle everything."

Elizabeth sighed again.

"I cleared up the house after the . . . What do you call it after a man dies and everyone comes to your house with food and easy phrases? A wake? Do they still call them wakes?"

"I've no idea," Elizabeth said. She still did not look at the woman so she couldn't see the quick smile on her face.

"Well, anyway, I'd just cleared the house, and I didn't want to think of anything, but a magazine cover caught my eye. I saw the title of your article on the cover, and it was as if you spoke to me. How To Be A Widow. Very hard title, I remember my friends saying that before Roger died. Such a cruel title."

"I meant it to be shocking," Elizabeth said. "Women know so little about what will happen to them, about their money, about their own lives." She was speaking with emotion now.

"I know I didn't. For instance, those two brokers. In the article, you warned me about them. The brokers who search the obituaries and call the grieving family and take over before anyone knows what is going on."

Elizabeth sat up a bit in bed. "I really got flack for that from other brokers."

"Well, I'm glad you wrote it and so many other things, about waiting and not giving anyone control of your money."

Elizabeth looked at her now. "I can't imagine you would give anyone control of your money."

"I would have then," Barbara said. "Then I would have done anything but face what was really going on. But you came into my home in that article just when I needed you, and every word was a blessing and a warning. I carried that magazine with me everywhere. I'd read it in the bath and I'd read it in bed, and I'd take it with me to work . . . when I finally went back to work. Last year I invested in a few of the things you recommended in that article, things that didn't rely on the stock market and secure things. I will never be able to thank you enough for it. You saved me. Not just financially, you did that, but in other ways. That article became my shield against a world changing too fast for me, a situation that I felt I had no control over. Thank you."

Elizabeth was sitting up and leaning forward a bit. Barbara's infectious eagerness and open emotions gave Elizabeth a sense that here was a woman like herself. "You're welcome," she said in real gratitude. "Sometimes, control . . ."

"Yes," Barbara said quietly, "sometimes things get out of our control."

Barbara stayed for over two hours.

# Nine

Elizabeth ate lunch alone in her room. She wasn't hungry, but she ate every bite. The aide took her tray, then came back in for the afternoon routine of temperature and blood pressure. This aide wasn't talkative, and Elizabeth was glad.

She only wanted to talk to Chris, and she didn't have any idea how to reach him.

Elizabeth and Barbara had talked a long time. Elizabeth didn't get any solutions to her problems, but she did, at least, get them expressed: loss of control of her life, not knowing what the next moment would bring, wildly fluctuating emotions. Nothing, absolutely nothing, was the same.

"Would you want it static?" Barbara asked.

"No. But I didn't request a roller coaster either. If it's going to be a roller coaster then I'd like to be the one running the ride, not the one helpless in the car!"

"You feel helpless?"

"Helpless and useless and out of control!"

"You've had great changes happen to you quickly, and you feel they were done to you rather than you choosing them."

"Exactly." Elizabeth felt someone finally understood her. "I have tried to stop reacting and make things go another direction, but it isn't working out that way. I seem to lose more control than before."

"The tighter you hold on the more it escapes."

"Exactly."

Elizabeth felt that Barbara understood. Chris hadn't understood; DeDe thought she could buy her way out of anything. And Elliot . . . What did Elliot think? Why did it matter what Elliot thought?

Elizabeth turned on the television set.

It was Oprah. Elizabeth had heard of the show but never seen it. Love at first sight.

She was soon on the phone calling De to discuss the program. When she was through, it was dinnertime.

How had the day gone by so fast? What had she done? What had she accomplished? She could hear Barbara's voice, "You feel like you had to accomplish something?"

Elizabeth ate and settled back with the book of pictures from Chris.

She'd accomplished one day in the hospital on full bed rest. *Good heavens, girl,* she admonished herself, *what more do you want?*

She slammed the book shut and said out loud, "Control!"

Television proved to be a narcotic to Elizabeth. It didn't put her to sleep, it made her want more. She had never had time to watch TV. Growing up she had only seen it if she went to town and stayed at a friend's house. The remote control was sheer pleasure. Complete control. Flip, flip, flip, flip. Don't like the guy's tie, flip; don't like the woman's voice, flip; don't understand Spanish, flip; country music, flip; rock and roll, flip; flip, flip. Total control and she didn't have to get out of bed.

"I like it," she said aloud. "This I like."

Jay Leno, David Letterman, Arsenio, late night movies, old TV, comedies she had never seen, PBS and English accents. Elizabeth would have watched it all night long if the night nurse had not come in and insisted she turn it off.

She woke early. She didn't even go to the bathroom. On went the television set. "Today," "Good Morning America," news in Spanish, country music, rock and roll, wrestling, an old movie, "I Love Lucy," "Gilligan's Island." Another news show, a program on business. She stopped at the program on business. A distinguished man she recognized was hosting. He was asking questions of a panel of people the camera didn't show.

"It happens more and more frequently. I don't think this is in the league of Michael Milken . . . nothing is even close to that, but it is still shocking. Don't you agree?"

Elizabeth sat up straighter in her bed and turned up the audio. She recognized the voice before the picture of the woman came on. Doris DesBarres. Doris, who hated Elizabeth March. Doris who came up with the nickname Wicked Witch, only she hadn't said "witch."

"No, I don't agree." Doris came into view. "Elizabeth March and her husband, well, nothing has been proven, it is only rumor. I don't think it is shocking when it is still only rumor."

*Doris DesBarres standing up for me?* Elizabeth rubbed her eyes and turned the volume up. *Can't be.*

"It's such a horrible thing to think of. Although I'm sure at one point or another all of us have wondered how she made such choices, such consistent winners. After all, she beat everyone. She would make a string of predictions, for lack of a better word, about some company making a profit or folding or. . . . Well, after all, how did she do it?"

*That's more like it,* Elizabeth thought. *Keep shoveling dirt, Doris.*

One of the men on the panel laughed and reminded everyone that Doris had come up with the Wicked Witch nickname.

Doris shook her head in mock dismay and said, "Who knew the name would stick or be so prophetic." She then quickly added, "Of course, if it's true." Her tone clearly implied that wardens were preparing a cell at the nearest Federal prison for Elizabeth.

Elizabeth reached for the phone and called Harry.

De answered. "Television! At this hour! God!" She gave the phone to Harry. He listened and turned on the bedroom set.

They watched together; Elizabeth silently in her hospital bed; Harry, barefooted and in pajama pants, on his side of the bed in his penthouse while De complained in the background.

When the short segment was over, although no one came out and said Elizabeth had done anything wrong, the impression was indelibly stamped. Elizabeth March, once considered a top expert and impeccably honest, was a crook.

"What am I going to do, Harry?"

"You are going to do nothing," he answered. "I'll handle this."

"I can't just let this go. She . . . *they* as much as said I am guilty."

"But they didn't." Harry told her to stay calm, he'd call or stop by later.

"Stay calm?" Elizabeth said. "Fat chance."

About noon, Chris peeked around the door as if he were afraid Elizabeth would throw something at him if she had the target. He found her absorbed by the television set.

"Look at this!" She pointed with the remote control to the street scene in vivid color. "There is this elephant thing and a big yellow bird and some real people, and they sing and count. Oh! The Count! He goes, 'I like a number I can hold in one hand.' It's so neat! I love this show! What is it?"

Chris raised an eyebrow as he answered. " 'Sesame Street.' You don't know 'Sesame Street'?"

Elizabeth looked at him like *he* was the

uninformed one. "Why on earth would I have ever watched 'Sesame Street'? "

Chris shrugged and shook his head. "I thought everybody knew 'Sesame Street.' "

"We didn't have TV. Was this around when I was a kid?"

"In the sixties," he said and gingerly sat on the edge of the bed.

"Oh, well, in the sixties I was going in to Denver every Friday and spending the night with my tutor. I'd watch 'Route 66' and some other show, I think it was called 'Hong Kong.' "

"I remember 'Route 66,' " Chris said. "I wanted that Corvette."

"I wanted George Maharis."

"Who?"

"The dark-haired one."

Chris shrugged again.

"I loved the guy from the other show, too. Rod Taylor! Whatever happened to them? Do they have their own series now?"

"I don't watch much TV now, except football occasionally."

DeDe and Harry came in. De leaned over Chris and planted a kiss on Elizabeth's cheek, but Elizabeth didn't notice;

she was too absorbed in the singing on the screen.

"Hello!" De chirped.

"What ever happened to George Maharis and Rod Taylor?" Elizabeth said.

De looked at Harry then hopefully at Chris. When no response came from either one, she was ready to offer an answer. Elizabeth, however, was off on another tangent, another channel flipped to by remote control. "How do you keep up?" De said to Chris.

"I'm just barely hanging on here by my teeth," he confessed.

Elizabeth cried out, "I know the answer or the question! The question is 'What is the European Group?' "

"Wrong, dear," De said.

"Oh." Disappointed, Elizabeth flipped the channels again.

Harry made a face at De, who then pulled at Chris's arm and said, "You want a cup of coffee, don't you? And whether or not you want one, I do. So come along."

Chris looked at Elizabeth to save him, but she was absorbed in another program: a row of men dressed in what appeared to be snakeskins. Then Chris saw they were all tattooed.

When they had left, Harry took the remote control from Elizabeth's hand and turned off the TV.

"I feel like I just dropped in from an alien planet," she said. "I had no idea what I was missing."

"You will have weeks to catch up. But we need to talk now."

"I didn't authorize or know about the trades."

"You can't tell me that you, a noted expert in finance and financial planning, had no idea what was going on when tax time rolled around. Surely you looked at the returns. Surely you studied the amounts and . . ."

Elizabeth jumped in. "I trusted him," she hissed. "I trusted my husband and signed everything."

"Elizabeth, you wrote articles that appeared in national magazines, women's magazines about that very thing, the trusting wife being lied to by her husband."

"I was my own worst client, Harry."

Elizabeth said it sarcastically, but the underlying betrayal was still there.

"I'm sorry if you *were* one of those trusting wives. If you did anything else in life but what you do, we could possibly, just possibly, get you out of this all together. But not you. Not the Wicked Witch of Wall Street."

"Well, thank you very much." Elizabeth didn't sound very thankful.

Harry sat in silence. Elizabeth felt his eyes on her. Although she was trying not to look at him, she finally did.

"What do you advise?"

"A public statement of the truth."

"What truth?"

Harry sat down and rubbed his hand over his brow as if he had a mighty headache. "What do you mean, 'What truth?' There is only one truth."

"Oh, come on, Harry, you're a lawyer. You know there is always more than one truth."

Harry signed. He leaned back in the chair and studied the ceiling.

"Elliot called and said he wanted me to represent him, because he's your husband."

"You said you wouldn't?"

"I said I was your attorney."

"I won't get him out of this," Elizabeth said. "When I left Colorado, I thought I would. But now I'm determined to clear my name first."

Harry sat up straight. "You can't get yourself out of this."

Elizabeth crumpled then. She curled up into a ball and turned her back on Harry. Harry wanted to reach out and pat her or hug her, but it wasn't in his carefully designed notion of a high-priced lawyer. He cleared his throat, and said, "We will call the SEC before they call us. We will tell them the truth. You will probably be lucky to pay fines, and never work in the field again."

From her rolled-up position, Elizabeth said, "And Elliot?"

"I'd say prison and fines."

"I won't pay his fines." Elizabeth sat up then and faced Harry. "I absolutely won't pay his fines."

"You don't have to."

"I know. I just want you to remind me when he comes begging."

Chris and De came back arm in arm.

They had charmed each other and behaved like two best friends.

"We've got to be going," De said and reluctantly let go of Chris's arm. "You dear boy, thank you so much."

"My pleasure," Chris said, and bowed.

De turned to Elizabeth and said, "Oh, dear, he'd be perfect if he weren't so trite."

Everyone was taken back for a moment.

"De!" Harry said, exasperated by his wife.

"Oh hush up!" De said. "We understand each other, don't we?"

"We do." Chris nodded in agreement. "We're two sides of the same coin."

"There he goes again! Isn't he cute?" De exclaimed.

"I'm the apple of her eye," Chris said. De hugged him and pinched his cheek. "She thinks I'm a babe in the woods when it comes to you."

Elizabeth joined in with, "I'm leading you down the rosy path?"

"Bet your boots," Chris observed.

"Enough!" Harry threw up his hands and then took his wife by the elbow and steered her out. They both waved goodbye.

Chris sat down in the chair and laughed. "She's something else."

Elizabeth agreed. "You really can't stop, can you?"

"A bad habit. But not one that hurts me or anyone else." He sounded a bit put-out.

"It's a lovely habit."

"Men aren't lovely." He was defensive and just a bit confused. "I thought after talking with Harry you'd be in a bad mood."

Elizabeth held her arms out to him. "I have been awful. But, come here. I won't bite."

"Cliché." But he stood up and went to her.

"Cut it out."

"Cliché," he said.

"A dose of your own medicine." She kissed his chin.

"Cliché."

She began to kiss his eyes and his nose and his temples and his lips.

Suddenly he was kissing her with all the pent-up passion he felt. Every fiber of his body went into that kiss. When they broke for a breath, Elizabeth stared at him with her eyes wide. "Go for it," she urged.

Chris held her again and kissed her softly. "Cliché and passé," he whispered before kissing her again. "Besides, I'm wearing cowboy boots, not tennis shoes."

"Shut up and kiss me," Elizabeth said.

# Ten

Chris held her and kissed her. Elizabeth lapped it up like a kitten with cream. She purred with delight, rubbing herself against him, kneading his shoulders and arms. She was so different from the last time he'd been here. Chris was stunned, but not stupid. He kept kissing.

Elizabeth spoke first. "I'm so glad to see you."

"Good to be seen."

Elizabeth laughed. "Say some more!"

"More what?"

She shook her head. "Never mind." Then she kissed him again. Over his shoulder, she saw the TV set, and she groped for the control and flipped the channels. "Look! Cartoons!"

Chris turned to see "Tom and Jerry"

silently doing their best to destroy the other. He chuckled and turned back to Elizabeth, who was mesmerized. He watched her, fascinated, as she watched the cartoons, fascinated. He turned again to watch and saw the same thing, the same cartoon doing the same thing.

A commercial came on and Elizabeth was equally mesmerized by the people cooking cake in a microwave. "I've used that," she said.

"Can't be as good as your home baked cake from the old stove," he said. "I loved the gingerbread and coffee cake you made." She ignored him for the new cartoon, a rooster with a little chick. She laughed and flipped channels. Chris got off the bed and sat in the chair. She made no motion to stop him. He sat through six more commercials and one more cartoon before he stood and grabbed the controller from her hands and turned off the set.

"Yoo-hoo! I'm here!" he said and stood at the end of her bed with his arms held out. "Ta-da! I'd do tricks but I don't know any." Then he shrugged and put his arms down at his side. He shook his head helplessly. "What is going on?"

"Nothing," Elizabeth said innocently. "I've never really watched TV, that's all. Really, that's all." She didn't look at him, then she scrunched down into the sheets and pulled her knees up.

"Don't pout."

"I don't pout."

"I don't understand what is going on. I come here; you seem glad to see me. Then you don't; then you do; then you don't!" He walked around to the side of the bed and took her hand from under the covers. "I don't understand and I want to. I really want to know what is going on in that beautiful, brilliant mind of yours."

"Flattery will get you nowhere," she said from her scrunched position. She sat up straighter. "Thank you."

"Thank you?" he asked. "For what?"

"For the books."

"Did you look at them?" He bent over and picked up one on nutrition and pregnancy from the box on the floor.

"Of course." She sounded tense.

"And didn't you wonder why I brought them?"

"Of course."

"But you didn't ask me." He sat down on the edge of her bed again.

She shook her head. "I can figure things out for myself."

"And what did you figure out about the books?"

"I'm not playing twenty questions with you!" She turned her back to him.

"Here we go again!" He threw his hands up and shook his head. "Elizabeth, talk to me. Ask me questions. Tell me something! Say something I can get a grip on."

Elizabeth turned over and stared at him, anger flaring from her eyes. "You brought me those books because you think I'm an idiot!"

"Oh." He considered what she said. Then he spoke quietly but firmly. "I brought you the books because I knew you were in bed for weeks. And because you are a brilliantly educated woman, I thought that books on babies and pregnancy and all that would be the perfect way for you to learn. After all, you do research all the time."

"Research," she repeated and sat up more.

"Research."

"Why didn't you tell me?"

"You never asked."

*George Templeton sat at Murlow's Point and smoked the pipe he only relished outdoors. The smoke swirled above him like a mist above a lake. Elizabeth could smell the aroma of cherry and tobacco. It was one of the things she always associated with her grandfather. Although the setting was beautiful and calm, not a ripple on the lake, not a wisp of a breeze, the moment was anything but calm.*

*"Do you think you could explain yourself?" he had asked. Elizabeth sat silently. No, she could not explain herself. She only knew she did not want her grandmother and grandfather to come to school for the awards banquet.*

*"I think we deserve at least a reason. Just screaming at your grandmother and me that you don't want us there, after we'd dressed. That isn't enough."*

*After they'd dressed! Elizabeth thought to herself. Her grandfather in his least tattered railroad coveralls and the sack-shaped jacket he called his "town clothes." Her grandmother in that faded dress that had to be from the forties, and those earrings with the feathers! And that hat! That ridiculous hat with the cherries and the veil! She thought all of this, but she could not say it.*

*"Since you don't want us there, we won't go. But if your feelings are this strong, you'd better be able to speak them out. Say them with conviction. If they are such as you want no one to know, then you'd best keep quiet." He sucked on his pipe and opened his mouth to speak again, but thought a moment and then didn't. The silence became like a heavy coat on a warm day.*

*"I . . . feel . . . strongly," Elizabeth said in a faltering voice. "I feel very strongly," she said with more strength. Then it became like a train downhill. "I am so tired of being poor!"*

*Grandpa took his pipe out of his mouth and tapped it on the rock he sat on. He pulled his tobacco pouch from his hip pocket and went through the elaborate gestures of re-filling his pipe. When he was tamping the fresh tobacco, Elizabeth began again. "They have teased me since day one. Every day of my life in school. Every year for eleven years. I go to school and someone says, 'Did you take a bath today?' They all know we don't have plumbing. Someone says, 'Whose clothes do you suppose she's wearing today? Did you donate that skirt to the church last week?' They tease me constantly about the truck, the clothes, our plumbing!"*

*"Lissy," he said quietly.*

*"No, don't stop me! You wanted to know! I'll tell you! I don't care!"*

*"I can tell," he said.*

*"No! You can't! I went to Denver for the tutoring for all those years just for this night! I got the scholarship to Wharton! I won! I did it! You didn't do it! I did it! To get out of here!"*

*Grandpa looked at her then, his eyebrows knit across his brow like a caterpillar dancing. "How did you do it?" he said in perfect sarcasm. "All those years, how did you manage?"*

*"It wasn't easy!"*

*He stood with the difficulty old age granted him. He tapped his pipe out on the tree beside Elizabeth, the ashes flying onto her new dress.*

*"Where did the money come from for your tutor? And the gas for the weekly trip to Denver? Where did the money come from for that dress?"*

*"Okay, so I didn't have to work at a job." Elizabeth swiped at the ashes smearing her rose dress to ashy gray on the hem.*

*"No, Elizabeth, that won't do."*

*"You gave me the money." Elizabeth sounded resentful.*

*"I worked for the money. My railroad pension wasn't enough to keep your grandmother and me, let alone a child!"*

*"It isn't my fault I was here!" Elizabeth cried out.*

*"Fault never entered into our thoughts when I went out and cut fence posts and rails. Never thought a thing about who's to blame when I went door to door selling firewood."*

*"Oh, and didn't I hear about that the next day when you'd been to one of my friend's houses. 'Elizabeth, your crazy old coot was at our door! Did you get dinner last night?' " Tears sprung into her eyes and began to fall. "I'm so tired of being poor!"*

*Grandpa turned his back on her and looked at the beautiful scene from the point.*

*Smoke was rising straight up from the chimney of the little cabin, spring flowers were blooming in wild blues and reds and yellows along the sides of the stream. It was heaven on earth to him. Somehow, he wanted Elizabeth to see it that way as well. He turned to her, bent down to touch her hair, but stopped himself. He held his hand a scant inch from her head and caressed her there. He said nothing more.*

*She finally quit crying. She wiped her eyes on her fists like she did when she was a toddler. He never felt so helpless. "We'd better be getting back. Your ride will be coming."*

*Elizabeth stood up and followed him to the truck. He opened the door to the rusty old cab, let her in and shut it carefully behind her. He stood for a moment looking at her. She was uncomfortable under his gaze. Finally she turned to look at him with fight in her eyes and defiance on her face.*

*He pulled a faded red handkerchief from his pocket and gave it to her. Waited until she blew her nose and then he said, "Elizabeth, we are proud of you." Then ignoring her new tears, he walked around to the other side of the truck and got in with great diffi-*

*culty. By the time they were back at the cabin, Elizabeth was through crying.*

*In the big, warm main room, standing by the bookcase filled to overflowing with encyclopedias and collections of great authors, her grandmother looked so small, so tired.*

*Grandmother poured a cup of hot tea for each of them, holding the teakettle handle with her apron. She noted the intimate sign language of people married for fifty years that they were not going. She said, "Well." Then placed the teakettle back on the big black stove. She put a smile on her face and sat down at the table to sip her tea. After a moment she put one finger in the air and said, "Oh! Your gift!" She went up the stairs slowly. The two sitting at the table heard noises of boxes being moved and the trunk lid at the foot of the grandparents' bed being slammed shut. Grandmother began the slow trip back down the steep stairs.*

*Elizabeth looked at her Grandfather, but he shrugged.*

*"It's for you." Grandmother held out an ornate frame, tarnished silver, deeply and floridly engraved with hearts and flowers and cherubs. In it was a picture of a beautiful woman in a graduation cap and gown. The*

*picture was hand tinted and it had faded to a lovely ivory and pale pinks and blues. It looked like a painting, but it was a photograph.*

*"Who is it?" Elizabeth asked.*

*"It's your grandmother."*

*"It's me, really it is," Alice said when she saw the disbelief on Elizabeth's face. "I graduated from college in 1910. I was twenty-one."*

*"Top of her class," George said with great pride in his voice.*

*"I didn't know you went to college," Elizabeth said. "If you went to college then what are you doing–"*

*"What am I doing here?" Alice finished the sentence. Elizabeth had the grace to blush. "I'm here because your grandfather is here."*

*"But you could have done anything!" Elizabeth cried out.*

*"I did do anything!" Alice retorted. "I taught school; I ran a store in Omaha, Nebraska, that carried school supplies; I ran the distribution of a school book and supplies company!"*

*"You never said anything." Elizabeth was shocked.*

*"You never asked."*

*Elizabeth put both her hands to her fore-*

*head and rested her aching head in them. "But if you did all that, why do you live like this?"*

*Again the sign language passed between the two old people. Alice nodded. "I live like this because I love George."*

*"Alice, that isn't all," George said.*

"No, it isn't." She up her thoughts into line before she spoke, "I was fired from the teaching job when I got married. I lost the store in Omaha during the Depression. People used a store a man *ran saying that he, after all, supported a family."*

*"But Grandpa? What was Grandpa doing?"*

*"We'll get to that," George said. He nodded to his wife to continue.*

*"After your mother was born, we moved to Chicago, and I got a job as a secretary in the supply house, and eventually worked my way to management. When your grandfather came out here to work on the railroad tunnels, there was nowhere for me to work. And I was elated!"*

*"I was getting my degree in engineering," George said. "I didn't finish. Your mother was born, it was the Depression. I don't believe your grandmother and I earned more than a thousand dollars for all those four*

*years in Chicago. Here, we made more. I bought this land, built the house."*

*"Then the accident," Alice said quietly.*

*"What accident?" Elizabeth said. "What are you talking about?"*

*"Minor, as accidents go. But your grandfather was pensioned off, let go."*

*"Your mother was your age. She ran off. Pregnant with you. Avery married her, at least she said he did." George looked at Alice and again the shorthand messages that only time can teach.*

*A car horn honked outside and Elizabeth got up and ran out. She came back in seconds and motioned to her grandparents.*

*"Come on! We can ride with Bruce and his dad. Tell me more!"*

*The two older people stood up slowly and pulled on coats, Alice handing Elizabeth a white sweater. "Why didn't you tell me all this?" Elizabeth said as she yanked on the sweater.*

*"You never asked," the two said in unison.*

Elizabeth had sat quietly for so long Chris became concerned. "Lissy?" he said. "Lissy, please come back."

"I'm here," she said, then looked at him with a pleading look. "Chris, I will be forty-five in a few days, and I am still the idiot I was at seventeen."

Chris held her to his chest and kissed her hair. "Lessons unlearned?" he asked.

"Never learned!" she insisted. "I was too blind, too stubborn. Even when it seemed I'd learned, I hadn't."

"Your grandfather would have said you had to learn everything the hard way."

Elizabeth was going to go on to another subject, one she could control. She caught herself. "Tell me about how you knew my grandfather."

Chris began immediately with the warm and happy reminiscence. If he noticed that the simple question had been a big step for Elizabeth, he didn't let on. She listened but she was mentally patting herself on the back. She had asked. A lesson learned.

"I stole his truck!" Chris happily related. "I was thirteen, and I saw this neat old truck at the edge of the National Forest. The engine was running, so I got in and took off. George Templeton found the truck and me not five miles later. I didn't know how to change gears. I was against the sign to the entrance to the National Forest."

"You're lucky you're not dead."

"I wasn't going that fast. I just couldn't see the road turning when I was watching my feet trying to figure out how to change from first gear."

Elizabeth laughed and said, "I mean you're lucky Grampa didn't kill you!"

Chris looked shocked. "Kill me! He taught me to drive!" Elizabeth looked shocked then. "You were afraid of him?" Chris asked.

"No! I just never wanted to do anything to make him mad."

"He was proud of you," Chris said.

"He told you he was proud of me?"

"Every time I saw him. Lissy did this or Lissy that or Lissy won this award or that honor. He was so proud of you."

Elizabeth sank back into her bed again. Chris looked worried. She patted his hand and said, "It's okay. Just a jolt of guilt."

"Because he cared so much?"

"No," Elizabeth said carefully. "Because I never wrote or phoned and told them anything once I left."

"Why not?" Chris asked. He was genuinely surprised.

Elizabeth shrank back into herself, putting her head on the pillow and turned away from him.

Chris took her shoulders and forced her to look at him. "Why on earth did you not talk to those two wonderful people?"

"Because I hated them. I hated all they stood for and I hated that I even came from them! I was so tired of being poor! So tired of being proud! I'm surprised he didn't have you thrown in jail for stealing his truck! I'm surprised you even knew him!" Elizabeth had begun and the rush of emotional words would not stop, not until she said all she wanted to say. "No one ever, ever came to see us, to see them. No one cared whether we lived or died or froze or starved, no one but the kids at school who made it their job to humiliate me on a daily, no, hourly basis!

"I didn't even come to my grandmother's funeral. Nor my grandfather's! I hated them!"

# Eleven

Chris was shocked at what Elizabeth just revealed. He said nothing directly to her, but he shifted his body so he was not touching her as intimately, and he looked away more often.

Elizabeth had learned a great deal about negotiating in her business life, and the eyes alone could tell her when a person was drifting away. Chris was not with her.

She shrugged out of his grip and turned up the TV. She was not going to be the one who was abandoned; she would do the leaving.

A hard thing to do when confined to a bed, but she managed.

Chris moved from the bed to the chair and watched the set with her. After a few minutes he looked at his watch and stood up to kiss her quickly on the cheek.

"I've got to catch my flight back," he said lightly. He wanted to add more, but Elizabeth merely nodded.

She then turned and smiled at him and said, "Thank you."

"I wanted to see you," he said.

"I'm glad," Elizabeth replied. She then turned back to the TV.

Chris studied her for a full minute. Her hair was in a ponytail, and she hadn't a drop of makeup on her face. She was in a hospital gown. He felt as if his heart would fly out of his chest if he didn't touch her. She paid no attention to him at all. It was as if she were in another room. *What am I doing?* he asked himself. *I hardly know this woman yet I fly half a continent to be shut out.*

Without another word or another glance, he left and went directly to the office of his friend, Barbara Ennis.

She was there and in between visits with patients in the hospital.

"What a surprise," she said, not sounding surprised.

Chris sat down on the love seat against

the wall facing the desk. Barbara came to sit beside him. "I'm glad you phoned me about her," she offered.

"Funny, I feel like some kind of rat. I wanted to find her here all better." He said it helplessly, hopefully. "You know, something hurts so you call the doctor and *presto!* It will be all better." He shrugged and leaned forward to put his head in his hands.

"You did the right thing," Barbara said.

"I've known her, known about her, most of my life," Chris began. "She was this wonderful fantasy woman. Perfect in every way. She was a success beyond most people's ideas of success. She was loved by people I loved, she was even better in the flesh." Chris shook his head and sighed. "What is happening?"

"Can't see the forest for the trees?" Barbara said, then when Chris moaned she punched him on the arm and said, "Sorry, I couldn't pass up the chance to cliché world's greatest cliché-monger."

"They are only clichés—" Chris began.

"Because they are so true. And in your case, more so." She stood up and walked to her desk and leaned against it, then she turned to face him and sat on the edge of her perfectly clean desk top. "It is so basic, I am surprised you don't know. Stress."

Chris looked up. "Stress?"

"Nearly every one of the major stress indicators, Chris! Divorce, job change, move from her home, pregnant! And then all the side issues. She remodeled a house. Do you know how often remodeling a house causes divorce, heart attacks, depression? The list goes on. The possible indictment, her husband lying not only to her personally, but on a business level. Money! She could possibly go to jail for what *that* husband did."

"I knew that," Chris said.

"And you suffer from savior syndrome."

"Savior syndrome?" Chris sounded skeptical.

"*I* can heal everything," Barbara said. Then she walked to the love seat and sat down. "You did help her. Now she has to deal with things herself."

"She can do it."

"Yes. She was doing it when she chose

to go back to her childhood. She has to let go of a lot of past."

"She has surprised me. I think I've got a handle on her, that I understand and . . . *POW!* She hits me with something else."

"How did you feel when you met her?" Barbara asked.

"Like I'd been hit by a lightning bolt. Like a fool, like a white knight, like a little boy, especially when I found out who she was."

"You didn't know?"

"Not until it was too late."

"An interesting way to put it," Barbara interjected.

"But it was, you see, too late. I loved her. It really can happen that way, love at first sight. Well, technically it was more like third sight or fifth sight. I knew her when I was just a kid, at church."

He looked at Barbara to see if she followed him, she nodded. "When she opened her eyes in the emergency room, when she spoke, when she came down the stairs, when she had on that silk dress." Chris stopped then and shook his head. "I never felt that way about anyone. Never in my life has anyone had this effect on me."

"Real love at first sight is rare, but it can happen," Barbara assured him.

"I've got to catch my flight." Chris stood and shook Barbara's hand. "Thanks."

"No problem-o," Barbara said with a wicked grin.

"That is just a fad, a passing phrase like 'Go ahead, make my day,' or 'Here come de' judge,' " Chris said with absolute seriousness.

"A true connoisseur." Barbara saluted.

Two hours later Chris was on his way back to Colorado.

Later that afternoon, Barbara met with Elizabeth.

"I never realized how good 'Leave It To Beaver' really was," Elizabeth said. "Of course I only saw it a few times when I was young."

"I had a crush on Tony Dow," Barbara admitted.

"Wally!" Elizabeth squealed like a teenager.

"He was so cute!" Barbara said. "Still is, you know they made a series just recently about Beaver grown up, and Wally and June."

"Really! What channel?" Elizabeth began to flip the channels.

"It was short-lived. But so much fun. Like going home, a family reunion."

Elizabeth stopped flipping channels and looked down into her lap.

"You don't have to answer me if you don't want to, but could you tell me why you went back?" Barbara asked.

"To escape the hurt," Elizabeth said. "Elliot hurt me very much."

"How did you meet Elliot?"

Elizabeth grinned. "It was cute. Really cute."

"Sounds interesting." Barbara encouraged her.

"I just moved to my own apartment. I'd always lived with a roommate. I was truly independent for the first time in my life. My first paycheck burning a hole in my wallet. I needed a bed. A mattress and box springs, the works, and I was on my way to buy that when I stopped in to a little art gallery. Spur of the moment! A painting caught my eye. Beautiful colors. Lines. It wasn't cheap. It was over $1,000!"

"When was this?" Barbara asked.

"Nineteen seventy-four. I bought it. Just pulled out my checkbook and bought it."

"I'll bet that felt good."

"It was scary!" Elizabeth said. "I had been poor, beyond mere poor, Barbara." Elizabeth stressed the words. "In college I lived entirely on the scholarship money and working in the cafeteria. I had nothing until I got the job with a major firm."

"You felt scared?"

"I should have bought the bed and put the rest into a savings account."

"You suffered from the 'should'ves' and 'ought-to-haves.' "

"Exactly! Then I left and as I was going out I changed my mind and turned back and ran into Elliot. He nearly knocked me over! So we both apologized and then we both went on our way which turned out to be the doorway to the art gallery and we both bumped into the other again." Barbara laughed and Elizabeth smiled. "He let me in first, then I let the gallery owner wait on him first, and found out he'd come in to buy the picture I'd just bought."

"I love it," Barbara said. "It is cute."

"For some reason his wanting the picture made me want to keep it. I showed him I had bought it, and I refused a two hundred dollar profit to sell it to him."

"Two hundred! You could have bought another painting and a mattress!"

"Well, it turned out I didn't need one. He moved in with his things about three days later."

"That was quick."

"He moved quickly when he wanted something. He didn't move as quickly about marriage. Four years."

"What made up his mind?"

"Taxes!" Elizabeth said. "We got married for the tax break!"

"How unromantic," Barbara said.

"It was." Elizabeth sighed. "It was the most unromantic wedding, unromantic marriage." She shrugged. "But we met cute!"

"So your marriage was unsatisfactory."

"Oh, no!" Elizabeth insisted. "It was just fine. That is, it suited us. We were comfortable in it. We made love, we talked, we had friends, we had separate lives and lives together." Elizabeth stopped a moment and tears welled in her eyes. "Except for not getting pregnant, everything was fine." She looked down at her abdomen and rubbed it softly.

"How do you feel about the baby?" Barbara took a risk in asking such a question. Any mention of the baby had immediately stopped any conversation in the past.

"I want it. I don't want it. I want it . . . I don't know."

"You have a right to feel confused," Barbara said.

"I don't know what I feel, let alone that I feel confused." Elizabeth chuckled and rubbed her tummy again. "When Chris told me I was pregnant, I thought he was kidding."

"He wasn't."

"Then, I was lost and didn't know what I was doing or saying or feeling and I latched on to him. I grabbed him and held him for dear life. When I saw him the first time, it was immediate. I felt—other than sick—I felt wildly in love!"

"At least you could tell the difference between sick and in love."

"Barely," Elizabeth amended. "Felt a little bit like the same thing. Only I got better when I was around him. But things kept happening. And then Elliot came back, and then this stuff with the SEC."

"I don't mean to get into legalities, but did you really not know what your husband was doing?"

"I didn't know. But I had developed a type of blinders toward him. Elliot had done many things over the years that were, if not outright illegal, at least shady. I got him out of trouble a number of times."

"But nothing like this?"

"He'd make a trade in a state not blue-skied, that means the trade wasn't legal in that state yet. Or he'd overspend in someone's account. Little, they could be fixed or arbitrated." Elizabeth looked at Barbara then and said, "Nothing like this. Nothing that directly involved me."

Elizabeth fidgeted around in the bed.

Barbara helped her with her pillows, and then they settled back.

"I couldn't believe this one. It can't be taken care of by paying a fine and a slap on the wrist. Not to mention what it has done to my reputation."

"But you went back to Colorado. You were out of the business," Barbara said.

"But my reputation! And . . . I guess it was just the surprise of it . . . the helplessness."

"You felt control slipping away," Barbara urged.

"Look at me!" Elizabeth yelled. "Look at me! I can't even control when I go to the bathroom! I have to wait until someone can come in and help me!"

"You are very angry about it."

"Yes!" Elizabeth cried out. Then in a quieter tone, "Yes. I don't like this. I never expected life to be perfect all the time. But I never expected this."

"We all worry about things and try to make sure that the things we worry about don't happen. Then what we didn't worry about is what happens," Barbara said. "I know I never expected my husband to be murdered. He was young, really. Only forty."

"No one ever expects murder," Elizabeth said. "How horrible for you. You must have been angry yourself."

"I was."

Elizabeth reached out and took Barbara's hand in hers and squeezed it. "I'm so sorry. My problems are small compared to what you went through."

Barbara accepted the words, took her hand gently from Elizabeth's and stood up. "You're going to be just fine, Elizabeth. Just fine."

"What makes you say that?"

"Because you can see other people's sorrow and not just your own. That is a very good sign."

After Barbara left, Elizabeth turned the volume up on the TV. She watched for a moment but was soon lost in thought.

*"Avery! Phone!" someone yelled from the dorm hallway. Elizabeth scrambled off her bed and ran to the pay phone. She answered and was surprised to hear her grandfather's voice.*

*She had not phoned or written for three years, and she had not gone home during vacations because of the jobs she needed to work to have money for next term.*

*"Lissy? Is that you?"*

*Elizabeth turned to the wall and put her hand up to cradle the phone, as if she wanted to hide. "Yes, Grandpa. What is it?"*

*"I have some news," he said and cleared his throat. "I . . . it's your grandmother."*

*"What? Is grandmother there?" she asked.*

*"No, Lissy." The old man made a strangled sound, then cleared his throat and said, "She died, Lissy. Alice died last night."*

*Tears welled in her eyes, but she willed herself to pull them back. "Where are you?"*

*"I'm in town. I'm at Doc's."*

*Elizabeth was silent. She pressed her lips together and closed her eyes tightly. She would not cry.*

*"What happened?" she said finally.*

*"She had a stroke. I could barely put her in the truck. By the time I got to Doc's, she was gone." Her grandfather tumbled the words out quickly then clamped his mouth shut so tightly Elizabeth could hear his teeth click through the phone line.*

*"I'm sorry, Grandpa."*

*"Can you come home?"*

*Elizabeth said nothing.*

*"Lissy, can you come home for the funeral?"*

*"I . . . can't. I have tests coming up. I just got the internship at Merrill Lynch; I've got my job . . ."*

*"I see," Grandpa said. He cleared his throat again. "We are . . . I am very proud of you, Lissy." Before Elizabeth could say anything, or cry, he hung up.*

*Elizabeth went back to her room, picked up her books and notebook, grabbed a coat and headed for the library. In one of the stacks, in a carrel all her own, she would cry. Where no one would see or hear.*

Elizabeth was transfixed by the television for the first ten days. By day eleven it began to have distinctly less appeal. Barbara came in three times; Chris called daily; De was there daily; the doctor came in twice a day. Other than that she saw no one, talked to no one but the nurses and aides and housekeeping people.

The afternoon Elliot showed up again, she was actually glad to see him.

# Twelve

"How do you do it?" Elizabeth said when Elliot came in. "How did you find me?"

"Nothing to it. I paid off a lady in housekeeping," Elliot said.

"Money handles everything," Elizabeth challenged. "I will get a restraining order if you don't leave."

"I'll leave. I need to talk to you, but I'll leave quietly if you'll just talk to me."

"I don't think there is anything to talk about." Elizabeth turned up the volume on the set, but then turned it back down when Elliot didn't leave. He stood at the end of her bed and stared at her.

"Elliot, go away." She spoke to him in her hardest voice. She suddenly realized that she had been talking to Elliot in that tone of voice for several years, hard and demanding and cruel. Wicked Witch. Her face must have shown the regret she felt, and Elliot jumped on the mood change.

"Are you all right?" he asked in his gentlest voice. "The baby?" He came around the bed to her side. Elizabeth turned off the set. "Is everything going to be okay?"

"I'm better. If I stay in bed, I will be fine. Thank you for asking."

He ran a hand through his hair and let out a long sigh. "I feel . . . Elizabeth . . . I don't know."

Elizabeth looked at him closely. His eyes were sunken into his skull, deep black circles under them. They were bloodshot and his face seemed to sag. She felt a great surge of some emotion, she searched her mind to find out what she felt. It wasn't love; was it compassion? Or gratitude that he'd actually found her again? "Thank you for caring," she said quietly.

"I do care." He ran his hand through his hair again and looked away. He licked his lips and looked at her again. "I've been up for about thirty hours," he said and looked away. "Jennifer had her baby last night. A girl," he said and then he scuttled from the side of her bed to the window as if he were afraid she would strike out.

"You told me she wasn't pregnant. You told me it was a lie."

"*That* was a lie," he said, staring out the window. "I need your help, Elizabeth." He looked down at his unkempt clothes, and his shoulders sagged. "I need your help."

*"I need your help, Elizabeth," Elliot said. His head was in her lap as they sat on the floor in front of the tiny fake fireplace in her apartment.*

*"Okay," she said.*

*He sat up and kissed her. "You really ought to ask what first," he said and then got up to pour another glass of wine.*

*"Okay, what?" Elizabeth was smiling. He had helped her; she would gladly help him. When she said she wanted a newspaper hadn't he run down and come back with six newspapers? If she said she was hungry, he*

took her to the most exclusive restaurant. If she said she needed shoes, he would return with a dozen pairs of the most beautiful shoes, all in her size.

He took a deep breath. "I need a little money. Just a bit until I get my quarterly from Grandmother's estate." He smiled at her.

"Okay," she said brightly. "When do you get paid at Burley's?" She mentioned the small brokerage he was working for.

"Ah, well, there is a small problem with that," he said and sat down beside her carefully to keep from spilling the wine. "I don't get anything for a while. I didn't make my draw this month, and so I have to pay them back with my commissions." He kissed the tip of her nose. "Just need to pay off a few credit cards and charge accounts."

"How much?" she asked. She pulled away from him and sat up on the sofa.

"Three thousand." He looked into his wine glass and swirled the contents around. "Just a little while."

Elizabeth looked stunned. "Three thousand. That is everything I have in savings."

"Just until I get my quarterly, Elizabeth," he said sweetly. "I'll pay you back."

Elizabeth stood up and went to her purse.

*She pulled out her savings account book and looked at the numbers. She then pulled out her checkbook and said, "I'll pay the bills. Why don't you give me a list and I'll write the checks, then I'll transfer the amount from my savings to my checking account." She looked at him as he stood up and came to her side. He took the book from her hand and kissed the tip of her nose. He put the book back into her purse and wrapped his arms around her and held her closely while he kissed her neck and cheeks.*

*"I'll handle it all. You don't need to worry about a thing. There is no need for you to worry about money and checks and bills. Just one little transaction, and I'll handle everything else." He kissed her. Elliot kissed beautifully. Especially wonderful for a girl who had been kissed three times in her life before Elliot.*

*The next day two dozen red roses were delivered to Elizabeth's desk at Merrill Lynch.*

*At dinner that evening, Elliot had prepared the table with candles and more roses, and he'd put dinner on her dime store plates and covered each plate with big bowls as if they were serving covers in a fancy restaurant.*

Elizabeth was ready to get angry at him for wasting the money on the roses and the dinner when he lifted a bowl with a flourish and said "Voilà!" *Under the bowl was a hot dog from the street vendor.*

*"Oh, Elliot," Elizabeth said. "You fool."*

*The real waste, she thought later that evening, was that they didn't even eat the hot dogs.*

"Nothing changes, really. Does it Elliot?"

"I don't know what you mean."

"I mean you are still asking me for help."

He was immediately defensive. "As if I never helped you."

"I could have bought your help at a better rate if I'd hired a butler," Elizabeth said. "I'm not going to help you. I'm not giving you one cent."

"I need money!" He looked wild.

"Nothing."

"Damn you!" he screamed. "You selfish, coldhearted bitch!"

Elizabeth pushed the button for the nurse, although she was sure they could hear his screaming at the nurses' desk. "Nothing," she said again. "Unless . . ."

He stared at her in anger then in interest. "Unless what?"

"Clear me," she said simply.

"What do you mean?"

"You know exactly what I mean. You take full blame, you take all of it on your shoulders. Clear my name from it completely."

"I'll go to jail!"

"Damn right!" Elizabeth said vehemently. "But you're going to go to jail anyway, only you're going to go poor. Clear me and I'll pay your attorney and give you an agreed upon amount." She looked at him with her best negotiating face, her eyes revealing only her expectation of the answer she wanted.

"Half a million," he said.

"One hundred and fifty thousand," she countered.

"Two hundred—"

She cut him off. "You have no room to negotiate Elliot. No comeback, no nothing. You take it or leave it."

Elliot ran his hands through his hair again. He paced the room and stood at the foot of her bed again, just as he had when he came in. "I'll go to jail," he said almost in tears.

"But your baby will be paid for," Elizabeth said. "And that bimbo will have some money so she won't have to sleep with someone else's husband to get by." She knew it was cruel, but she didn't regret it. She had played victim long enough. Now she held all the cards. She could see why people acted this way. It felt powerful.

"Pay all the SEC fines," Elliot demanded.

"I always did." Elizabeth answered.

"I tried to love you," Elliot said.

"You failed at that as well," Elizabeth said just as the hospital security came in her door. They looked from Elizabeth to Elliot, who didn't look so much like a problem as he did a beaten, starved kitten.

"You can escort him to his wife's room," Elizabeth said. "He was confused."

The next morning on the front page of *The Wall Street Journal* was a full interview and confession from Elliot March. He cleared Elizabeth, heaped praise on her, and stated that it was only because she had trusted and love him that she had not known what he'd done.

It did not make Elizabeth feel as she thought it would. She lost that feeling of power over another and the feeling of relief. All she felt was empty.

DeDe phoned before Elizabeth was through with the article.

"Harry is jumping up and down on the bed, dear," she said. "Whatever you did, he's happy."

"I did what I always did. I paid him off."

Harry got on the line. "I don't care about the price, my dear, it was cheap."

"Harry," she said, "I'm easy, but I'm not cheap."

Midnight, Christian was just getting through with his shift at the ER. He said good night to the sheriff who'd brought in a drunk and the social worker who was with an abused woman who'd been beaten senseless by her banker husband.

The automatic door opened and the phone rang. Before Chris was out the door, the nurse called him back.

"Dr. Hanford," Chris said into the phone.

"Christian," a breathy childish voice said.

He recognized it. Chris almost hung up the phone, but didn't. "Casey."

"I'm in town." She sounded happy and full of guile.

"I'm going home," he said and immediately wished he'd kept his mouth shut.

"I'll meet you there," she said with a lilt in her voice. "You didn't change the locks, I bet."

"No." He wished he could think of something to say, but he couldn't. "No," he said again.

"I'll be waiting."

"If you brought back the sofa, you could have a seat," he said but she'd already hung up.

He slammed the phone down, apologized to the nurse for jarring her with the noise, and then he left.

* * *

A Lincoln Town Car sat in front of the house. All the lights were on as if she'd gone from room to room.

She met him at the door. She was the epitome of a ski bunny. Long, lean, blonde, blue-eyed. Her hair had always been short, but she'd let it grow. Now, it flew about her head in little curls like a child's doll.

She was dressed in blue tights and a long cream ribbed sweater. She had her shoes kicked off and was barefoot with bright red polished toenails. She had no polish on her fingernails because she always chewed her nails to the quick.

Chris did not hug her hello when she reached out to him, consequently her thumbnail was in her mouth in seconds.

"Take your finger out of your mouth." The words were automatic. He'd said them to her thousands of times over the years.

She put her hands behind her back like a reprimanded child and then followed him to the small love seat, the only piece of furniture in the huge room. He sat down and stretched out, leaving her no room to sit. She sat on the floor at his feet and looked up at him like an adoring teenager, which is what she had been when she moved in with him all those years ago.

"What are you doing here?" he said.

"I came to see you. Don't you want to see me?" She had one deep dimple which made her look younger than her thirty years. Her tanned skin hadn't yet begun to show the damage that continual suntanning would show. Her eyes sparkled in their deep sockets. Her eyebrows were dark and straight. She looked fresh and clean . . . and conniving.

"I don't think so," Chris said. Then he pulled off one cowboy boot, shoving her out of the way so he could put it down where she was kneeling.

"Christian, don't act like that," she said in her little girl voice. "I don't act like that to you." As if that was all that was wrong with their relationship, *she* was not harsh with *him*.

"No, you don't," Chris agreed. "You pack up all the furniture and leave me the trash and a note and disappear. But you don't do this." He threw his other boot as hard as he could and it hit the sliding glass doors, luckily nothing shattered.

"Christian!"

"Don't pull that, Casey," he said in a bored voice. "I have never hurt you, and I never will. Now get out." It felt good to finally be able to tell her to get out. The way she had done it, deserting him that way, he'd not been able to say those words.

"I can't," she said in a whispery little voice that cracked a bit on "can't." "Daddy said."

"I don't give a damn what your daddy said," Christian said, but felt goose bumps form on his skin as he said it.

Harrison Richardson Merritt, who owned twenty or so hotels around the world, was not a man to whom one said you didn't give a damn. No one knew how he got the money to build or buy the hotels. Although the speculation was that he was with some form of illegal syndicate and the hotels washed the money, nothing was ever proved. He was an ugly little bullet of a man, who talked crudely, acted crudely, and ran the most elegant hotels in the world. He'd ignored his daughter and hated his son, who killed himself three years before Casey and Christian met. When she insisted she was staying with Chris and moved in with him, her father disowned her. She had not spoken to him or seen him since. Her mother, a long-legged model who'd moved to Texas and stayed permanently hidden there, seldom talked to her daughter.

Chris had only met the man briefly all those years ago, and had never seen or heard from him since, but the impression stayed. He was a vicious, cruel, cold man, and he would just as soon kill Chris as deal with him.

"Daddy says he'll set up your own clinic," Casey said hopefully. She reached out to Chris and put her hands in his lap. When he didn't immediately brush them away, she placed her head in his lap and whispered, "Please, Chris. Please take me back."

# Thirteen

The next morning Elizabeth lay back on the pillows and placed her hands on her swelling abdomen. The baby was content, she thought, not kicking or punching or whatever it was they did as the floated around in there. What did they do? She saw the box of books in the far corner of the room. In all those books there had to be an answer. She rang for the nurse's aide. When she came they went through the books until they found one with pictures and words that seemed understandable. Elizabeth began to read.

DeDe and Harry found her engrossed in her book when they got there a few hours later.

"What time is it?" Elizabeth said when they came in.

"Nearly lunch," De said and snapped her fingers. In came a uniformed waiter with a huge cloth-covered tray. Harry gave De a quick kiss and told Elizabeth he had to go. De and Elizabeth ate a beautifully prepared salad and range-fed beef tips over sourdough toast, with asparagus spears. They luxuriated in cheesecake for dessert. "I feel human!" Elizabeth declared. "The food here is fine, but not this good."

"Good is not good enough!" De cried out. "We celebrate victory over your ex-husband."

"It was a hollow victory," Elizabeth said. She folded her napkin and looked so sad that De came to her side and hugged her, rubbing her back and arms as if she were rubbing circulation back into them. "Isn't winning supposed to feel good?"

"Maybe you didn't win," De said.

"What do you mean?"

"Maybe you just didn't lose."

"It was definitely not a win-win situation," Elizabeth agreed. "But at least it was my choice."

"All is our own choice," De said. "I

am old." She raised a perfectly arched, perfectly made-up eyebrow. "And I won't tell you how old either, but I have learned in all these years that we have choice."

"You don't believe in fate?"

"I am a realist."

Elizabeth shook her head but respectfully listened. There was very little "real" about DeDe Steinberg. Not her hair nor her face, not her teeth nor even her breasts. Realist seemed a farfetched way to describe herself.

"Yes. A realist. My hair goes white, I look at that fact and find the best colorist. That is real. My face wrinkles, I look at that fact and find the best plastic surgeon. That is real. These are the facts; what can I do about them? The result is fact and becomes real. Therefore I am a realist."

"It works for me," Elizabeth said and meant it. No more sitting around in this bed feeling sorry for herself. The fact, the "real," was that she had to stay here, she could do things with that. What would the best thing be? To read these books, these wonderful books that a loving, kind, and generous man gave her; learn, make this reality a different one. "I think I've got it," Elizabeth said to De with a beaming smile on her face.

"By George, I think you've got it," De agreed.

"Thank you," Elizabeth said.

"No, thank you," De said as she swirled on her coats and scarves and prepared to leave. "Now, get better. I have a shopping spree in mind that will make real how beautiful you are when you are pregnant."

Elizabeth said goodbye, then she settled back once again with her book. But she couldn't read it. All she could think of was Chris saying she would make a beautiful mother. She had never thought of herself pregnant. She was beginning to see it. Beginning to see the reality. She dialed the hospital in Vail, hoping to find Chris there. She wanted to talk to him, to tell him what had happened. She wanted to tell him she loved him. Before the phone rang, she put it back down.

Where had that come from? That need to tell Chris she loved him? She knew she wanted him, she knew he made her feel wonderful. But, could she put her heart on the line by telling him? When did she grow courageous? When had it become *real?*

She dialed the number again, but the desk said he wasn't on today, so she called his home. The phone rang several times and with each ring Elizabeth felt her heart fill with more and more of this love. She couldn't wait for him to get on the line. She couldn't wait to tell him she loved him.

"Hello?" A childish woman's voice answered the phone.

Elizabeth looked at the phone as if she could see through it to see who was at the other end. "Dr. Hanford?" she said.

"He's in the shower," Casey said. "Can I take a message?"

Elizabeth was frozen.

"It's okay," the childlike voice said. "I'm his wife. I'll tell him." Casey smiled at her deception.

Elizabeth could hardly speak. She started to say something twice but choked on the words. Finally she said, "I'll call him at the hospital."

"He won't be going in," Casey said.

"We're going out of town for a few days. Oh, here he comes now. Honey!"

Elizabeth hung up.

So, that was who had left him. So selfishly caught up in her own things, she had never even bothered to ask him to share his emotions about the empty house and the plans for the woman who had left.

She felt more ill now than she had all along. She felt as if someone had run a truck over her. She felt . . .

"Damn it!"

"Who was that?" Chris asked. He was drying his hair with a towel. "What are you doing here?"

"Must have a been a salesman," Casey said. "I'm here to kidnap you." She giggled.

"Casey, I'm not going anywhere with you." Chris sounded bored.

"Christian, please. You've got to come with me. You've got to talk to Daddy." She was pouting. With her new curls she managed to look like a five foot, seven inch moving Shirley Temple doll.

"I don't want to talk. I didn't talk to him while you lived here and now that you don't live here I am not about to talk to him."

"Christian!" she wailed. "Daddy will give you a million dollars! For your clinic! No strings!"

"What clinic?" Chris said as he put on his boots. "Since when will he help me start a clinic?"

"Since now. Please. Let's go talk to him."

Christian sighed. "Okay, where is he? At the Lodge?" He mentioned the hotel in Vail her father owned.

"New York," Casey said.

At the mention of New York, Chris became more interested. He could see Elizabeth. He could find out about this money *and* see Elizabeth. "New York," he said. "I'll call the hospital."

"I've already taken care of it," Casey said.

"I'll bet," Chris said and went for the phone. He called the hospital and found out that another doctor would cover for him for two days. Since this was his day off anyway, he had three days.

"Okay, three days. I get my own room."

"Three days, and you get the penthouse," Casey said.

Less than an hour later they were on their way in Merritt's private jet.

"I'm so glad we're together," Casey said.

"If you mean together in the jet, yes, we are together. But if you think I'm taking you back, you're wrong."

Casey looked upset for a moment, but she quickly smiled and shook her curls. "I mean here!" she said. Daddy had told her what to say and how to act. She absolutely must do what Daddy said. "I have always hated public transportation. This is so much better."

Chris looked at her again. He had never understood what she had seen in him. They had never had anything in common. Never had anything to talk about. She didn't like his being a trauma doctor. She would have preferred him being something less dramatic, less demanding of hours. A radiologist.

Chris looked out the small window at the white clouds. They were over the great plains now. Occasionally he saw through a break in the clouds the patchwork quilt of farmland below.

Why had he let Casey into his life? *Because it was easy,* he answered his own question. *I didn't have to win her or woo her; I didn't have to make her parents like me; I didn't even have to like her myself.* Chris stared out the window while Casey chattered away about her new hairstylist and the latest clothes she'd bought. He had never listened to her. At least not since the first year.

He'd tried. It was exciting at first. She didn't know how to drive; she couldn't cook. Later he'd found out she couldn't read. She had dyslexia, and her string of private schools had let her keep on passing from grade to grade as long as Daddy gave money and food and donated equipment. No one had noticed or maybe it was just that no one cared that Casey Merritt could not read and could barely write her name. And, above all, Casey Merritt was so lonely she hooked on to the first man who didn't care whether she had money and she never let go. She was loyal. To survive her disability and family situation, she'd had to learn a lot of tricks to get by.

*I should have gotten a dog and sent her home.*

He was immediately ashamed of the thought and looked quickly at her to see if she could read his mind. She was talking about the new bell-bottom pants from the designers.

"I should have gotten a dog," he said aloud.

"Do you have a dog? I like kittens, puppies and kittens. I don't like them when they grow up." Casey was off on a story about a kitten she had. Chris looked out the window. She couldn't read his mind. She couldn't read a street sign.

Elizabeth could only have been more surprised when Chris walked in the door that evening if he'd been carrying a chimpanzee with him.

"What are you doing here?"

"I came to see you."

Elizabeth folded her arms across her chest.

"So how's it going?"

She looked out the window and refused to look at him. "Don't you read the papers?"

"Not lately," he said.

"I'll bet."

"Lissy, you are driving me crazy!" He spun on his heels and was about to leave when he changed his mind. "Do I go buy a few hundred copies of newspapers or do you tell me?"

"Too bad there isn't a newspaper that can tell me about you."

He hit his forehead with the flat of his palm. "Of course! I'm supposed to tell the newspapers I'm working double shifts to pay back my friends who have covered me."

"I'm not talking about that," she said. "I'm talking about a wife."

"Whose wife?" he said and held his arms out. "Whose wife am I supposed to know about?"

"Your wife."

He stood at the foot of her bed. He looked as if he had found his way into a big blank wall in a maze and had no idea where to go.

"Your wife," she said again. "The one

who answers the phone and says you're in the shower."

"That was you." He looked as if he understood now. "That wasn't, isn't, *never* was my wife." He shook his head and put up his hand to stop her. "That was Casey. We did live together. We did not marry."

"She said she was your wife." Elizabeth was not going to let up. "She said she was your wife."

"She isn't." He was tired of this. "Tell me what was in the papers."

Elizabeth thought about it first. She wasn't satisfied with the answer. In fact, it didn't answer anything. But she told him about Elliot.

"That's great! That's wonderful!" He was genuinely happy for her. "Now, get on with your life!"

*"Grandpa?" Elizabeth was surprised he was calling. It had been nearly five years since her grandmother had died. How he'd found her, she wasn't sure. She wasn't going to ask him anyway.*

*"Lissy. It's so good to hear your voice." He*

*sounded weak, tired. "I need to talk to you about a few things." He could barely be heard. Elizabeth strained to hear him but she was being buzzed on her intercom. "Lissy–"*

*"Grandpa, I've got to go. I've got a meeting. Can you give me a number? I'll call you back in an hour or so."*

*He gave her the number and a room number. Elizabeth didn't ask why there was a room number.*

*"Lissy!" he said.*

*"Yes, Grandpa?"*

*"Now, get on with your life!" He said it with real effort.*

*"I will. Bye." She hung up and went to her meeting. Two hours later she called and was surprised to learn it was Denver General Hospital. When no answer came from the room number, she called the main desk.*

*"I'm trying to reach my grandfather, George Templeton."*

*"And your name?" the nurse said.*

*"Elizabeth Avery."*

*"Yes, you are to be told." The nurse cleared her throat and said in a very gentle but straightforward voice, "Your grandfather died about forty-five minutes ago. I'm so sorry."*

*"But I just talked to him!" Elizabeth felt*

*a lump in her throat big enough to make swallowing difficult.*

*"He'd been having a series of heart attacks," the nurse said. "If I could just get some information from you. Who should we call for the funeral home?"*

*"I'm in New York. I don't know any funeral homes."*

*"I'll put you in touch with a social worker here. She can help you make arrangements."*

*Elizabeth made the arrangements, paid for it all with her credit card, but she did not go back. She did not go home.*

"Take me home, Chris," she said suddenly. "Please take me home."

He came to her side. She looked up into those lion's gold eyes and reached out her hand to his cheek. She wanted to touch him. She wanted to hold him. He bent over her and kissed her softly.

# Fourteen

Chris held her closely. He stroked her hair and kissed the top of her head. But his mind was elsewhere.

Harrison Richardson Merritt, Dick Merritt, met him and Casey at the airport. The limo was discreet but distinctly a Merritt possession with the logo of the hotels in gold on the door. Dick kissed his daughter and slapped Chris on the back. "Good to see you again," he said as if he'd seen him months ago, not more than a decade.

"Good to be seen," Chris said. It was the last sentence he got to finish for the rest of the ride.

"It's gonna be a great clinic, son," Dick began.

"Well, let's just—"

Dick interrupted. "It will be called the Merritt Clinic, but you will be the head of it."

"But I—"

"Don't you worry about a thing, I won't interfere. What do I know about a medical clinic?" He laughed one hard *HA!* "I know about business though, and makin' people comfortable. It will be the most comfortable damn clinic in the world, I can tell you that."

"It—"

Casey interrupted this time. "Daddy said I can be the business manager." She snuggled up to her father like a kitten to a warm spot. "Didn't you, Daddy?"

"You want—"

"Yes, I did. Son, you've done a world of good for my little girl here. Frankly, I always thought she had the brains of a duck." Casey laughed and kissed her father on the stubble-darkened cheek he presented. "Used to call her 'Duck,' didn't I, babe?"

"Yes. And I hated it," Casey said, but she didn't sound as if she hated it.

Chris gave up trying to speak. For the rest of the ride to Park Avenue, he listened as the man and his daughter changed the whole course of his life for him.

The limo pulled up outside the hotel and Chris opened the door, jumped out before the doorman or driver could help open the door. He hopped into a cab waiting for another fare. The cab took off in a squeal of tires and honking horns. Chris looked back to see Dick waving his fist and Casey batting her father on his substantial, if short, body with her purse and stomping her feet.

He had escaped. He'd wanted to escape since the end of the first fourteen months with Casey. Now he had done it overtly, not just in working hard and long, or in all the mental ways he had escaped her for all those years. He had actually, physically escaped.

"Where to, man?" the cabbie asked.

"Colorado," Chris said. When the cabbie turned completely around in his seat and looked at Chris, even as he drove, Chris said the hospital name. The cabbie swung into another lane, spun around a corner on two tires, and, amidst more honking horns, deposited Chris at the wrong hospital.

Chris thanked him anyway, paid him, and found another cab. This one knew the correct hospital.

"I'd love to take you home. I want to take you home. I can't take you home," he said.

Elizabeth hugged him harder. "I know I can't go right now. I have to get that doctor to say I can go, but I'll do that." She sounded as if she knew she could do it. She sounded like she had no doubt she would be going home in a few days.

"Elizabeth, I don't really know how to tell you all of what is going on, so I might as well begin at the beginning."

"Good place." Elizabeth reluctantly let go of him and let him gently push her back into the pillows and tuck the covers around her. "Stalling?" she said.

"Yeah," he admitted.

"You don't have to stall with me. You don't have to hide anything or make up things with me."

"Thank you," Chris said. He sat down

on the edge of the bed and took her hand. "I feel I do. You are here for one reason and one reason only. The amount of stress in your life is jeopardizing the baby and your life."

"I'm learning," Elizabeth said.

"I don't want to add to the stress." He kissed her fingertips. "You mean too much to me."

"You mean a great deal to me, too. What are you getting at, Chris?"

"You asked me if I was married."

"You said you aren't."

"I never married her. But Casey and I lived together for over ten years. She left me the night you came over." He looked at her and she nodded. "I wasn't as disturbed by her leaving as some might have been. Actually I was relieved. I felt as if I'd been a baby-sitter and teacher to her all those years. She always said she was madly in love with me. She always said she couldn't live without me."

"How interesting." Elizabeth was visibly angry, and it was beginning to come through her voice. "Please go on."

"I don't love her."

"Where have I heard that before?" Sarcasm dripped from her voice.

"Lissy," he pleaded. She didn't respond so he just went on. "She was back when I got back last week."

"I'm not surprised."

"I was," Chris said simply. "She had a proposition for me."

"I'll bet." Elizabeth was not going to ease up.

"Her father is very wealthy. They did not speak the whole time she lived with me. All of a sudden she is back with the news that her father will build a clinic, a million-dollar clinic."

"A million doesn't go very far these days," Elizabeth said. "I ought to know."

"Casey came to Vail in her dad's jet, offered to fly me back to New York. I took the offer and now I'm here, and I don't know what to do." Chris got off the edge of the bed and threw his hands up in the air and paced the room.

"I don't want Casey. I don't ever want Casey. I don't want her old man looking over my shoulder. Believe me, it was far better when he hated me instead of calling me 'son.' "

"Cut the long story," Elizabeth said. "What do you need from me?"

"Need?" Chris stopped pacing and stared at her, confused.

"Need. Do you need money for your clinic? One million wouldn't put in enough of today's equipment for an average office, let alone an average clinic. Well, how much do you need? Do you want me to put you in touch with some investors? I don't have that kind of money. Anymore." Elizabeth began her tirade, ignoring the reaction she could see on Chris's face.

"I used to have money, but I'm going to lose most of it because of the last man who needed me. So, what is it? Money? Approval? Do you want my approval for you to go back to this moron you used to live with? Approval? You got it. Go back. But, frankly, I'd hold out for a hell of a lot more than a million."

Chris stood at the end of her bed, stunned. He couldn't believe what he was hearing. He silently pulled his emotions together. Elizabeth looked anywhere but at him. He stared at her in thought.

"First, she isn't a moron. I've called

her that myself, and I can't believe I'm saying this, but she isn't a moron. She was ignored, shuttled around; a miserable child who could not read or write, and all the money in the world couldn't change that." He was so quiet, she had to listen. "I won't let you call her a moron. It took a great deal of intelligence to get as far as she did."

He went to the window and stood watching the boats go up the river. Neither one spoke for a few minutes.

Elizabeth broke the silence. "I'm sorry. And I'm ashamed of myself."

Chris was holding her before she got the last word out. "No, no, no. I'm sorry. You don't need to be ashamed."

They each excused the other and then they held each other again.

"I don't need your money or your investors," Chris said. "I do want you to know what is going on."

"I'll listen," she said.

"Her father can afford to give a million to a clinic. There are areas in Colorado near the resorts but not in the resorts, you know? Places where they really need a clinic. I need some testing equipment, nothing major. I need a nurse; a million would be enough to do this."

Elizabeth sat back again. She looked at Chris as if she'd never really looked at him. She admitted to herself that she hadn't. Other than his undeniable and very noticeable good looks and wonderful body, she had not looked at this man. She knew nothing about him except he was kind and tender. And she loved him.

"This is something you have always wanted?"

"My father . . . do you remember my father?" Elizabeth blushed and admitted she did not. "He was the doctor there until the big money took over Vail and turned it into the place it is now. He used to be paid, like an old country doctor, very little money, but we got chickens and beef and beaver pelt. You name it and Dad got paid in it." Chris was smiling at the memory. "We were so damn poor!" He laughed out loud, and Elizabeth was surprised as she laughed with him.

"So were we," she said.

"I went to med school on scholarship.

My dad died while I was in school. Vail grew! God, how it grew!" Chris shook his head. "But the people, the ones who worked there and lived there, they got shoved out."

"Shoved out?" Elizabeth asked.

"Do you know that most of the people who work in Vail, Aspen and so on, don't live there. They can't afford it. They live in little towns as far as seventy miles away. They don't live in great ski lodges, either. There are a lot of immigrants, aliens. I know of one family from Guatemala. They have a mom and a dad and six kids and aunts and uncles and cousins, and they all live in one trailer that is twelve by thirty."

Elizabeth took his hand and held it close to her heart.

"I see them all the time in the emergency room," Chris continued. "It's their only place to go, really. And we never get paid."

"How would you get paid at a clinic?"

"That's what I want your help on," he said.

"My help?"

"I don't want him to just give me

money. I want him to set up an endowment and let the money fund it."

"You want him to put the money in an investment and the earnings pay for your staying open," she said. He nodded. "Well, I think he must have people who can set that up for you."

"Probably," Chris agreed. "What I want is help in making him do that."

"I don't see how I can help," Elizabeth said.

"Oh, yes, you can. You have the skills I need. You work up the proposal the way it should be, and I'll give it to him. And then you can teach me how to negotiate."

"Work out a business proposal? Yes, I'd love to. I'm bored to death. Television is not as wonderful as I thought. But as for negotiating, I think you had better rely on your own self."

"Why?" he said simply.

"Because, at the moment I couldn't negotiate my way out of a—"

Chris finished the sentence for her. "A paper bag. Cliché!"

"It may be, but I couldn't. Who is this man anyway?"

"Dick Merritt."

"Merritt Hotels!" Elizabeth visibly brightened. A look of interest lit her face. "His stock is ready to go sky-high. They have opened up Russia! One of the first luxury hotels!"

"There, see!" Chris said. "You know that kind of thing."

"That doesn't mean I'm going to teach you to negotiate."

"Why not?"

"Because there are several things that you need to clear up for yourself."

"What?"

"What does he have on you?"

"I see," Chris said. "What can he use to get me to do this his way?"

"Right. The first and actually most important thing in negotiating is homework, know the other side of the table. Know more about them than they know about you."

"That's easy. I don't think he would have even known who I was if Casey hadn't been with me and said this is Chris."

"A great deal is known about Dick

Merritt. But this is personal. This has to do with his daughter."

Chris moaned. "Oh, he wants her to be the business manager."

"So his motivation isn't philanthropic," Elizabeth said.

"Far from it."

"But your motivation is. And I bet he thinks the two of you want this clinic for the same reasons."

"That's about the size of it," Chris said. Then he kissed her. "You were helping me. I just had to say it," he said in a taunting voice.

Elizabeth smiled. "Maybe I was, maybe I wasn't."

"No, you were helping. I can tell helping when I get helped."

"Okay. I was helping." She took his hand and held it again. "I have so much to think about and worry about. I'm sorry I blew up."

"You know, you never ask me about me," Chris said. "I'm not saying that I wanted you to give me the third degree, but I did wonder why you never asked me anything."

"Shall I say I'm sorry again?" Elizabeth asked.

"Just tell me you love me," Chris said. He looked into Elizabeth's eyes and searched there for the answer she wasn't giving.

"I . . . think . . . I . . ." Elizabeth couldn't put the words together in a sentence. She coughed and looked away then looked at him again. She knew she loved him. She had loved him since she first opened her eyes in the ER. She knew she loved him. *Just say it,* she said to herself, *you know it's true, just say it.* She couldn't.

"Too soon?" Chris said. "Yeah, too soon." He looked outside to see that it was getting dark. "I've got to go make an appearance. I kind of ran away."

"Yes," she agreed quicker than she intended. "I mean, you have things you have to do."

He kissed her again. It was sweet and soft with his tongue running lightly along the line of her lips. It sent the most thrilling shiver up her spine, and she blushed again. Could a pregnant woman feel such an urgent rush of desire? Should she?

"I'll be back later, but maybe not until the morning," he said. She nodded and kissed him again, pulling him down onto her. She held him to her as if she might never see or feel him this way again. "Hey. Really, I'll be back," he said.

# Fifteen

Barbara pushed open the door to Elizabeth's room with her foot. In her hands she carried an uneven two-layer homemade birthday cake with pastel pink frosting and lit candles. Just two in the shape of a four and five.

"Happy Birthday!" she sang out. "And many more."

"How did you know?" Elizabeth was smiling from ear to ear. "Who told you?"

"No one told me. I looked it up on your chart." She placed the cake on the bedside table and said, "Now, make a wish and blow out the candles."

Elizabeth did as she was told. She took Barbara's hand and held it tightly. "Did you bake that yourself?"

"I did. And it was the first cake I have

baked in four years. So no jokes. My oven must be uneven." She held it up, critically examining what looked to be a flat on one side. "I don't know how the candles keep from falling off." She put it down again and shrugged. "Oh well, the best laid plans of mice and women who don't cook often go astray." Barbara leaned over and gave her a quick, strong bear hug. "Happy birthday," she said again.

"I have never had a birthday celebration," Elizabeth said quietly.

Without missing a beat, Barbara said, "I should have put a big number one on the cake then."

Elizabeth laughed. "No, I'm definitely forty-five."

"You don't look a day over whatever age will make you feel younger," Barbara said diplomatically.

"Thank you kindly. I think I will settle on a permanent thirty-five." Elizabeth rang for the nurse's aide. While they waited, lightning flashed and thunder growled.

"It has rained all day for days!" Elizabeth said. "It barely clears up, and then it rains some more. I don't believe how quickly I forgot about the gray cloudy days and the rain. Fall in Colorado is so different. The mornings are sunshine-filled, and if it rains it's in the evening."

"I have been told about Colorado sunshine. More sunshine days than Miami or Los Angeles."

While they waited for the aide, they talked more about the change in weather. It was cloudy all day, and morning rains signaled the change of season. It would be fall soon. Humid, hot, Indian summer, followed by more wind and rain and finally the gray winter of New York City. No beautiful drifts of gleaming white snow, but the black and brown and gray crud of city snow.

The aide arrived with paper plates and a knife and forks. She also brought two cans of fruit juice, and she wished Elizabeth a happy birthday as well.

"I haven't had this much attention on my birthday for as long as I can remember."

"Not much was made of birthdays in you family?" Barbara said.

"I don't remember," she said. Then

she tilted her head to one side and said, "Grandma made waffles for my birthday breakfast. And I would get a small gift that evening before bed. A new notebook or pens, something I needed." Elizabeth became quiet. It was not a happy memory. It embarrassed her to think of the simplicity. No, the *poverty* of it.

She searched her mind for something to brighten those years. She raised her eyebrows and nodded her head and smiled.

"In high school, my extra tutoring in math and college entry courses were always my gift." She smiled a very stagey smile. One that said "No, I'm not happy but I'm smiling anyway."

"No balloons, no party of girlfriends dressed in ruffled dresses? No ice cream and cake?"

"No. No girlfriends. I only had one friend, Barry Cavet, who lived about four miles away. He was only a friend until we both became teenagers. Then he tolerated me when he had to." She was back in the dumps again. Damn, why did she only seem to remember the bad things.

"It sounds as if your grandparents did

the best they could. But what a lonely life."

Elizabeth began to answer her. Her words tripping over her tongue as she tried to explain herself, her life, and how she felt about it. She couldn't get words to form and finally she blurted out, "I hated it!" Then she quit trying and shook her head.

"Then, why did you go back?" Barbara said. "Why run back to a place you hate?"

"I had to," Elizabeth said. "I just had to."

"Do you think that is the answer?"

Elizabeth cut another slice of cake and settled back against her covers. She ate the slice in a few bites, and Barbara did the same. Elizabeth put the plate back on the bedside table. She folded her arms across her chest and looked past Barbara to the window and the pouring rain.

"I don't know why I went back. I did it quite spur of the moment. I picked up the phone in my office here in New York and found a realtor in Vail who found out that the land was available. I bought it, sight unseen—and believe me I got the surprise of my life when I did see it—sold everything and went back within a few weeks of Elliot leaving me. I just did it."

"That was a very powerful thing to do," Barbara said as she cut another slice.

"Three slices!" Elizabeth cried out in surprise.

"It's birthday cake, no calories in birthday cake," Barbara assured her.

"In that case, baby and I will have another slice."

Barbara smiled as she cut the slices. Elizabeth had included the baby. *Very good,* she thought.

Elizabeth ate a few bites. Barbara could see that she contemplated the next words she was going to say with each bite. Elizabeth then asked, "Why do you think it was powerful? I never thought of it as powerful. Just something I was compelled to do. Forced actually."

"It was extremely powerful!" Barbara assured her. "How many women, or men for that matter, do you hear about who buy land, sell everything they have, and move away from the city and a successful career? Not many!"

"Not many can," Elizabeth argued. "I'd bet if you gave that nurse's aide enough money and told her she could go live in paradise—" Barbara's eyebrows rose at the description. "She would jump at the chance," Elizabeth concluded.

"Why do you call this place that made you so miserable paradise?" Barbara said.

Elizabeth began to describe the beauty of her cabin and the little valley. The mountain peaks surrounding it like points on a tiara. The lake and stream, the wildflowers, the aspens turning gold like treasures of Spanish coins. And the wildlife, her raccoon, the deer, the wild goat. She talked a long while about the moon on the snow making it look as if the snow were melted sapphires flowing over the land. Or the sun on a snow frosted morning making each flake look as if it were a diamond. And if you just reached out and cupped a handful, preserved the diamonds and sold them, you would be the wealthiest human being on earth.

She wound down eventually. Barbara

was smiling at her with a very gratified look on her face.

"Sounds like paradise to me," Barbara agreed.

"I think I went back because I needed to find the part of me I left there. I don't think I can go on until I come to grips with the abandoned child, no mother and no father, who grew up there." Elizabeth looked down at her plate and said quietly, "And ran away."

"You did the most powerful and wonderful thing. You actually went back. Most of us settle for just going back in our minds."

"I've done that, too," Elizabeth admitted. "Some word or smell or emotion will take me back. I always blocked that before. I never went back even in my mind." She looked down at her abdomen and rubbed it in small circles. "Do you suppose she is making me do it?"

"Well, if she is, congratulate her for me. It is something we trained people can't always get someone to do," Barbara said. "Did you know Napoleon Bonaparte and Lawrence of Arabia were born on your birthday?"

"No! good heavens! What two strange, exciting people to share a birthday with!"

"I can't think of two better. You are very much like them."

"Elliot used to call me a little Napoleon. I never asked him why. I just assumed it was an insult."

"Do consider the source. But in this case he was right. You are a Leo. Leo the Lion."

"Right now I feel like I'm a very poor excuse of a lion in some tatty fleabag circus show confined in a horrid padded cage."

"But coping," Barbara said gently.

"Yes, we are," Elizabeth agreed, rubbed her abdomen again and smiled.

Christian took one look around the hotel's penthouse and immediately wanted to bolt as he had when the limo arrived.

He was so impossibly out of place in the entryway. From what he could see of the rest of it, he would be like a fish out of water.

It looked like a cross between a mad

collector's museum with no theme—"Just if it's old and massive, I'll collect it"—and a movie set. A riot of color and furniture and art made one's eyes dart from place to place, trying to settle. They couldn't, however, forced as they were to go on to something else, desperate to find a place to rest, but unable to, even for a moment.

He was feeling a bit wobbly in the knees when Casey emerged from one of the rooms. She looked so clean and white and uncluttered in a simple white dress, he was actually glad to see her.

"Is this where you grew up?"

She looked at him with disappointment in her eyes. "Silly, I told you! I went to boarding schools from the time I was seven. I really lived there. I only visited here." She walked closer to him and tried to hold his hand but he shrugged off the attempt. She sighed.

"I told you," she said again.

A note of sadness crept into her voice, and Chris changed the subject. What the hell, he was going to make her sad no matter what.

"Where's your dad?"

Casey looked around as if she might find him behind a massive Chinese vase or standing next to a Michelangelo reproduction. Then she shrugged and smiled. "I forgot. He went to Paris."

Chris found a chair that looked like it wouldn't matter if he sat in it. He crossed his ankle over his knee and kept beat with some unheard music with his toe.

He stood up and went back to the elevator doors, thought again and came back in to where Casey stood looking confused and hurt. *Damn it!* he thought. *She always looks hurt and confused!*

"I thought he wanted to talk to me about a clinic."

"He thought you did. You are the one who disappeared." She said it without malice, just a trace of sarcasm.

"Casey, I don't . . . I'm not the one . . . oh, what's the use." He went back to the elevator, and it opened for him. He pushed the lobby button, and as the doors closed he shook his head.

He had never been able to really talk to her. They had never developed an intimate level of communication. Sex—yes. Communication—no. Him telling her or listening to her. But no dialogue. Monologues for each of them; to which, apparently, the other did not listen.

Casey had made no further move until the doors closed. It was so like him. He'd speak without saying anything she could understand and then walk away. She was always looking at his departing back. Or her father's back. Or her mother. Someone was always walking away from her.

She walked to an ornate Louis the XVIII desk and pressed a button on the panel indented on the desk. "Follow him," she said. She then went back to the center of the room.

Once on the street, Chris turned first one direction, then turned around and began to walk in another, completely ignoring the doorman who tried to get him a cab.

# Sixteen

"What do you mean you lost him?" Casey asked the two men in front of her. They looked at the intricate carpet design and shuffled from foot to foot.

"Well, Dennis here, he saw him go into a store and when we waited outside for him he disappeared."

"*Now* you didn't lose him. He disappeared," Casey said.

"It's like Jerry says. I saw him and he went into this little store and I stayed outside the door, see."

"Yeah, and so I went round back only there was no back door or nothing," Dennis added.

"And, like he never came out," Jerry said. "I went in after an hour and nobody is there but a lady."

"Nobody came out of a one-entrance store." Casey didn't believe him for a minute.

"Well, yeah people came out and went in and came out . . ." Jerry said.

"But *he* didn't come out," Dennis said.

Casey sat down at the ornate desk and picked up a pen and tapped it on the desk top. "You lost him."

"Nobody like him came out of the place!" Dennis insisted. "Gotham Costumery. Nobody came out like him."

Casey looked at the two men as if she would like to squash them under her foot. "Dennis, what does costumery mean?"

The two men looked at the other and shrugged in the way of New Yorkers.

"You're fired," she said and stood up to lead them out. "Get out."

"Because we don't know a word?" Dennis sounded astounded.

"Jeez-sus!" Jerry said. "If I'd a know that I'd a read a damn dictionary!"

Standing by the elevator, Casey folded her arms across her chest. "Just tell me who did leave."

They looked at each other and Dennis said, "I didn't see anybody, he saw 'em."

Jerry said, "Jeez-sus! All I seen was two women come out with big boxes, and a man who had a little kid with him and a cow." He shrugged again.

"A cow?" Casey was dubious.

"Yeah, a cow." Jerry said it in a "so there!" tone of voice.

"Do you mean that someone came out wearing a cow costume?" Casey demanded.

"Well, ah course! What do you think, I don't know a real cow from a guy dressed up like a cow? Jeez-sus! What do you think I am . . . stupid?"

Elizabeth opened her eyes from a nap so deep even the sounds from the TV set couldn't wake her to see Elsie the cow standing at the side of her bed, pink plastic udders flapping as she danced to the music on MTV.

"Who are you?" She shook her head and knit her brow. Was she dreaming?

The cow stopped dancing and performed an elaborate and clumsy bow.

"I'm the singing birthday cow. Actually I used to do TV commercials but I was an 'udder' failure." The cow shook with laughter and its cowbell clanked. "Udder failure! Get it?"

Elizabeth recognized Christian's voice. She was sitting up in her bed and laughing. "You idiot!"

The cow put hooves on hips and swaggered around the room. "Hey! Either you got it or you don't. And I, for one, think I've got it."

He turned around and made an exaggerated swish of his rump so the tail flew in nearly a full circle.

Elizabeth was shrieking with laughter. "You got it!" she agreed.

"They don't call me the queen of the cow patch for nothing!" He swished his tail again and the unbelievable udders shook like water balloons dangled from a window.

When Elizabeth could talk again, she said, "I thought you were a singing cow!"

In bovine character he began to sing, "Happy birthday to M-o-o-o! Happy birthday to M-o-o-o!" By now nurses and aides and cleaning staff and a patient or two were in the room or in the hall, all of them laughing at Chris's antics. On each "m-o-o-o" he shook his tail and udders and the cowbell rang. "Happy birthday dear . . ."

"Don't you dare!" Elizabeth called out.

"EE-LIZ-A-BETH." Everyone sang out with Chris. Elizabeth put her hands over her face. She was vivid red.

"Happy birthday to M-o-o-o!" Chris added a real flair of a finish on this one. He bellowed.

When the crowd finished applauding and Chris bowed them out of the room, he shut the door. Then and only then did he take off the cow head.

"It's you!" she said in mock surprise.

"Aw! You're just saying that." He looked down to his plastic hooves and kicked one hoof against the other. "You're just trying to make me feel like less of an idiot."

"No, no, no, no," Elizabeth said. "I want you to fully enjoy being an idiot. Nobody I know could be quite as good an idiot as you. It was the best idiot I've ever seen. And don't forget I worked on Wall Street, tons of idiots on Wall Street."

He bowed again. "Thank you kindly, ma'am."

In absolute seriousness, Elizabeth said quietly, "No. Thank *you.*"

"Happy birthday, beautiful lady," Chris said and leaned down with much shifting of udders and clanking of cowbell to kiss her tenderly, then more passionately until his costume rode up so high the neck was about to cut off his chin.

Chris rummaged around under his suit and brought out a small silver wrapped package.

"Open this now or later, but I want out of this suit."

"I'll open it now!" She tore it open quickly. It was a velvet ring box and she opened it eagerly. Inside was a gold and platinum ring of hearts entwined with a heart-shaped three-carat diamond in the center.

Tears sprang to her eyes. She began to shake and she dropped the box onto the sheets and blanket. "Oh, Chris. I can't."

"I love you," Chris insisted. "Of course, you can."

"Oh, Chris!" She was reaching for him and in spite of the costume he held her as she talked into the spotted brown and white fabric. "I'm pregnant!"

"No kidding!" he said and leaned back to look at her in mock surprise. "I thought you were just glad to see me."

"Chris! I'm not kidding!"

"I'm not either! I love you. Marry me! Let's raise this baby together and make more babies!"

She looked at him as if he'd lost his mind. "I'm not going through this again for anything or anybody!"

"Okay. That's fine, too! I just want to marry you and live with you forever. I love you!"

Elizabeth sighed, picked up the box, and opened it again to look at the ring. Chris took it from her and put the ring on her finger. Then he kissed the fingertip and then every fingertip.

"We have right now, Lissy. What happened in the past, even what happened just this last second, it doesn't matter. We have now. The future doesn't matter unless we waste now. Casey and Elliot have our pasts. This baby is going to have our future. I love you. *Now,* Lissy. It's all we have."

Elizabeth looked into his lion's eyes and she reached her hand up to trace his cheekbones down along the jaw to his lips and back. She leaned forward and kissed him. "I love you."

His reaction was immediate and startling. He attempted to turn a cartwheel, but thought better of it. He lowed like a cow in heat; he ran around the room; he swished his tail and he laughed. They both laughed. "She loves me!" he'd crow in between gyrations. "She loves me!"

"You idiot," she said with great, tender, sweet love in her voice.

"Well, yeah! But I'm an idiot in love! Move over." He tried, cow suit and all to climb in bed with her, but there was no way. She was laughing so hard tears were running down her cheeks. He kissed her again and rained kisses over her eyes and cheeks. "Better be happy tears," he demanded.

"They are. Happiest."

He let go of her reluctantly and began to scratch in strange places. "I've got to get out of this suit!" he cried and went into her bathroom and shut the door.

"Modesty?" Elizabeth called out.

"Udderly!" he called back.

She laughed and settled back on the pillows. She held her hand out in the time-known fashion of a girl with her engagement ring, trying to catch the light on every facet, trying to see the love in it as if it were *in* the ring, not with it.

"You know, we went about this a bit backwards," she called out to Chris.

He stuck his head out the door and wiped a towel over his face. "Backwards?"

"We made love before I knew your name. You knew me naked before I knew your name!"

"There was a nurse in the room the first time," Chris said as he sat on the bed with her. "Doesn't count."

"I mean it. We are going about this all backwards. Not that I don't do everything that way."

Chris looked thoughtful. "Yes, we did do it backwards, but not until we'd done it frontwards and sideways and every which way but loose."

She punched him on the arm. "Not that."

"Ow!" He rubbed his arm and then

he put the spot in front of her face. "My mother always said that a kiss would make it better."

She ignored him.

"Very few people know this about me," she began. She turned her head from Chris to look out the window. "I do my work backwards."

"Uh, huh," Chris said as he tried to position himself for another try at getting her to kiss his arm.

"You see, I'm not a very good analyst really. I don't really understand why a P/E ratio or Book Value ought to matter."

Chris gave up trying to get kissed. "Okay. So how did you get so many hot ones?"

She looked at her ring once again and held up her hand to the light again. "I felt it."

"You felt it?"

"Yes. I ran my hand on the paper, prospectus, newspaper article, whatever. I felt it. If they were good, it was hot."

Chris looked at her and said "OOOOHHHHOOO! So, you really are the Wicked Witch of Wall Street!"

"That is why the name really hurt me. No one knew that I was doing *that* first. Then I'd go backwards and do the analysis. I very seldom missed. But it didn't work the other way. If a company looked good on paper, but didn't feel good, it didn't make any difference what the paperwork added up to. It failed."

"Are you kidding?" Chris said.

Elizabeth shook her head and blushed.

"You mean you could pick stocks and companies and bonds by touch?"

"You don't believe me." Elizabeth was upset. "Oh, please say you believe me!"

"I believe! I believe!" Chris said. "You do things by touch, backwards! Works for me! We found each other, you are going to marry me."

"I said I love you. I didn't say I'd marry you," Elizabeth corrected him.

"Oh, great. On everything else, you work backwards, on marriage you want to go the other way."

"I'm confused," Elizabeth said.

"Well, to follow the way you usually do things, you should touch me, decide I'm hot, marry me, and then decide to marry me."

Elizabeth considered what he'd just said. She shook her head. "Nope. I married the last time the very same way. Nope. This time, I'm going to know why first."

"Because you love me and I love you, and we feel damn hot together!"

"Give me some time, Chris. After all, I'm still stuck here in bed."

"Right where I want you."

"I refuse to be barefoot and pregnant."

"Too late!" Chris kissed the tip of her nose.

# Seventeen

De and Harry were the next to bring birthday wishes.

"Don't you have a home?" De asked Chris.

"Home is where you hang your horns," he said, holding up his cow head.

That stopped De for a moment. "I do believe you are the only person I ever met in my entire life that left me unable to think of what to say next."

"Come visit more often," Harry said in a stage whisper.

Pretending to ignore the two men, DeDe kissed Elizabeth's cheek. "Men can be so trite," she said. "Happy birthday!"

She put two small boxes on the bed and demanded Elizabeth open the smaller one first.

Elizabeth tore the package open; inside were two tiny tennis shoes. She was speechless as she twirled them from their wee laces and started at them.

"I couldn't resist," De said. "Aren't they the cutest things you've ever seen!"

*"Elizabeth!" Her intercom squawked. "There's a man here to see you." It was the second week in her very own office instead of being out in the bullpen with the others. She shared a secretary who called everyone by a first name. Elizabeth stood and was about to go out the door when the secretary said, "He says he's your father!"*

*She stopped, her hand on the knob. She felt the breath being forced by instinct into her lungs. She wanted to sink into the floor of the thirty-second floor and not surface until China.*

*Her hand shook as she opened the door and went into the bullpen. As she threaded her way to the reception area, she worked out what she would say. About how she hated and despised him, about how she never wanted to see him, and to get out of her life. About how deserting her and her mother was the worst thing any man could do, and she hated him. And then she saw him.*

*He was sitting in the corporate office, looking like a crushed-up brown paper lunch bag. Everything about him was wrinkled, brown and tan, and shabby. His hair was long and thin, and his tanned scalp showed through the gray hair. His corduroy coat was tan; his pants were khaki tan. He wore a turtleneck in brown and brown ornate cowboy boots with white and green insets. The cowboy boots embarrassed her immensely. They seemed to scream at her that he didn't belong here. His face was deeply weathered and tanned. She cringed when he looked up at her. She had his eyes. There was no doubt. She had his eyes. His face lit up and he stood immediately, dropping a small white paper box from his lap. He bent over and picked up the small box, held it out to her. When she did not take it, he put it in his jacket pocket where it bulged.*

*"I'd know you anywhere," he said in a drawn-out southern drawl. He blushed, the leathered skin turning a deep wine-red. "I . . . I mean . . . You are Elizabeth Templeton Avery, aren't you?"*

*She did not want to take him through the*

*bullpen, so she asked the receptionist if the board room was open.*

*She led him to the massive room with its fourteen-foot-long teak table and the deeply cushioned chairs. The board room carried out the corporate stark modern look, but it had windows that warmed the room with the view of buildings and sky and clouds. It was an impressive and intimidating room. Elizabeth felt comfortable in it. Her father, if he was her father, also seemed to be quite comfortable.*

*Elizabeth sat at the head of the table; her father sat three chairs to the left of her. She put her hands on the table, and her right hand held the ring finger of her left hand. He did much the same thing.*

"I know this must be a shock to you," he said. His voice was one of too many cigarettes and too many scotches. "I am *your father." He looked at her hopefully. She leaned back in her chair and put her hands on the armrests. He did the same.*

*"I think I would be shocked as well if somebody just came up and said they were my old man." He smiled and the very way his eyes crinkled up in the corners was exactly the way hers did. "Hell, I never met my old man, come to think of it."*

*"What do you want?" Elizabeth said. Her voice had recently begun to sound tough. At times, Elliot said, she shrieked.*

*"Why, I don't want anything. Not a thing." He looked at her with a gentleness Elizabeth could feel, as well as see.*

*"I don't know how you found me." Elizabeth leaned forward in her chair. "I don't want to know. I owe you nothing and you will get nothing from me," she warned.*

*He leaned forward and put his hands back on the table, open, pleading. "Baby, I don't want a thing."*

*Elizabeth jumped up from her chair and leaned across the table to put her face in his. "Don't you ever call me 'baby.' No one calls me 'baby'!" She was surprised at how vehemently she said it. "Say what you came to say, and then go away." She stood up as tall as her small frame would allow. He somehow seemed so much more of a presence in this room than she did. She felt her heart flutter an extra beat, stop beating and start again with a surge. "Well?"*

*He looked up at her, and he smiled again. He pulled the small box from his pocket and put it in front of her. "They're yours," he said. "Go on. Open it. I don't want anything from you. I just want you to have them."*

*Elizabeth stood where she was for a long while, her arms across her chest, trying to control her breathing and her erratic heart-beat.*

*"I want to give them to you. I don't want anything from you," he said again.*

She took the box and lifted off the top. She held up a small scuffed pair of white baby shoes; they dangled from the wee laces. Tangled in the laces was an unbelievably small fine gold chain with a small gold charm. She turned the charm and read E.T.A. 9/15/48 Daddy's Baby *in fine etched script.*

*Elizabeth thought she would faint. All the saliva in her throat threatened to choke her. Her hands were too weak to hold the small, nearly weightless things. They dropped to the table and she sank to the chair. Huge tears welled in her eyes. for once she did not try to force them back. Elliot had once said to her in the middle of a fierce fight they were having that she was going to drown in all her unshed tears, and she felt as if this just might be the time to do it.*

*Her father gently came up from his chair*

*and came to her. He knelt at her side and gingerly put an arm around her.*

*"Unfair," she sobbed. "This is unfair!"*

*"That's true," he agreed. "It's damn unfair."*

*"Why are you doing this?" she asked between sobs. He handed her a clean white handkerchief with the initial "A" discreetly embroidered on a corner. The thread was brown.*

*"They told me you were dead," he said.*

*She blew her nose loudly and then did it again. "Who told you?"*

*"The state."*

*"What state?"*

*"Where your mother died. She died in Nebraska. I was in Alaska at the time. When I found out your mother died, I came back. The state social services told me you both died of tuberculosis."*

*Elizabeth wiped at her still overflowing eyes. "I was at Grandma's and Grandpa's in Colorado."*

*"I know that, now," he said gently. "I should have gotten in touch with them somehow. But hell, old George, he hated me." He winced and slowly straightened up and sat in a chair closer to her. "I should have faced*

*the old bear, but I didn't do it." He looked down and blushed again. "God, that old man hated me."*

*"How did you find me?"*

*"Well, I got myself a detective. After I saw your picture in the magazine, I thought there can't be two Elizabeth Templeton Averys in the world. So I got a detective to follow the trail, so to speak, as if it were just the day I went to Alaska. He found out the state had mixed up the records. Another little girl of three had died that same day as your mother, and the file was in with your mother's. He found yours, too. And found out about Colorado. How good you were in school and all. About the full scholarships." He stopped then. he looked into her eyes and smiled again. "I'm real proud you turned out so good."*

*Elizabeth blushed. "Why now?" she asked quietly and without anger.*

*"Hey! I finally struck it rich!" He flung his hands into the air and shook them. "I finally did it! I hit oil!" He shook his head in disbelief at his own good luck. "I been searching out that damned black stuff for nearly sixty years, and I finally did it. Texas! Of all the places!"*

*"There's lots of oil in Texas," Elizabeth said, as if it were obvious.*

*"Hell, yes! But me, I'm* from *Texas and I run all over the whole damn world, chasing and chasing, and I mean I been* everywhere! *I go home and strike oil." He shook his head and laughed a wonderfully infectious laugh. "I go home to Nocona, Texas, and decide to put in a water well on the old dirt farm. Damned if they didn't find oil!"*

*She was smiling with him and soon was laughing along with him, as well. Suddenly, she stopped smiling and began to cry again. He came over to her, but instead of kneeling down he pulled her up to him and patted her on the back. He hugged her as she sobbed into his soft jacket. When she could talk again, she said, "I . . . don't know your name." He laughed at her in disbelief.*

*"You don't know my name? How could you not know my name?"*

*"I only ever heard Avery. Nothing else." She looked up into those eyes that were her eyes, and he smiled back.*

*"My name is George Jefferson. Call me Jeff. My mother liked to call all of us after her favorite presidents, but she already had a*

*Washington and a Thomas so I was George Jefferson Avery."*

*"I have uncles?" She was excited at the prospect of a family.*

*"No, baby. You don't. That is, they are dead now." He sighed and patted her once again. "I'm sorry, baby. I've got to be sitting down." He sat heavily, a little of his presence in the room seemed to dim.*

*"Ain't life a bitch?" he said without apology for the crudeness.*

*"And then you marry one, as Elliot says."*

*"I heard about you being married to some blue blood without a cent to his name."*

*"He'll have money when his mother dies."*

*"So what's he do for money now?" She could tell he already knew the answer.*

*"He's a broker, a good one." She wondered why she felt it necessary to defend Elliot.*

*"He's a vulture, you'll pardon me saying so. Old George probably used to say worse about me."*

*"He never said anything about you."*

*"Naw, maybe he wouldn't." He visibly perked up. "Say, let's go get us some lunch and talk a bit."*

*Elizabeth picked up the shoes and chain and held them out to him. "I'd love to have lunch with you. But I want you to keep these."*

*"Oh, baby. Those are yours. I bought 'em for you and they belong to you."*

*Elizabeth put them into his hands. "They are yours. I give them back. They are yours."*

*Something in her voice and the look in her eyes, so like his, made him nod in agreement. "Thank you. I* will *kind a miss 'em. They brought me some luck, I'd say."*

*He died three weeks later, back in Texas, of emphysema and congestive heart failure. Although she never saw him again, they had talked almost daily. He did not tell her he was dying. The oil well, once pumping twenty-five barrels of oil a day, dried up two years later. Elizabeth invested the money in a company that cleaned up oil spills.*

"Lissy?"

She heard Chris call her, and she wanted to come back from the memory. But she also wanted to stay there, feeling guilty for not loving her father.

"Lissy?"

She looked into his deep set brown

eyes and she jumped back in time to the first time she saw those eyes. She reached out and pulled him to her and kissed him.

"I want to go home," she whispered. "Please take me home."

# Eighteen

Chris returned the costume and walked back to the hotel. It was dark and he was tired and disturbed by what Elizabeth had said when he left.

"Take me home. I've got unfinished business there," she'd cried.

He hadn't asked what she meant. He'd kissed her and wished her happy birthday again. He'd held her tightly and while they were together he'd felt a funny little push. He knew he'd felt the baby move, and it had affected him as deeply as Elizabeth's plea.

And now he had to face Casey and probably her father as well.

Frankly, going back to the emergency room and facing the many traumas of life would be welcome, compared to what he was going through here. At least there, he felt as if he knew what he was doing, and he had a more than fifty-fifty chance at predicting the outcome. In his own life, things weren't that easy to foretell.

One of the bars in Merritt's hotel was a small, cozy, wood and leather place with hunting prints and waiters in fox hunting gear. The bartender wore the "Pink" jacket which was really red. He had an earring in his left ear and a long ponytail under his hunting cap. He was nice and didn't ask a lot of questions as Chris drank one beer after another and followed each beer with a shot of whiskey.

After four of these, Pinky, as Chris had begun to call him, finally said, "I think you've had enough." He offered to get him a cab.

Chris looked up at the mirror behind the bar and saw two—no, three—of himself. "I do believe I am drunk." Chris had never drunk much, but he was a friendly and even helpful drunk. "No need to call a cab, Pinky, old Pinky, old guy. Just aim me to the penthouse elevator. Just point the way. Just show me the way to go home, and I'll get there myself. It isn't my home, you understand. I just said that. My home is not there. I've got to take Lissy home. But Casey is in that home, and this home and . . . aw, hell . . . just get me on the damn elevator." He stood up from the stool and sank to his knees.

Pinky came around the bar and with the help of one of the green-jacketed waiters put him on the elevator. He called up to the penthouse to let them know he was on his way.

"You shouldn't have done that, Pinky. I thought you were my friend. How could you have done that? To me! What did I ever do to you?" Chris rambled on as the doors shut. When they opened, he expected to see Casey standing there, arms folded across her chest. That would have been bad enough. It was worse than that. Casey's father met him. Dressed in a tuxedo and velvet slippers, all so incongruous on the bulldog body of the man. Chris smiled. Then he passed out.

Dick Merritt did not suffer drunks gladly. He half-dragged, half-carried Chris to the master bathroom. With amazing physical power for a man of his age he threw Chris fully dressed into the shower and turned on full blast the double jets of water to ice cold.

"Wake up, kid," he shouted. "Wake up, NOW!"

Chris was having a hard time catching his breath from the shock and stinging needles of water that seemed to pierce his shirt and jeans. "I'm . . . I'm awake! I'm awake!"

Dick turned off the water and handed Chris a huge fluffy towel and pointed to the terrycloth robe. Chris nodded. Dick said, "In the kitchen. Five minutes." Chris nodded again.

Five minutes later Chris walked barefoot into the kitchen area and smelled coffee brewing and bacon and eggs cooking.

Dick Merritt had taken off the tuxedo jacket and rolled up the sleeves of his silk shirt. Massive ham-like fists and hairy arms were preparing plates of food for both of them. He nodded in the direction of the glass table and Chris sat.

"Drink," Dick said, and Chris picked up the heavy mug of coffee. The coffee was so hot and so strong it nearly took the skin off his tongue. "Now, eat," he demanded and sat down across from Chris. The two ate in silence.

Surprisingly, Chris felt better. He still had to talk to Dick Merritt. He still didn't want to, but he felt like he could.

"I don't drink much," Chris began. "I suppose if I did I could have handled it better."

"I'm damn glad to hear you don't drink much. And you probably didn't eat much either." Dick sounded tough, but not angry.

"No," Chris agreed. "I had a piece of cake. That's it."

"Was this before or after the cow costume?" Dick asked as he poured another mug of coffee for them both.

Chris grinned. "I had no idea I was so important."

"Ha!" Dick was genuinely amused, a big grin split his face. He said it again, "Ha! You aren't. But my girl is."

Chris drank the coffee and then looked up at the tough older man who had been so absent yet so important in his life with Casey. "Mr. Merritt—" he began. Chris was told to call him Dick. "Dick, I don't love Casey," he sputtered out in one breath. He took a deep breath and began again. "I have cared for her, taught her, I hope, been tender and kind and giving to her. But I don't love her."

"She doesn't think you love her either. So she ain't . . . isn't . . . stupid."

"She is far from stupid," Chris agreed. "I have a great deal of respect, and even awe, for what she has done." Chris put his elbows on the table and leaned forward. "She can't read, she can't add, she can't follow even basic instructions. She couldn't drive, couldn't read a recipe."

"Her mother and I thought we did the best for her, good schools. Expensive schools." Dick defended them.

"I'm sure you did. But nobody seemed to notice these things happening. She isn't stupid, but she sees things differently. Where you and I see 'dog' she sees 'Pob.' What the hell is 'Pob'? " Chris threw his hands in the air and shook his head. "Do you realize how hard it is to get through life when nothing is what it is supposed to be?"

Dick put his elbows on the table and

shoved aside the plates. "You sound like you love her."

"I do *not* love her. I respect her." Chris did not back down or stop his impassioned tone of voice. "This clinic you want to build. That's nice. Nicer still making Casey the manager. Buy why do it?"

"Why not?" the older man challenged.

"Because it makes no sense."

"You have told Casey many times about how you'd like to have a clinic in Vail."

"I would. And, I wouldn't." Chris leaned back in the chair, back on two legs, precariously balanced.

"Explain," Dick demanded.

"That used to be a dream. I would work in the ER for a while, then open a clinic. Save the world. I know better now. In fact, I've learned a lot these last few weeks. I love the ER. I love the whole thing. Even when I hate it, I love it. I like to help. I like to make things better when it seems like no one else can, when it's hopeless. Like I felt about Casey."

"You can make things better no matter

where you are," Dick argued. "You can make things better in a clinic."

"It's not the same." Chris slammed the chair down on all four legs and leaned on the table once again. Dick leaned forward as well. That is how Casey found them three hours later; two warriors deep in conversation and happily oblivious to the time.

"It's nice to see my two men enjoying themselves." She went to her father's side and kissed him then to Chris. Her father stopped her.

"Casey, honey. Sit down." Even when he was saying the sweetest of words, it was barked like a command. Casey sat between the two.

She looked from one man to the next. She smiled at first. That soon faded. "What is it?" she asked quietly.

"Let me." Chris held up a hand to stop Dick. "Casey, our lives together haven't been good for about the last three years. I know you agree with me on that, after all, you left me."

"I came back," she said.

"Casey, I've been gone. Even when I was there, I was gone."

"Daddy!" She turned to her father, pleading. "Make him stop!"

"Honey, nobody could stop me, and I'll be damned if I'm going to stop him." He said it gruffly, but he patted her hand, rather ineffectually trying to comfort her. "Baby, you weren't exactly honest with me about the two of you. It's been over for a while."

She stood up so fast she tipped over the kitchen chair. "Damn you!" she cried to Chris. "I don't want to be nobody!"

Her father stood then, taking hold of her shoulders and making her look at him. "Honey, you could never be a nobody. Why, you are my baby. My child! I did the wrong thing in saying you couldn't be in the family if you wanted that ski bum . . ." He turned his head to Chris, "You should pardon the expression." Then back to Casey, "Look, you don't know what I was going through then. Maybe someday I can tell you. But I was wrong, and I'm sorry." He shook her a little bit, but she ignored him. He put one big beefy hand on her face and turned her face to him. "Listen to me. I'm grateful to him. You hear me. I'm grateful. He got you back to me. He taught you. He made you see you ain't . . . aren't no dummy! I'm glad you're here. I'm glad you're back."

"Daddy," Casey whispered. "I just wanted you to love me. Like you loved Terry." She mentioned her late brother. Dick winced when she said his name and let go of her. He sat back down in the chair and put his head in his hands.

"I'm sorry, Daddy," Casey whispered.

"Casey, honey. I'm the one who is sorry."

Chris picked up the fallen chair and gently pushed Casey into the seat. He began to ease his way out of the kitchen.

"Casey, baby. I should have know you were the strong one. If I'd have known. You are a strong lady. You are! Why, Chris says you are so smart!"

"He did?" She sounded happy and tender.

"Oh, listen, he says you could run a clinic. So I'm thinking, why not a clinic to these kids who can't read and write?"

"Adults, too!" Casey said.

"Of course, you can decide. You can do anything you want . . ."

Chris left them talking. They never noticed he was gone. Chris went into the first bedroom he found. It must have been Casey's from the amount of makeup and clothes tossed around. He fell onto the deep wide bed and fell into an exhausted, somewhat drunken sleep.

When the doctor left that evening, Elizabeth was only slightly happier. In spite of the grandest birthday she'd ever had, she was sad. The doctor had agreed to let her be on "mere bed rest." She could get up and go to the bathroom and shower, she could wash her hair, and if she dropped something she could get it herself and not have to buzz for the nurse's aides.

"You have done very well. Your blood pressure is good, heart rate good and everything is coming along fine. Now, if you do as well on this you will soon be able to go back to that secluded hut in the mountains." The doctor teased her.

"You make me sound like a hermit."

"In about three months, you will never

be a hermit. There will be someone with you always."

"Now, that I can't wait for!" She perked up. "She will be so much fun!"

He looked at her over his glasses and smiled. "And she'll throw up on your best sweater and make acres of dirty laundry."

"Killjoy."

He ignored her jibe. Instead, he patted her toes and said, "You're my best patient."

She called De and would have called Chris, but she had managed, once again, to not ask him where he was staying. Old habits were hard to break. If she had any hard lessons to learn, the first one was to ask! She had spent forty-five years not asking. Not having a real conversation with anyone. Not learning about another person except what was their net worth, how much risk were they willing to take, and how much would she make.

*I wasn't quite that bad,* she amended in her own self-condemnation. *But I did not care about any personal part. Not about their lives or their beliefs. I didn't even get ad-*

*dresses. At first I left that to my assistant and then Elliot.*

How did we ever last as long as we did?

*Three* A.M. *and Elliot wasn't home. Elizabeth had to get up and call Hong Kong in ten minutes. Then into the office for the London opening. Three* A.M. *and Elliot was still not home. If she'd ever been a smoker, she'd have had a cigarette now. Coffee. She'd get up and go make coffee. What was ten minutes one way or the other when you'd been awake all night waiting for your husband to come in. To come in from going out to get a newspaper. Seven hours ago.*

*She got out of their king-size bed and put on the hand knit robe she'd bought herself on her thirty-fifth birthday. It was once a perfect fit, but it sagged a bit now and the rear was stretched. Still, she loved it. Her hair was tied in a messy ponytail. She hadn't slept and her eyes were showing dark circles and puffs on the upper lids.* I look like hell, *she thought as she caught a glimpse of herself in the hallway console mirror.*

*She made coffee, then a coffee cake. She made her phone call, talked to some idiot who assumed if she didn't speak the Queen's English she must be a moron. Arranged the trade, took out the coffee cake. Ate all of it. It was four forty-five when the lock turned and the door opened to admit Elliot.*

*She met him at the door to the kitchen.*

*"Good morning," she said.*

*He nodded. He took off his overcoat and hung it over the back of the hall chair. He began to go toward the bathroom, but she beat him to the door. She flung herself in and slammed the door in his face. She locked it, turned on the shower, and sat on the toilet and cried. Just before all the hot water ran out, she jumped in, rinsed off, and then dried herself. She took an extra long time doing her makeup and hair. They only had one bathroom. She hoped to high heaven he had to go to the bathroom in the most dire of ways. She hoped he suffered as much as she had suffered all night.*

*He stood up from the hall chair when she came out. He looked pale, but not uncomfortable. They nodded to each other as they passed each other. She did not ask and he did not offer to tell her what had happened to him when he went out to buy a paper nine hours ago.*

# Nineteen

Harry sat very quietly beside the hospital bed. He attempted to begin speaking, but would get only a syllable or two out before he would shake his head and quit speaking. Elizabeth flipped the television stations over and over and over. That began to irritate Harry, combined with not being able to say what he wanted.

"Would you stop that!" He finally got out one whole sentence.

"Sure." Elizabeth settled on a soap opera.

Harry cleared his throat and began to speak. "I have talked with your doctor, and he has said that it is all right to go ahead."

"Go ahead and what?" Elizabeth said.

"The attorneys for Elliot and the federal attorneys for the SEC want to do depositions."

"I expected that," Elizabeth said.

Harry sighed. "I expected it as well. But I thought they would accept a blanket deposition. You knew nothing, period."

"They won't?"

Harry shook his head. "Each and every item. Everything. Fifteen years. Day, time, everything."

"Good," Elizabeth said. "It will be boring. But I will finally know just what is going on."

"You might as well call it your job. It will take weeks and weeks."

"I'm not doing anything right now, Harry," she said with a lilt in her voice. "Will they start tomorrow? The sooner the better."

"You amaze me, Elizabeth," Harry said genuinely. "Do you have any idea how much this is going to cost you?"

"Your fees?" she asked. He nodded. "Harry, you're worth every penny."

"Elizabeth, I know your financial situation. With the deal you made with Elliot and now this, you'll be broke."

"I've made money before, and I'll do it again." Elizabeth tried to sound unconcerned, but nothing he had said before had upset her as much as that revelation.

When Harry left, she allowed the fear to settle over her like clouds on a rainy day. *No money.* The entire reason for her whole life, the entire focus of her functioning had been to never again be without money.

And now, her baby would come into the world as she had. Poor, without money.

*Don't panic. Don't get upset. Don't, don't, don't! No money! History repeats itself! The only thing I will have is the cabin in the mountains of Colorado, and we'll be poor!*

She could feel her heart beat faster, feel the bile rise in her stomach. She could feel her breathing become shallow and fast.

*Take a deep breath! Take another! Another! Slow down. Think clearly. Take another breath. Relax. Think calmly. Think of Do, not Don't. Take another breath.*

* * *

*"Elliot, I tried to use my credit card today and it was denied."*

*Elliot looked up from the book he was reading in front of the wall of stereo equipment he had amassed over the years. He reached for his remote control and lowered the volume. "I'm sorry. What did you say?"*

*"I tried to use my credit card and it was denied. I haven't used the card since Christmas. I called and they said you had been using it."*

*He shrugged. "You said I could."*

*"I didn't say you could use ten thousand dollars!"*

*"Take a deep breath, Elizabeth. Lower your voice. You are shrieking. I hate you when you do that."*

*Elizabeth did take a deep breath. But when she opened her mouth, she still sounded strident and shrill.*

"What in the hell did you do with my money?"

*Elliot glanced up at her as if she were the most boring person he had ever met. Then he put on his patrician voice, looked down his thin nose at her, and said, "What do you want me to do about it? I have no money as you know perfectly well."*

*He sat that way for several minutes. Elizabeth tore up the bill and flung it in his face. "I'm not paying it," she said as calmly as she could.*

*He shrugged. "It's your credit." He sounded so bored.*

*Elizabeth felt her heart beating faster, her breath getting shallow and fast. She could barely swallow. When she felt she could speak, she said, "Never again, Elliot."*

*He stood up and let the book drop to the floor with a thud. He walked to her with his lonely, pleading puppy look. "Just until the next quarterly check, darling." He put his arms around the unmoving Elizabeth. "You know I always run short just before the quarterly. I'll pay it." He kissed her forehead and eyelids and lips.*

He never paid it. None of the times did he ever pay it back.

The phone rang. It startled Elizabeth and that startled the baby who began a rowing contest. Holding her stomach and reaching for the phone, Elizabeth got a mental image of what she must look like. She answered the phone laughing.

"Hey! I like it!" Chris said.

"Where are you?" She was proud of herself for asking, but that was quickly quashed by his answer.

"I'm at the airport. I didn't have time to come back in and see you before I had to leave. But I'll call you from Denver, and I'll call you when I get to Vail. I'll call you every hour on the hour if that will make you laugh like you just did."

She laughed. Just to please him.

"Elizabeth?"

"Christian."

"I love you."

"Thank you."

"Thank you? Didn't anybody ever teach you what you are supposed to say when somebody says 'I love you'? "

"I guess no one ever did."

"I'll have to work on that when you get back," he said. "I've got to run. Call you in about three hours."

He hung up before Elizabeth could say anything else.

She really didn't know what she was going to say, anyway.

*How do I tell him that I'm poor? How do I say that, at the moment, his love was nice, but I feel useless and worthless?* She sighed, scrunched down into the bed, and turned up the soap opera.

*These people haven't a clue how bad life can really be,* she told herself. *My life would make a great soap opera. But who'd believe it?*

Harry called twice about the records in storage. De came by with a new T-shirt and lots of juicy gossip about people Elizabeth used to know. It was amazing how quickly Elizabeth seemed to no longer care. She listened anyway.

After a shower Elizabeth felt more like her old self. She didn't have to avert her eyes while someone she barely knew washed her. She could wash her hair. Blow dry it! She could walk from the bathroom to her bed whenever she wanted. It was amazing how good that felt.

Barbara dropped in with a friend of hers. They'd just had lunch together and were discussing some of the articles that Elizabeth had written over the years for both business and women's magazines.

"I want you to meet Angeline Graves." Barbara introduced the gray-haired, grandmotherly beauty to Elizabeth.

"Angeline, meet Elizabeth March."

Angeline held out a soft, dainty hand which shook hers with an iron strength. "I'm so glad to meet you."

Elizabeth looked flustered and blushed. Barbara said, "I should explain. Angeline and I shared a lab table when we were in college. I was nineteen, Angeline was forty. We have had a very long relationship, and we talk or meet each other weekly." Barbara smiled at Angeline.

"She helped me a great deal when my husband died," Angeline said.

"And you were there for me when my husband was killed," Barbara reminded her friend.

"Hardly the same situations, but the support was invaluable."

Barbara nodded and Angeline spoke again. "Well, we began to talk about my latest project. I am starting a magazine for women. *Really for women!* As if we need another women's magazine that tells us how to dress or cook or get a man! No! Mine is for women who, for one reason or another, have money to handle for the first time in their lives. There will not, I swear, be a single line about diets or the latest trend from Paris, unless that trend is financial."

Barbara interrupted. "Besides, she has one of those already." She named a top women's magazine.

"I think it's a wonderful idea," Elizabeth said. She looked from woman to woman. "What does it have to do with me?"

Barbara looked shocked. "It has everything to do with you!"

"Okay." Elizabeth sounded unconvinced.

Angeline addressed Elizabeth directly. "You see, you gave me the idea about six years ago in an article you did for a magazine. I used to be the editor. At that time I had a marketing study done, but it just wasn't time. Now it's time!"

"It's time for what?"

"For this magazine!" Angeline was excited, her pale blue eyes glistened and her pink cheeks glowed.

"Perhaps it is," Elizabeth agreed.

"Baby boomers divorcing; retirement amounts bigger or smaller in some cases; widows, always a factor."

"And you have been writing about it for years!" Barbara said.

"I still don't see what it has to do with me."

"I want you to write it for me." Angeline sounded as if it ought to be obvious.

"Write it?" Elizabeth couldn't believe her ears. "Are you talking about a glossy paper, hundreds of pages magazine? I can't write a whole magazine!"

Angeline shook her head. "Not just yet. At first, a newsletter format. Subscription cost, mailing cost, low. focus, pinpointed. Word of mouth, high."

Elizabeth was intrigued. "You want me to write a newsletter about money and investments, aimed at women who never really handled money on their own." She really was intrigued.

"Do you know how often women, intelligent women, absolutely can't understand how to handle their own money?" Angeline said.

Elizabeth and Barbara looked at each other and laughed.

"I'll say I do!" Elizabeth said. "Begin with me!"

"Very few women admit it. Men, too. If they would only shut up and climb down off that high and mighty pedestal they've put themselves on. Oh, very few people understand economics, not even economists understand finances!" Angeline said. "I've got a list of possible subscribers that will knock your socks off. I think it's time. Seize the day!" she cried out, her fist held high.

"You can write it from anywhere, that is if your cabin has a computer," Barbara encouraged.

"It doesn't, but it will." Elizabeth was raring to go. "I know just what the first topic will be."

"What?" Angeline and Barbara both asked.

"Ladies, beware of your husbands!"

The SEC panel that came to the hospital room were, at best, coldly polite. At worst, which is what they were, they were incensed they had to come to the hospital rather than making Elizabeth come to them.

Two men and a woman. Gray suits and red ties, the woman dressed in the female version, soft silk tie at the neck, but severely tailored gray suit. For just a flash, Elizabeth thought of the woman calling the men in the morning to discuss what they would all wear. It was ridiculous, but it helped her lighten up as she dealt with their strict and angry personae.

The preliminaries were soon over and the questioning began.

The more they asked, the angrier they got. It made no difference what they asked. She denied knowing about anything.

"On March 19, 1984, did you buy and sell three-hundred shares of DIMV at a profit of $7,850?"

"I know nothing about that."

"You do know that day trading is against the rules and regulations of the SEC," the woman said in a monotone.

"Oh, yes," Elizabeth agreed.

"This trade was made in your account," one of the men said.

"But I knew nothing about it," Elizabeth said again.

And so it went.

"Did you trade four hundred shares of Walt Disney into account number 3391 on the morning of April 24, 1988, and buy it back the next morning for the account number 8331?"

"Did you trade knowledge about a merger with . . . ?"

"Did you knowingly take a margin account . . . ?"

"Did you make a day trade . . . ?"

On and on and on.

Elizabeth held up better than the three interrogators on the first day.

By the end of the three weeks of investigating, she was even stronger and they were angrier than ever.

And for the entire time, Harry sat in the chair next to Elizabeth's bed and quietly took his own notes. He, as well as the SEC, also tape-recorded the entire proceedings.

On the final day, Harry arranged for a small, simple cake to be delivered. He also ordered a small carafe of coffee. When the cake and coffee were delivered at the end of the day, the SEC trio stood and began to leave.

Harry stopped them and said, "Won't you please share our cake and coffee?" It was the first thing he'd said other than "good morning" and "good afternoon" in the entire three weeks.

The woman looked up and carefully considered the possible ramifications. The two men dove in. In a few minutes all were acting as if it were the most normal thing, for people who had treated her as a liar and conspirator to be eating cake and drinking coffee with her.

But, what really made Elizabeth sit back and shake her head was what they said as they left. All three agreed: "This whole thing could have been handled with one phone call."

It had cost Elizabeth thirty thousand dollars for what could have been a two dollar phone call.

*Article idea number two,* Elizabeth told herself. *If you can do it the hard way–don't.*

# Twenty

"How am I doing?" Elizabeth asked her doctor after he examined her chart. "Blood pressure? Weight?"

He put the chart down and smiled at her. "Very, very good. Under the circumstances, very good."

"May I go home now?" She asked him everyday.

"How many more days of the depositions?" he asked her, referring to the attorneys who congregated in her room for four to five hours a day.

"Today was the last day."

He thought for a few moments then answered, "I'll make you a deal. You need to rest a few days now that this SEC business is all over. I want one twenty-four hour period of good behavior. Then you can get up and go to your heart's content."

"That is not much of a deal. That adds up to six weeks. Just what you said when I came in."

"That is the deal," he said.

"Done," Elizabeth said and shrank down into her bed. "I'm going to be like some sailor on dry land, you know, my legs won't work."

"They'd better or you'll be back here," he said as he patted her toes, winked, and left the room.

She phoned Chris immediately. He wasn't available so she left a message. She called DeDe next, who screamed with delight. Harry understated, "That's nice."

She made a few calls to Denver. There were a few things she wanted to do when she got back.

Barbara and Angeline would be coming in to have dinner with her that evening so she waited to tell them.

Six weeks. She had survived. The baby had survived. She was going to have a job that would make her a living. Her worry about money, although not completely gone, was at least eased.

*What could go wrong?*

She immediately stopped that thought. *What an immensely stupid thing to think. If you don't know by now that anything can happen!* she thought.

*The alarm went off, it stabbed their eardrums and Elliot rolled over to turn it off. Elizabeth moaned. He missed the button and the alarm kept up its piercing buzz that seemed to make the heart panic and the adrenaline pump. It was the most annoying alarm clock they had ever had. They both needed something annoying to get them up. The radio alarm had not worked, they both liked music and they would roll over and fall back asleep unless it was put on an acid rock station or something else they both hated. And that was sacrilege to Elliot. So they got an old-fashioned one from a junk store. It was wound at night, and it clattered everyone awake in the morning. Elizabeth threw it one morning, so that was the end of that. This one worked. Now if Elliot could just find the button.*

*He found it and they both took a deep breath and closed their eyes again. Elliot got up and went into the bathroom. Elizabeth stayed in bed to wait for the sound of the running shower when she would get up and start a pot of coffee. While he drank coffee, she would shower and dress. Then they were at the office before most of the world was up. Five A.M.*

*But this morning there was no shower. Elliot came back to bed and began to make loving noises and soft sounds.*

*They had been married for fifteen years. The act was done on automatic. No thought required. He ran his hands along her body, caressed her breasts and nipples with his fingertips and then teased them with his tongue. Elizabeth responded. Gratefully. It had been at least three months since they had even so much as kissed each other.*

*She was so glad he was touching her that she sighed and moaned in the way he always liked, said the words he liked to hear. He responded with more intense sucking of her breasts and rubbing his hand down her flat belly and to the deep cleft between her legs. She was ready, had been ready since he first touched her. She opened her legs; he was on and in her so quickly she hadn't caught her breath before it was over. He kissed her breast one more time, got off her, and went into the bathroom again.*

*She lay there as the shower started. She tried to think of how wonderful it had been. She said over and over to herself that he loved her, all was fine, life was back to normal.*

*She put on one of his T-shirts and went into the kitchen. She prepared the coffee, ground it freshly and put it in the drip coffee maker, turned it on and went back to the bedroom then into the bathroom. Elliot was in the walk-in closet, dressing. When she was through and dressed, she came back out to the kitchen and poured herself a cup of coffee. Only then did she see his suitcases.*

*"You forgot we have to go sign the tax papers," she said.*

*"I did not forget," he said.*

*"Good." She looked at the suitcases, but she said nothing.*

*"I'm not very good at this kind of thing," he said. He stood up and put on a raincoat and picked up one of his suitcases. Elizabeth felt her heart pounding, and she could hear it in her ears.*

*"Actually, I've never done this before," he added as he walked to the front door and put*

*the suitcase down. He went back to the kitchen and picked up the other suitcase. Elizabeth stood just where she was. He took a deep breath. "Not that it matters to you, but I'm leaving you."*

*She still said nothing. Her throat was so constricted she thought she might choke on her own tongue. She could not make a word come out.*

*"Well, I didn't think it would matter to you, but I think I will tell you why." He actually gave her his most charming smile. "You'll appreciate this. Remember Jennifer in records?" She shook her head. "Christmas party? Gave out copy machine copies of her naked breasts as Christmas gifts? Painted the nipples red with markers?" Elizabeth stood stock still. She thought she was going to throw up. "Well, she and I are getting married. She's pregnant. Isn't that amazing? The fantastically perfect Elizabeth Templeton Avery March can't get pregnant, and the brainless bitch from records drops her pants and I'm going to be a daddy." He walked to the door and picked up his other suitcase.*

*Elizabeth didn't remember leaving the kitchen, but she did remember pulling on one of his suitcases. Pulling and struggling with him. "Stop it! Elizabeth!" he yelled at her and shoved her from him. She fell against the hall table and slowly sank to the chair. Still she said nothing. He opened the door and threw out both of his suitcases and then slammed the door behind him.*

*Elizabeth felt deaf and blind. She hadn't heard what she had just heard; she couldn't have seen him leave. It hadn't happened.*

*She got up and put on her coat, found her briefcase and handbag. She went to work. She called Harry and told him what had happened. He told her to come in and after she signed the tax forms they would start divorce proceedings. He told her that Elliot had already been in and he'd not said a word about the situation. He told her to hold on and everything would be fine. He said it was a straightforward divorce case. What could go wrong?*

It was just another moment, another proof that she was not someone who could be loved. She was easily abandoned. Easy to walk out on. No matter how good a person, or even how bad, people left her.

Chris phoned and the call brought Elizabeth back to the moment.

"I didn't have time to tell you. But my personal problems seem to be cleared up." He told her what had transpired. "I think I helped, at least I did no harm."

Elizabeth heard the question in his voice. The genuine hope that he had done the right thing. She was so lost in her own memory, so in pain from it, that she said the first thing that came into her mind.

"You must not make very many mistakes," Elizabeth said.

"Why do you say that? Of course, I make mistakes. Plenty of them."

"But you are so concerned that you did the right thing."

"Of course I'm concerned!" He was surprised at her words. "I'm always concerned. What are you getting at?" She wasn't saying what he had expected her to say. She wasn't even acting like someone he would know.

"Maybe it's just that I'm older than you," she said. "But I feel that my mistakes were the best I could do at the time with the knowledge I had at the time." Elizabeth wasn't thinking of Christian and his problems. She was thinking of her own. His angry response at first made an impression on her own thoughts, but the hard tone of his voice slowly got through to her.

"Oh, that's real good, Lissy. You, the great avoider of asking questions, the all-time champ of not being aware of other people, their lives and their problems. You are trying to tell me . . ." He broke off.

"Look, Elizabeth." She could hear him take a deep breath and practically tick off numbers from one to ten.

"First of all, your age and my age aren't factors in any of this. Secondly, take a close look at your mistakes and the reason they happened. Then, and only if you really think you did the best you could, give me advice."

He said goodbye and hung up before Elizabeth could say another word.

To the silence on the line she said, "I have been."

She held the phone in her hand for a while before she hung up. She thought of trying to call him back. Angeline came in.

"You look like you've just had very bad news. Should I come at another time?"

Elizabeth shook her head and put on her old smile, the one that said "I don't feel like smiling but I'm going to anyway." Elizabeth was soon caught up in the further planning for her newsletter. She would examine her relationships later.

Or, maybe it was supposed to be that she drove people away. She shrugged and got on with her work.

Chris had never hung up on someone before. He didn't know why he just did. And to Elizabeth of all people! The one woman he loved more that his own self. He loved her even more than his work! He'd hung up on her! He hit his forehead with the palm of his hand and started to pick up the phone to call her back.

He thought again. *I wasn't wrong. I wasn't* tactful, *but I wasn't wrong. Using her own methods, I did the best I could with what I knew.*

He'd call her later and talk with her. He'd do the right thing. He stood up and left the doctors' lounge.

*Hey! It works!* he thought. *I did the best I could with what knowledge I had at the time.*

In his heart he knew that what he really felt was fear. Fear that she wouldn't speak to him again. Fear he would never hold her again. Fear that she would never admit she loved him.

He knew that he could not play the role of white knight and save her from herself. He'd learned that lesson the hard way, but he didn't want to lose her.

Christian thought of her the first time he'd seen her in the ER and when she'd run out of her cabin as if ghosts chased her. He smiled. She thought she was so independent and didn't need anyone. He thought he wanted someone who didn't need him totally, someone who could pick out her own clothes, decide what to eat, and pick a restaurant without his guiding hand.

He'd no idea that someone could be so frustrating. Barbara was right, he suffered from savior syndrome. He wanted to help, and if they didn't need his help he was frustrated. Elizabeth made her own decisions; she didn't need or want to know his. She was what he'd always wished for.

Now, he steeled himself to buck up face the music. Or, would it be more appropriate to say, "Be careful what you wish for you just might get it"?

He went into the first examining room, the patient had a bloody scalp from an accident with a tree, a chain saw and a six-pack of beer. "Hey, fella!" he said. "Anybody ever tell you don't drink and drive a chain saw?"

Elizabeth couldn't sleep. She and Angeline had talked a great deal about the newsletter and how Elizabeth could keep up with the news when she didn't live near civilization.

"A satellite dish for all the cable channels, a computer and modem, a fax machine. That ought to do it," Angeline said. It was all so simple now. In her beginning journalism days, a manual typewriter and a phone were all the lucky writer had to depend on.

Elizabeth ran a mental tab on the cost. "I can't do all that," she said. "I don't have any idea how much I have left at the moment, but I can't do that." She was blushing from the tips of her toes to the roots of her hair. She was burning with embarrassment. Money always seemed to stop her. Not having it caused her pain, and having it had caused her pain.

Angeline let none of it bother her. "The company will lease them. Don't give it another thought." She looked at Elizabeth and saw her very real distress.

"Haven't you any money, really?" she said in disbelief.

"I haven't what I thought I had." Elizabeth sounded angry. "I have always been very conservative. My money is in conservative funds and bonds and a very few growth stocks. I have been selling off to cover everything, and a forced sale is a sure way to lose money. I can't wait for an opportune time, I have to sell regardless. I've lost well over two-thirds of what I had."

Angeline, although probably in her seventies, had a very young voice and face and body. Her whole air was one of graceful and beautiful disregard for being in the last third of her life. She suddenly looked her age. She sank into herself. The taut skin folded into accordion-pleated waves, and her hair looked faded. She let her voice get tired.

"Don't you believe in your own abilities?" She sounded so weary.

Elizabeth looked at her in shock. No one had ever asked her that. Never. Her abilities had been what she and everyone else had believed in. How could she. . . . And then she reached out her hand to Angeline.

"I have never believed I was anything but a sham. A fraud. I have thought that I was faking it all along. But I know better. I see it now. I am very good. I am. And your asking me to do this newsletter is what made me realize it." Elizabeth took the older woman's hand and shook it.

"Let's make a pact. I will not doubt that I will do my best, and you won't doubt your choice of editor."

Angeline came back into bloom. They

had both faced their own doubts, and came out on the other side in fine shape.

"Done." Angeline smiled.

# Twenty-one

Midnight. Chris was half-asleep on the little love seat in the huge, nearly empty room. He'd been thinking in a half-hearted way of getting up and going upstairs to bed when the phone rang. He always sprang fully alert whenever the phone rang. He looked at his watch and thought the hospital must have had more than it could handle.

It was Elizabeth.

Just the sound of her voice made his body react with desire. He was sorry she was so far away. If she'd been nearer, he would have gone to her immediately just to see her, to touch her, to tell her he loved her.

He looked at his watch again. "Hey, it's two A.M. there! What are you doing calling me at two A.M.? You ought to be asleep!" He wondered why he couldn't tell her how he felt. Why was he holding back his desire for her?

"I'm awake. Wide awake." Elizabeth said. "Chris, we just had our first fight!"

He held the phone away from him and looked at it. They had? Then he put the phone back up to his ear and spoke. "Lissy, we did not have a fight."

"Okay, we had a misunderstanding, and I'm calling because I can't go to sleep until I tell you I'm sorry."

Chris shook his head and smiled. *God, how I wish she were here so I could tease her and touch her.*

"Are you going to be one of those women who says you can't go to sleep until the argument is over?" Chris sounded wary. He wished he could take back the tone of voice, but it was too late.

"No," Elizabeth said, "but I am going to be one of those women who admits she was wrong when she finds out she is wrong."

"Admirable quality. But you weren't wrong," he said gently.

"It was insensitive and blind of me to say what I did."

"Oh! That! Yes, you were," Chris teased. "You were definitely those things. But you were also right."

"Chris, you are arguing with me." Elizabeth sounded shocked. "I call to apologize and you are arguing with me."

"I am not!"

"You are!"

"Not!"

Silence on the other end.

Finally Elizabeth said, "Are you joking with me?"

"Can't you tell?"

"No."

"Well, you'll have years and years to find out if I'm joking or not. A whole month of Sundays."

Elizabeth laughed. "Now that's the Christian Hanford I know and love."

"Go to bed," he said.

"I can't go anywhere else." Then she remembered. "Oh! I forgot to tell you! I get released in two days!"

"Great! Call me as soon as you have your flight information. I'll pick you up in Denver."

"You can pick me up in Vail."

"I want to drive up with you. I love you," Chris said what he had wanted to say ever since she phoned. He waited for her answer.

"Thank you."

"God, I've got a lot of work to do on you." He shook his head and sighed. "I said I love you and you say . . . what?"

"I'm working on it. Are you going to be one of those guys who demands the right response every time?"

"Yes."

"Well, if I have to."

"You do. Now. I love you."

"I love you." Elizabeth said it like a speaking computer.

"Go to bed," he said in his most medical voice.

"I feel like a teenager talking to my boyfriend. Did I tell you I never had a boyfriend when I was a teenager?"

"No, but I could figure that out for myself."

"How?"

"Go to bed," he said again, followed by a gentle laugh.

"What? Do I have a label or tattoo

somewhere that says 'NEVER HAD A BOYFRIEND'?"

"Say good night, Gracie!" he said.

"Who's Gracie?"

"I forgot, no television education. I've got a lot to teach you."

"All right. Good night," she said.

He hung up and leaned back on the sofa.

For the first time he really wondered what he was doing. He'd asked himself that from the very first time he saw her in the emergency room. But this time, he had some more insight into not only her, but himself.

Each one of them suffered, but in a different way. Opposites yet the same. It was her own pain that flayed Elizabeth; the pain of others that did it to him. But now both of them felt the raw burning touch of love for the other. Still, Chris had to deal with his problems and make sure he wasn't adding any to Elizabeth's.

What was it Barbara had said about him? Savior syndrome. Make it all better.

Come to the doctor and he'll fix everything.

He'd just been in—and just let go of—a relationship that was nothing else *but* those things. Was he about to get into the same thing?

*Too late. Sorry doctor or savior or whomever I think I am, I am in too deep now. And it's right where I want to be.*

Elizabeth put her hands behind her head and looked up at the dark hospital room ceiling. She could hear a buzzer go off, another patient calling for help in the night. That was just what she had done. She had called Chris for help in the night. And she was certain he would give it. For the first time in her life, she knew she had someone who could help her in the night.

The *second* time in her life, she corrected. She had always been able to call on her grandparents. It was herself who could not be relied upon. She was the one who was never there in time of need.

She lowered her arms to encircle the

growing child. *I'm learning, daughter. I'm learning.*

"Let's go shopping! Bloomingdale's is just screaming for us to spend, spend, spend!" DeDe came into the room with her usual exuberance. "And don't you say one word about money, it's mostly yours anyway." De was referring to the huge amounts of money Elizabeth paid to Harry.

"Worth it at any price," Elizabeth said. She had on a blue jean jumper dress and a red T-shirt De had brought the night before. She was also wearing good walking shoes with support. She had been up less than two hours, and she was already tired.

"I have arranged everything," DeDe said. "The limo will take us there, and then you will sit."

"I can't believe I'm saying it after being flat on my back for six weeks, but that sounds good."

They checked her out of the hospital. Once they were settled in a dressing room with sandwiches and fruit juice, the fashion show began.

It was amazing. Suits for the executive with more style than what Elizabeth wore *before* she was pregnant. Dresses with great thought to fashion, evening gowns so magnificent Elizabeth couldn't believe they were for pregnant women. Sports clothes for every possible situation. Nightgowns and underwear, accessories galore! Elizabeth couldn't believe when they even came in with a wedding gown for the finale. It was beautiful, but a shock.

"Good heavens! Why are you shocked!" De said. "An unbelievable amount of marriages take place with the baby as the marriage broker!"

Elizabeth chose several sports outfits, jeans, sweaters, and lounge outfits. She chose one suit and one dress because DeDe insisted. And just because she couldn't help herself, she chose an evening dress. It was off the shoulder, red silk, beaded heavily with gold and pearl bugle beads. It was so beautiful, she had to have it. She even tried it on. The dress fit like a glove, but she was assured it could be let out for her increased growth. Elizabeth knew she was being silly to want the dress so much. And where on earth would she wear it, she had no idea. But she loved it.

With underwear and several pairs of shoes and other accessories, it came to over seven thousand dollars.

"For clothes I'll wear for a few months!" Elizabeth was shocked.

"You can wear them again next time!" De assured her.

"NO NEXT TIME!" Elizabeth was adamant.

De shrugged her shoulders. But the overall mood was, want to bet?

# Twenty-two

Before she left New York, Elizabeth arranged to have lunch with Barbara.

"At a real restaurant!" she told Barbara. "Real food! Real waiters!" She was so excited she even added, "And I'll be wearing clothes!"

"Now there's an exciting prospect!" Barbara laughed. "Listen, let me choose the place."

"Done." Elizabeth agreed to meet Barbara at a deli.

When they met, Elizabeth was dressed in her new suit. "I decided it's the only time I'd get to wear it," she explained.

"It looks great. This is a celebration so go all out. I'm having pastrami on rye with swiss and hot mustard."

Elizabeth ordered the same. "The baby

may have nightmares from this, but I'm going to love it. I'm glad you chose this place. The food couldn't be more unlike hospital food!"

"Well, we could have done tandoori or maybe Greek," Barbara said, "but I think this is *so* New York."

"I never miss New York," Elizabeth admitted. "The first months I was back in Colorado I missed plumbing and electricity and bathtubs, but once that was taken care of there was nothing I missed at all."

"You were extremely busy, extremely emotional, and not truly aware of a lot then."

"I still don't think I'll miss much." Then Elizabeth laughed. "Actually, I will miss take-out and delivery of Chinese food!" They both laughed. "I can just see me calling up the nearest Chinese delivery in Denver and giving them directions. Fourteen miles north past the Vail exit! Look for the lake and the raccoon!"

They were still laughing when their order was called, and Barbara got up to get it. When she did, Elizabeth saw Elliot, Jennifer, and the baby, sitting two tables from them.

In a city the size of New York, and with a population as big, she could not believe the coincidence of seeing these particular people in this deli.

She had not realized that it would hurt her, make the whole happy moment come to a screeching halt. Tears sprang into her eyes. How she hated all these damn tears!

They had not seen her. If she thought she could have, she would have melted into the chair. Anything to keep them from seeing her.

Elliot took the baby from Jennifer while she ate her sandwich. He held the baby gently, not as if he were afraid in any way. Typically of Elliot, he seemed to fit right in with the father role. No unease. The baby spit up a small bit of milk, and he casually wiped it up and continued to eat his own salad.

Elizabeth could not, even though she wanted to, tear her eyes away from the vision of family togetherness. Elliot was smiling, Jennifer was smiling, the baby was sleeping. Perfect family scene.

She didn't look at Barbara when she returned to the seat and blocked the view. She looked down at her plate. Barbara noticed immediately.

"What's happened?"

"Cold, harsh reality," Elizabeth answered. She told Barbara about them.

Barbara put her hand on Elizabeth's arm. "We can leave. We don't have to stay if you don't want to."

"I don't have a clue what I want to do, other than melt into this damned uncomfortable plastic chair. Or go blind."

"No one wants to see these things," Barbara said.

"No, but there it is," Elizabeth said with an edge as cold as a frozen Colorado lake.

"Now, you have to cope," Barbara stated quietly, allowing no room for an alternative. Coping was the only answer.

Barbara picked up her sandwich, piled far too high for the average human mouth. She tried to stretch her mouth to open and bite. She made a mighty effort, making Elizabeth giggle. She managed to get a small bite out of a corner. With mustard on the corners of her lips, she smiled broadly. "I got cheesecake, too," Then she pushed forward a plate with a four-inch square of solid New York cheesecake.

Elizabeth smiled . . . and coped.

Elliot and family left a few minutes later. If he had noticed Elizabeth there in her suit and ponytailed hair, he did not acknowledge her. She had coped, and the crisis had passed. Except for the memories. .

*"I'm sorry," Elizabeth said. She sat in the big soft chair in front of their gas log fireplace. The log provided the only light in the apartment. Elliot sat at the dining-room table. "I am truly sorry," she said.*

*"Stop it, Elizabeth," Elliot said. "It isn't your fault."*

*"It seems to be. I don't seem capable of getting pregnant."*

*"We don't know that," Elliot said. As if ten years of trying weren't enough proof.*

*"No," Elizabeth agreed with him. "We don't. And I'm not willing to go through the testing and surgery to prove it one way or the other." She stood up and went into their bedroom.*

*Elliot stood up, walked to the door of the bedroom but did not enter.*

*"It would only take you away from the office a little while," he said soothingly.*

*Elizabeth came to the doorway. "You don't understand. I will not go through all that. I refuse." She looked up at him and added, "I'm sorry."*

*Elliot's reaction was swift and terrifying. He slapped her so hard her teeth rattled, and she cut the inside of her lip on her teeth. She could taste the salty blood.*

*"Don't bother lying to me." He said the words as if they were poison being spit from his mouth. "You aren't sorry, and I'm not sorry I hit you."*

*He grabbed his overcoat and left the apartment. He came back hours later and joined her in bed, making swift and, for them, passionate love.*

*Elizabeth never cried over the incident. She never told anyone, and the two of them never spoke of it. He never hit her again. She never lied . . . if she spoke to him.*

Chris put his house for sale. The real estate agent was a squawky, loud man with a bad hairpiece, but he was sure they'd sell it for the price Chris wanted.

"Could you possibly put furniture in? Maybe rent some? A place does better if it looks like somebody lives there and likes it." Chris said no.

The man sighed. "Okay. Maybe it knocks the price down a few thousand."

"I'll manage to put up with the loss," Chris said.

They finished the paperwork, and Chris gave him a key.

"Call me first," Chris said. "If I'm here, I'm asleep."

As if he had cursed himself, Chris could not sleep that night. He lay awake, looking at the ceiling. The sound of the breeze through the pine trees and aspens whispered to him. Ordinarily it was a lullaby. Tonight it kept him awake.

"Lissy," it whispered. Over and over again. "Lissy." He rolled over and tried to sleep on his back. He punched his pillow and twisted it to fit under his head as he tried to get comfortable on his side. He ended up in the kitchen making an omelet and drinking milk just about ready to go sour.

He stood at the kitchen sink and ate the food right from the pan. He'd purposely made too much, thinking that if his stomach had major demands on it, then the blood would all rush there and he'd go to sleep.

His brilliant strategy backfired. A fierce stomachache, a headache, and nausea were his rewards.

Morning arrived, and he was in worse condition. He had a fever, and he was more than having difficulty keeping food down. He was sick. Self-diagnosis: flu.

He called in sick, something he had never done for real, although he had often said he was sick to go skiing. A typical disease in Colorado ski country. But this time he was really ill.

"I'm making a fortune working for you," his friend who always covered for him said.

"If you only knew how sick I really am," Chris answered.

"Well, you must be. There's no skiing yet, and you aren't flying off to who knows where," his friend joked.

"I only hope when you get this sick I'm around to rub it in."

"How sick are you again?"

"I'm so sick I can feel the hair grow on my cheeks."

"Ugh. Don't worry. Three-day flu at the most."

Three days. Elizabeth would be back on the third day. He had to feel up to driving by the third day.

Feed a cold? Starve a fever? Starve a cold? Feed a fever? He never could keep that straight. He was ravenously hungry, but he couldn't keep it down. He drank lots of weak herbal tea, lots of watered-down lemonade. He drank watered-down kids' fruit drinks. He heated hot water and lemon juice, hot water and kids' fruit drink. He even drank heated gelatin. The lemon-flavored wasn't too bad, but the strawberry-banana was horrid.

He took tepid baths, then took hot ones because he was shivering. He sat in the sauna, took a cold shower, and sat in the sauna again.

He took aspirin and seltzer.

He worked so hard at making himself well, that he exhausted himself. He needed that. The night before Elizabeth was to fly in, he finally slept hard and deep.

So deeply that he didn't hear the phone ring in the morning. It was the realtor who assumed Chris wasn't home. He brought the prospective new home owner to the house and began showing them the place. He spent a great deal of time apologizing for the condition of the house. Chris had not cleaned up after himself, and it was a replica of a hurricane disaster. By the time they found what looked to be a long dead and forgotten body—Chris—in the bedroom, the woman shrieked insanely. The realtor was ready to give up on ever selling the house with a maniac living in it. Chris, however, felt like a new man. Physician, heal thyself!

Chris met Elizabeth at the airport. He was still weak, a little pale. She noticed and was proud of herself for asking him if he was feeling okay. He told her he'd been sick, described it in detail, and made Elizabeth wonder if it really was a good idea to ask after all.

She hugged him tightly, but kissed him gingerly. She didn't want to get sick.

"It's not the lips that spread disease," he told her. "It's these." He held up his hands and wiggled the fingers at her. Then he tickled her.

"Stop it!" she cried. "We're in front of all these people!"

"That is my next fantasy," he said and raised his eyebrows in an exaggerated sexual leer. She looked doubtful, then she smiled.

"Actually, that is a fantasy of mine, too. But not when I'm this fat!"

They got her bags. Chris was shocked at how many she had.

"I should have hired a truck."

"Don't be silly! It's just a few clothes," Elizabeth insisted.

"Speaking of clothes, are you tired?"

Elizabeth looked at him in complete confusion.

"Really, are you tired?"

"No, not at all," Elizabeth assured him. "What about you?"

"I'm fine. Let's go to Babe's."

"Babe's?"

"Baby furniture and baby clothes for the best-dressed child in the West."

Elizabeth thought about it for a moment. Then she said, "I have a very strict budget. I lost everything, you know."

"You have a strange concept of losing everything. Do you mean everything in the sense of destitute, no roof over your head, or do you mean that instead of living in luxury for the rest of your life you can only live in luxury for two years?"

"Are you joking with me again?"

"No." Chris looked at her in all seriousness. "I am saying to get your priorities straight."

"I think I have been."

"Good. So which is it?"

"I can live moderately for two years. I've a salary coming, and I'll invest again. Soon I'll be fine."

"Or you can let me buy this stuff, pay bills, and—"

"Hold it. I pay my own way."

"So do I. And you have to admit that is a first for both of us. Our usual pattern is to pick people who use us, need us. We are both capable and willing to support ourselves. Breath of fresh air, don't you agree?"

"Let's go shopping," Elizabeth said with a happy smile on her face.

They bought out the store. Crib and bassinet and changing table and dresser. Blankets and sheets and diapers and toys. Clothes—she insisted for a girl, he threw in a few that were unisex. Pictures for the baby room and a baby album for photos. A stroller, a highchair, a car seat, and a walker. A gate to put in front of the stairs and light socket protectors. Bottles and ointments and more clothes. Chris paid for it all while Elizabeth made the arrangements for delivery.

Back in the car, they were heady with elation. Buying for the future had made them happy. Both of them were people who loved to buy for others, give to others.

Chris started the car and turned to Elizabeth. "Are you ready?"

She knew what he was asking. "Yes. It's time."

# Twenty-three

On the drive to the cemetery Elizabeth thought about what she planned to do when she got there.

Like all children, she had taken her family's devotion to her for granted. For months now she had been going over her life and seeing it with the new eyes, the new heart and mind that had developed when she came back to Colorado. She wanted to tell her grandparents about all these emotions and all the fears and pain she'd been through. She wanted to talk to them as if they were there, beside her as they had been, even when she was so selfish and ignorant of it. She wanted to tell them she now knew so much more than before.

She wanted to tell them that she realized their love for her had not been such a natural thing as a parent for a child. They had raised their child. She wanted to say to them that she saw it as a rare gift to her. She wanted to explain that their selfless generosity had made her what she was, and her gratitude, although too late, now flowed freely.

It was undoubtedly sheer luck that social services so many years ago had put her grandfather in the same cemetery where he had buried her grandmother. She said that to Chris.

"Luck!" he answered. "How can you even think that? You who make your stock choices by touching a piece of paper to feel the vibes? Luck! It's pure fate! Pure fate! Guiding angels or spirits made it work!"

"You mean that?"

"I mean that, and I think we were meant to meet the way we did. Pure fate." Chris turned into the gates of the cemetery on the hill overlooking South Denver. It was one of the cemeteries that had no headstones above the ground. Nothing but plaques in the ground.

She looked at the map the mortuary

had given her with her grandmother's and grandfather's plots circled in violet ink. They were four rows apart at opposite sides of the other. She had talked to the mortuary about moving them together, and the arrangements were made rather easily.

Chris found her grandmother's grave first. He helped Elizabeth from the car and took her hand to walk with her to the site.

*Alice Gorasch Templeton*
*6/16/1889-5/20/1970*

Elizabeth asked Chris to help her to the ground. He did, then she asked him to leave her alone for a moment. He said he'd find George's grave site.

Elizabeth sat with the wind lightly blowing the long strands of her hair that had escaped her ponytail across her eyes and face. She reached up to brush the strands away and found tears on her cheeks. All thoughts of what she would do were erased. All she could do was sit there and whisper over and over, "Thank you. Thank you."

She looked up and saw the white frosted mountains to the west above the rooftops of the south suburban houses. The line of the peaks continued south to Pikes Peak which rose high and beyond the rest. It was beautiful. The sky was clear, crystal blue. The grass, even though it was fall, was still green and had just been mowed. That fresh green scent was so clean, like her grandmother.

Chris came back, and Elizabeth held out her hands to be helped up.

"Are you ready?" he asked. She nodded yes.

*George Allan Templeton*
*12/12/1899-4/24/1975*

Elizabeth looked at the dates again. She shook her head.

"What is it?" Chris inquired.

"It says he was younger than my grandmother."

"Hey, look at that! Ten years? How about that!"

"I didn't know." She felt her heart break. There was so much she didn't know. So much she could have known.

Chris took her arm and helped her down to the ground. He began to walk away, but she called him back. "Please stay. I think I need you here."

"Okay." He stood behind her, his legs touching her back. She liked the feel of him there. He ran his hands along her head and brushed back the blowing strands. She felt so much love in that gesture.

It was so silent. No sound but the wind and the occasional bird and the flapping of the massive flag that flew from the center of the cemetery.

"Grandpa, I love you," she said it very quietly. Then she leaned back against Chris's supporting legs and said it again. "I love you!" A feeling of warmth flowed over her. It was as if a huge warm coat has been buttoned around her. She could not feel the wind or hear the sounds. She was completely enveloped in the warmth.

She sat for a long time. She didn't know how long. Finally Chris asked, "Aren't you getting cold?"

It brought her back to reality. She saw that the wind had brought clouds, and the sun was hidden. It looked like a storm was coming. The thick heavy clouds were loaded with snow. You could smell it in the air.

"I bet it's snowing at home," she said.

"Early opening," he said, meaning the ski slopes would open when there was enough real and manufactured snow.

"I'm ready," she said.

Back in the car she realized she had done and said none of the things she had so carefully thought out. But she felt wonderful.

"Is there any chance you could get the new addition in before it's too deep in snow?" Elizabeth was pleading with the contractor over the phone. "I'll pay you double, anything if you'll just get it in before the snow is too deep."

"Ma'am, I'd love to take you up on it, but the best we could do is get the foundation dug, and that is iffy." He sighed. "I can get the foundation poured and the satellite dish delivered before it's bad. That is all I'm going to promise."

"Good enough," Elizabeth said. It was really all she wanted. Just get the dish in so she could start relaying her newsletter. "Ask for the impossible and when that isn't possible, the possible *is,*" she said when she hung up. Life was going wonderfully well, now. She was in good health, the baby-to-be was doing well. Miraculously enough, Chris had sold his house.

"Fate?" she said.

"Absolutely. If I'd tried to do it any other time, it would have sat like an albatross around my neck."

"You don't feel that way?" Elizabeth was suddenly in a panic. *What if Chris feels I am that albatross? And the baby! Two albatrosses! Albatrossi?*

*Good heavens!* Elizabeth thought to herself. *Why am I thinking of such stupid garbage? Why am I not thinking about Mutual Funds versus playing the market? Why am I not focusing on options and maybe entering the money market buying foreign funds against the dollar?*

Then she thought again. *Because this is much more fun!*

Chris was fully moved into the cabin. His move consisted of transferring the drawers of clothes and maybe ten things on hangers. He had his personal mementos in two metal trunks. He had three sets of skis and nothing else.

"You certainly travel light," Elizabeth said.

"It isn't that," Chris explained. "I used to have a great number of possessions. My family had, I mean."

Elizabeth helped him put away his clothes. "Go on," she encouraged him.

"We really did lose it all," he said quietly. "The house burned to the ground. We got nothing out but ourselves and at that, just barely. My mother was burned badly. She lived a few more years after that, confined to a wheelchair. My parents really never recovered from it."

"I'm so sorry." Elizabeth felt weak with anguish for him. It was a new feeling for her. Anguish for the devastation of someone she cared for.

He opened a trunk and pulled out a small box. "Here, this is all that we saved when we went through the ashes." He held it out to her. She opened it and found a child's alphabet book charred on the page ends and smelling, still, of acrid smoke. She gasped when she saw the ugly blob of greenish metal and white leather. Chris looked over her shoulder and laughed.

"My bronzed baby shoes."

A simple silver frame held a picture, cracked and browned, of two handsome people. "Your parents?"

"On their tenth wedding anniversary," Chris said and took the frame from her. "They went out to dinner and I terrorized the baby-sitter. She was in tears when they got home, and my mother swore she would never leave me again." He traced their faces with his fingertip. "That worked for about two weeks. Then I guess we both forgot the promise because they went to a medical convention, and I broke my arm and Mom had to come back from Florida. God, was she mad at me." He smiled.

"You're smiling because your mother was mad at you?" Elizabeth couldn't believe that he was so happy remembering how mad his mother had been.

"I enjoy my memories," he said. "I have a lot of good ones, and they help make up for the not so good ones. Like the fact that Dad had this thing about yard work and shoveling snow."

"What was that?"

"He didn't do it. He had a son, and that was the son's job."

"Sounds pretty reasonable." She thought to herself all she had done was take care of herself and help set the table and cook. Not exactly hard physical labor.

"Not in the winter in Vail. Usually over eighty inches of snow, a mile-long driveway, and a father who was a doctor and had to be able to get out at any time. I felt like a slave!" He was smiling broadly. Elizabeth couldn't understand why he was so happy. She asked again.

He laughed. "I was just thinking of the time I'd refused to do it, and he got a call to go help a rancher who'd had a steer fall on him. I felt so awful out there with the snow blower in the middle of the night."

"I guess you would," Elizabeth said.

"Not because I was shoveling snow or blowing snow. But because I was causing my father a great deal of delay, and it could have been the difference in saving or losing a life. That was the last time I ever complained about it."

"Did the man live?" Elizabeth was sitting on the bed now.

Chris sat down beside her and pulled her to him. "Yes, the man lived. I lived. To shovel again! And I have learned the value of *things*. They have no value at all. Our hearts and minds hold the value, and that can never be lost or burned or die." He kissed her tenderly.

Since she had been home, they had cuddled and kissed and held each other frequently. She had spent the long hours of the night in his arms, being held. She woke to his holding her. She was grateful for it. But she suddenly wanted more. She pulled his head down to hers again and kissed him passionately, and he returned the kiss with equal heat. He kicked the rest of the things to the floor and lay out beside her.

"Make love to me!" she begged.

"Are you sure?"

"I want you!" she said in a deep breathy whisper. "I love you. Please, let's make love." She kissed him with every word. "Now!"

He helped her remove her T-shirt and the jeans with their panel for the expansion of her stomach. He took her bra and panties off then stood beside the bed to remove his clothes.

He leaned over the edge of the bed and said, "You are the most beautiful woman I have ever seen. I love touching you." He ran his hands along the swollen abdomen and up to her breasts. They were beautifully full and the nipples and areolae were darkening and widening. He bent to kiss them, and Elizabeth sighed. The sensation was unlike any other time in her life.

He lay down beside her, his manhood rigid and trembling and hot against the skin of her thigh. She reached down to touch him there, and he gasped with tension. His hands touched every inch of her, and his tongue and lips trailed his hands, leaving Elizabeth shivering with chills of passionate desire. She had never felt so sexy, so sexual, so passionate. Chris had always made her feel sexy and sexual. But this was as if it were from somewhere else. Something inside her made her feel *more.*

Every touch was heaven, every kiss was paradise. Every move they made, one against the other, was unlike any other time. Blissfully they reached the release they both wanted. It was beautiful and passionate and tender and wildly satisfying.

"Thank you," she said.

"You are thanking me for returning your love? Lady, you still need some intense therapy." He began the process all over again. This time it was slower. The position they were in, Chris on his side behind Elizabeth, made it less strenuous. Once again, Elizabeth said thank you.

"What am I going to do with you?" Chris said. "I admit, I'm superman. But I don't think I can keep on going until you figure it out."

"Figure what out?" Elizabeth kissed his chest and began to draw her tongue along his belly.

He pulled on her ponytail gently and said, as she came up to lip level, "I love this ponytail."

"Figure what out?" Elizabeth said between more kisses.

"That you don't thank me for loving

you. You just love me back." He pushed her gently around until they were spooned against each other. He kissed her neck and whispered, "Go to sleep." And promptly did so himself.

Elizabeth smiled as she slept. She felt the most secure, the most loved, and the happiest in her entire life.

When Elizabeth heard Elliot's voice on the phone, she felt so sick she thought she might faint. She sank down into the nearest chair, the rocker from upstairs she had moved down to the main-floor bedroom. It creaked as she sat in it, and that noise helped her to calm down.

"Why . . . what do you want?"

"I didn't want you to find out from just a paper," Elliot said.

"Find out?"

"You will be getting some papers soon from my attorney." He cleared his throat. "I have thought a lot about this, and I think it would be best if I gave up my rights as a parent to our child."

Elizabeth couldn't believe what she was hearing. Give up? Rights as a parent?

She said nothing. This was not something she could deal with.

Elliot spoke after there was no response from Elizabeth. "It really would be best, Elizabeth. I make no claim that the child is mine. The child has no claim to me. It's for the best. The child can't come within one hundred yards of me and vice versa." He cleared his throat again. "Believe me. I have no rights to any estate the child may have, and it has no claims to mine. It's best. Believe me."

"I'm . . . I'm sure . . ." Elizabeth was still too stunned to speak. She had never thought of Elliot as having any rights. Never thought of the child as having any claim to Elliot. It was shocking to hear it put in these terms.

"At any rate, I went to court and gave up the rights. The child is all yours. I'm not responsible."

Elizabeth took a deep breath and said, "No, Elliot, of course you aren't responsible. You had nothing whatsoever to do with the act that made this child. God only knows who you thought you were making love to, excuse me, it couldn't be called making love, could it? No, it was really just a last act of hate against me."

"You are getting upset!" Elliot sounded pretty upset himself.

"You're damn right I'm upset!" Elizabeth was screaming now. "You son of a bitch! I'm glad! Do you hear! I'm glad!"

He hung up. Elizabeth sat holding the phone for a long time.

When Chris came home, she told him what had happened.

"It's good," he said. "Really good. I'll adopt her."

Elizabeth held back tears. Since she'd been pregnant, she had either cried or laughed or loved or hated to such extremes that she thought she'd break if she cried again.

"Don't stop me this time," Elizabeth demanded. "Thank you."

Chris put his arms around her and held her. The baby chose that moment to shove hard and reposition herself. Chris grunted.

He held Elizabeth tighter. "See! She is so happy about the whole thing she can't wait to get out and shake my hand!"

# Twenty-four

Ski season officially opened. Chris, who had already taken off more days during the summer and early autumn than he usually did the whole year, was anxious to get out and ski. The weakness of the flu bug he had in September seemed to still cling. He hoped if he just got away from it all—skied and relaxed—he'd feel better.

He had two days off in a row. Although he usually spent every hour of every free day with Elizabeth, he said that this time he was going to ski all day and all night . . . and all the next day if he could.

Elizabeth thought he was kidding.

"Nope! For real. When I was a kid, we would ski by the full moonlight. It was free at night." He looked at her questioningly. "I can't believe you lived here your whole childhood and never skied!"

"Well, I didn't. And what is more, I don't want to ski. Ever." She rubbed her huge belly. "Nothing could make me go out to stand in line and freeze my you-know-what off just to end up at the bottom going through the whole thing again. No. Give me a book, a warm fire, and a hot drink." She looked at him tenderly and then lifted her lips for him to bend down to kiss. "Are you sure you feel all right?" she asked. He seemed strained and pale.

"Just let me ski, and I'll feel like a new man."

When the call came from the hospital, Elizabeth expected to hear he'd broken his leg or crushed himself against a tree. Amy's news stunned her.

"He has a fever of 105 degrees, he's having difficulty breathing. They are putting in a tube now. I think you need to get here."

Elizabeth flung Chris's big parka over her sweats and drove to the hospital.

Amy met her at the door.

"He is very ill," she began. "They are thinking of sending him to Denver in the Flight For Life helicopter."

"What is happening?" Elizabeth begged for answers.

"We don't know. We just don't know."

In the emergency room, Chris had oxygen going into his lungs from an incision in his throat. He was hooked up to so many wires and tubes that it frightened Elizabeth to think of what they were. When the doctor came in, she was so pale and distraught he put her into a room of her own in spite of her cries not to leave Chris.

Amy stayed with her. "He doesn't know you are there." She tried to comfort Elizabeth, but it only added to her panic.

"Can't someone tell me what happened? He left at dawn to go skiing. What happened?"

"He never got to the slopes," Amy told her. "He realized as he was driving that he was losing it." Elizabeth began to shudder uncontrollably. Amy held her and called for a physician to order a mild sedative. Pregnant or not, Elizabeth was falling apart. "He came in and passed out at the desk."

"He didn't say anything to me!" Elizabeth was trembling and sobbing dry tears. "He said nothing!"

"You have to calm down," Amy said. "You must!" She was no longer a sweet-looking cheerleader. Amy was worried for her friend's health, and she was a nurse in full charge. "If you don't relax, you will be of no help to Chris, and you will damage the baby." Elizabeth nodded. "Now, get into control. Do it. If you have to pull every bit of strength you ever had to do it, *do it!*"

Elizabeth took several deep breaths, and Amy got her a drink of water.

"I want to go back in," Elizabeth said.

"Not unless you can handle it. I can't have you hysterical, the doctor can't have it, and Chris, least of all, can help you."

Amy struck a chord with that. Chris always helped. He needed her help. And she wanted to be there for him. "I understand," Elizabeth said. "Will they let me back in?"

She and Amy went back into the examining room. Chris still looked deathly pale and was sweating profusely. The beeping and lights and the sound of the oxygen, at first, swirled around in Elizabeth's head. She had to take a few deep breaths. Harriet Clough came in.

"Are you all right?" she asked. "I don't want to have to give you *anything.*" The concern and caring amazed Elizabeth. She had only seen this woman twice.

"It is taking some getting used to, if you ever do get used to it," Elizabeth said. She looked over at Chris. "I'll be okay." She let Harriet put her arms around her. She was grateful for the gesture.

The doctor came in and nodded to Elizabeth. "You're the famous Elizabeth?" he said sweetly and lightly. Then his face and voice changed to reflect the severity of the situation, as if he'd just used up all his bedside manner. "We don't know what has happened. It must be a virus. The quick tests don't show what it its, just the symptoms. Some viruses can never be found. We are going to get him to Denver to the Jewish Hospital. It will take about fifteen minutes. They do remarkable work on this type of thing."

Amy stepped up and said, "I'll drive you to Denver." And before Elizabeth could say anything, she was gone making arrangements.

A moment before, the room had been full of people. Now it was just Elizabeth and Christian and the equipment. He looked as if he were a robot run with hydraulics. Hoses and tubes and plugs everywhere. She had been here for a half hour, and this was the first time she had been able to get close to him. She took his hand and kissed it. She held it up to her cheek and rubbed it there. His hand was hot and papery. It didn't feel like the last time she touched him. Could it have been only four hours ago? A lifetime ago.

"Chris? I'll be there. I'll be with you." She spoke as if he were conscious and able to talk back. "Amy is taking me to Denver, and I'll be at the hospital as soon as I can. You will be there without me for a while, but *I will be there!*" She leaned down and kissed his brow, rubbed her cheek against his cheek. She heard the helicopter, and in moments the crew was getting Chris prepared for the trip.

Amy took Elizabeth to her car and said, "Do you want to go home first and get anything?"

At first Elizabeth thought, no. She changed her mind. Amy took her to the cabin, and Elizabeth was in and out in a few moments with a small box.

"Is that it?' Amy said. "You don't want any clothes? No suitcase?"

Elizabeth shook her head. "This will be all."

Chris was in the Intensive Care Unit. The rooms were around a circular desk with many nurses and doctors consulting computer readouts, screens, and charts.

There were rules. Never before had Elizabeth so violently hated rules. She could see Chris for fifteen minutes every hour. Otherwise she had to wait outside in a visitors' lounge. It was not time for her to see him, and all she had seen when she got there was the end of his bed, his fingertips, and all the equipment.

She had thirty minutes to wait. Amy went down to get them a drink. The waiting room had coffee and tea. Elizabeth drank neither.

A woman doctor, who looked younger than Chris, came into the waiting room and asked for Mrs. Hanford.

Elizabeth did not answer, but she looked up at her. The doctor said, "Are you Elizabeth?" Elizabeth nodded.

"I'm Dr. Bette Barnette. I'll be the primary doctor for Dr. Hanford. Can you tell me anything about the days preceding this incident?"

"He'd had the flu a few weeks ago. He said he was better. I thought he was pale and drawn-looking." Elizabeth looked down at her belly and then looked back at the doctor. "Actually, our thoughts have been more on this," she rubbed her belly, "than on anything else. I should have noticed."

The doctor shook her head. "*He* should have noticed. But doctors are the worst at this kind of thing. They are either hypochondriacs or ignore even the most obvious signs of illness." She reached out to take Elizabeth's hand. "Come on, we can go see him."

Elizabeth followed. Chris was more pale. His chest seemed to be working very hard even with the assistance it was getting in breathing.

"He has been awake twice and wrote notes to us." She pointed to the yellow pad and felt-tip pen on the bedside table. "He asked for you and he told me that his IVs were wrong." Dr. Barnette smiled. "I ignored the second message."

Elizabeth looked shocked. Dr. Barnette assured her, "They weren't in yet. They couldn't have been wrong." Elizabeth smiled then, and at just that moment Chris opened his eyes.

"I'm here!" Elizabeth said and went to his side to take his hand. He pointed for that tablet and pen and wrote in a spidery script, "I love you. I'm okay! I love you!"

Elizabeth kissed his hands and brow. The doctor spoke to Chris. "We are doing blood workups and sputum. We think it's a viral pneumonia of some sort."

Chris wrote on his pad. "No kidding."

"We've got you on antibiotics just to stop the secondary infections and your oxygen—"

Chris held up a hand and wrote on his pad: "I feel better already—you're doing great. THANKS."

"No problem," she said and left them alone.

"Amy brought me. She's here," Elizabeth said.

He nodded and blinked his eyes. He tried to write on the pad, but he was getting weak. Elizabeth stopped him. "You should rest."

She took the pad and pen from him and leaned down against the side of the bed to try to hug him. It was difficult. There were so many tubes and wires. He held her arm as tightly as he could. She was shocked at how weak he was.

A moment later a nurse came in to tell her time was up. Elizabeth went back to the waiting room and saw Amy standing there.

"Oh, Amy!" she cried. "He's so sick!"

"Sit down and drink this," Amy said, handing her a can of fruit juice. "I talked to the nurse, and he is actually upgraded already. The antibiotics have only been going in for three hours but he *is better.*" Amy looked so confident that Elizabeth drank and sat quietly for the next forty-five minutes.

Back in the room again, Chris did not wake up, and Amy and Elizabeth each held a hand for the entire fifteen minutes.

Returning to the waiting room, Amy said, "They have family rooms here. Shall I make arrangements or would you like to go to a hotel?"

"Do what you think is right," Elizabeth said. "I can't think right now. My mind is an absolute blank."

"He's getting better!" Amy said.

"I've never been around sickness. I've never been sick myself except when I got pregnant. I don't know what to do or how to act."

"There is no right way to act, so don't worry. Just take it easy on yourself."

Amy went to make arrangements for the two of them to stay at the hospital, and it was time to visit once again.

Chris was awake. The nurse was changing an IV bottle, and he wanted to direct what she was doing. The nurse would not give him the tablet to write on. Elizabeth did.

"It's running too fast!" he scribbled.

The nurse stopped and counted the drops. "No, it isn't. This is how fast Dr. Barnette wants it to go." She turned to Elizabeth and said, "Doctors are the worst patients."

Elizabeth smiled at Chris. "That is considered a cliché," she said to him. "You must feel right at home."

He took her hand and held it to his cheek. She stood there beside him the whole visiting period.

The rest of the day went on in that way. Chris was either sleeping or awake, telling the nurse or doctor what to do or telling Elizabeth he loved her. By evening he actually had some color in his pale face.

Amy and Elizabeth ate and went back to the Intensive Care Unit. Dr. Barnette was waiting for them.

"Good news. We've got it under control. He is on demand oxygen, not forced. In fact, tomorrow the tube comes out if he keeps going this well."

"Thank you." Elizabeth could barely speak for the choking she felt in her throat. She had come to recognize that feeling. She wanted to cry, but was not allowing herself to.

Amy let Elizabeth go into the room alone for the last visit of the night. Elizabeth took in the little box she had brought along. It was Chris's mementos. She put his melted baby shoes and the singed child's book on the tray table. She set up his parents' portrait on the bedside table.

"Chris, you will need these," she said. "Good memories, remember?" He was sound asleep.

She slept quite well that night. She had coped once again. *This might become a habit,* she thought as she drifted off to sleep.

# Twenty-five

Elizabeth showered and put on her sweats. She waited for Amy to get ready. They ate quickly in the hospital cafeteria. They were up in the Intensive Care Unit by 7:30 A.M.

Elizabeth had just told Amy that she knew Chris would be sitting up waiting for them so they should hurry.

When they turned the corner and saw the main desk, they both knew that something was wrong.

Chris's room was filled with doctors, nurses, and technicians. A nurse headed for them as soon as they were in view. The two were led back to the waiting room.

"I'm sorry. He took a turn for the worse last night about two," she was saying. Elizabeth felt her world spin around at an odd angle, and she had to sit while Amy asked more technical questions.

"Elizabeth, it's a temporary setback," Amy assured her. "His fever spiked, went higher. He had convulsions. It was pretty touch and go." Amy did not hold anything back. "He is back down to just 104 degrees, and they think it will get better today."

"Who are all those people?" Elizabeth asked.

"They are taking more samples and making more tests. Also the therapist is there for—"

"Therapist?" Elizabeth interrupted. "What is that for?"

"He needs to move his body. The therapist is doing arm and leg movement for him."

Elizabeth went white. "Is he paralyzed?"

"No! But he is unconscious. They are just making sure, Elizabeth. They are just doing everything they can." Amy took her hand and squeezed it tightly.

There was a phone for the family in the room, and Elizabeth disengaged her hand from Amy's and dialed Barbara in New York. She quickly told her what was going on and then burst into tears. Amy left the room. Elizabeth listened to Barbara as she spoke, giving one word answers when necessary.

Until Barbara said, "When did you come to the decision that you don't deserve to be happy?"

*Elizabeth sat with the headphones on and her eyes shut. She wanted no interruptions from the stewardess, fellow passengers, nothing. She wanted to hide. The headphones were not on, and the ruse worked. She was left entirely alone for one-hour forty-five minute flight from New York to Denver.*

*No music, no movie. Just her own thoughts.*

*She was doing a good job of beating herself up. Elliot had left her because she was a barren, tough, old bitch.*

*Elliot had no reason to stay with her. She had never made him happy, except when she gave him money. He was always so grateful and good to her then.*

*He had really hated her.*

*It was all her fault.*

*He was from such a wealthy family.*

*It was doomed from the beginning.*

*The jet took a quick dive from hitting an air pocket. Elizabeth opened her eyes and smiled at her seat companion, then quickly shut them again.*

*She was doomed.*

*A jinx.*

*She was doomed from the moment her mother died and her father abandoned her. No, he lost her. She was a lost child. An abandoned child.*

*Well, she wouldn't be lost or abandoned anymore. She was going to buy her security, once and for all. She was going home. She would own her security. The jet landed in Denver. She took a cab to the nearest auto dealer and paid cash for her four-wheel drive. It was waiting for her. Money did that kind of thing. She wanted it, she bought it.*

*She stayed at The Brown Palace in a suite. she was treated like a queen. They even gave her room service at three in the morning and found the address for the furniture store at that hour, as well. Money made sure those things happened.*

*She had taken her hard earned money, hers and no one else's, and bought back her family home. The only home she had. Not because she was a good person who deserved it, but because she had more money than anybody else.*

*No. Elizabeth Templeton Avery March may not deserve love and family or even decent treatment. But she could buy decent treatment.*

*The hell with love and family.*

*The next two weeks she spent money and prepared to go to the cabin. She offered big money, paid big bonuses for getting exactly what she wanted, and tipped delivery people more than they ever dreamed of. All of them treated her well.*

*When she arrived at the cabin, she realized that she could hire a staff to do the cleaning. She chose to do it herself.*

*She ended up in the emergency room in the hospital at Vail.*

*It was exactly what she deserved.*

Elizabeth hadn't realized she'd hung up. She was not aware that Amy was trying to get her attention.

She'd suddenly had one of those moments. The eureka! The Ah-Ha! The now-I-see-it-all!

She came back to the present with a slam of reality.

"Elizabeth! He's conscious!" Amy was crying out. She stood, and they both went to the room. Chris was looking right at her. He smiled.

She went to his side and took his fingers to kiss, but he stopped her.

He motioned for his pad and pen. She handed them to him.

He wrote slowly and with great effort, "You're here! I dreamed you were back at the cabin."

Elizabeth nodded. "I'm here. I'm not leaving." She said it gently, but there was no doubt that she would not be forced to leave.

"I'm getting better," he wrote.

"Yes, you are. Don't write anymore. Just let me hold your hand."

He fell into a deep sleep. When the visiting time was up, he did not wake or notice her leaving.

Amy's husband called them in their room. He would be up that evening to take Amy home for one day.

"I'll be back. I'll bring you some clothes and things. Can you make me a list?"

"Yes, I'll give you a key. Oh, would you pick up the mail as well?" Elizabeth welcomed the practical thinking. Lists and mail and other thoughts. Anything but what her mind was thinking: She loved someone, and they were leaving her.

She made out her list with detailed directions on the location of each thing. Amy looked at the list, and her eyebrows rose at one item. Elizabeth saw this and said, "Trust me. I need it." Amy smiled and came over to give her a quick hug. The two pregnant women laughed at the difficulty they had getting their arms to reach.

"A few months and we'll both be holding babies in one arm and hugging each other," Amy said encouragingly.

"I can't believe it," Elizabeth said.

Amy's husband was waiting. "I'll be back tomorrow evening, and then I'll stay as long as you need me."

"You've been wonderful," Elizabeth said.

"It's easy when it is for two unforgettable people."

"He *is* unforgettable," Elizabeth said proudly.

Amy left but was back in a moment. "We may not forget Chris, but we did forget your key." Elizabeth laughed and got the key for her. They hugged again. When Elizabeth was finally alone, she lay down on the bed and turned on her side with a pillow under her belly and fell asleep.

She woke up two hours later. She had missed two visiting times. She grabbed a cup of hot soup in the cafeteria and took it to the waiting room. She had ten minutes before they would let her in. She ate and for a short moment she felt as if everything would be all right.

"Chicken soup heals a great deal." Dr. Barnette came in and sat down beside Elizabeth.

Elizabeth smiled and held up the empty cup. "We could have eaten more. It was actually good!"

"We have a few test results." Dr. Barnette went right to the point. "The antibiotics have taken care of the sideline infections, and have caused a few problems of their own, nothing we can't handle," she quickly assured Elizabeth. "But what happened, which virus, we still don't know. It can take weeks for those to be identified, and even then it may be some new or mutant strain." She sounded discouraged and realized it.

"I'm sorry to sound this way, but we can't always find out all the answers. His fever is down to 101 degrees and has stayed there for three hours. His heart and blood pressure are doing well. He does have a hard time breathing, and we are going to keep assisting him until he can make it on his own for several hours." She looked away and then looked back into Elizabeth's eyes, firm and direct.

"It's frustrating for all of us. But mostly for you. We get to be around him all the time, and we know from moment to moment what we are doing and his response."

Elizabeth nodded. "You have all been very good at telling me. And I had Amy here. She is a nurse, and she explains it all to me. I'm a stock analyzer, not into the medical field at all. I've never even had a cold!"

The doctor looked closely at Elizabeth and said, "Stocks? Are you *that* Elizabeth March?"

Elizabeth nodded and looked down at her ballooning figure. "Hard to believe!" she joked.

"I thought I recognized you!" the doctor said. "When I got out of medical school, I had so much debt. And to be honest, I'd never even written a check. My existence was cash-to-pocket-to-grocery-store-to-rent-to-gas. In one day and out the other. I read an article you wrote for a medical magazine."

"I don't think it was me." She didn't remember writing for a medical magazine. "Unless it might have been a reprint."

"Well, it did a world of good for me. It was basic and easy to understand. And poor as I was, I did what you said. I paid *me* first. I put money into retirement, even though I was just starting out. I even put it into one of the funds you recommended."

Elizabeth was smiling. She felt intensely proud and blushed.

"I've about paid off my debt, but I've also got money in place for retirement and for emergencies. God forbid should I not be able to work anymore, I'm covered. Let me shake your hand." Dr. Barnette held out her small slender hand and shook Elizabeth's firmly. "Thank you. You really made a difference in my life, and I appreciate it."

"Thank you. You just now made a difference in mine," Elizabeth said sincerely.

"Let's go see Chris." Dr. Barnette led the way.

Chris looked much the same, but he was conscious. He attempted a smile and reached for his paper and pen.

"We can't make him shut up," Dr. Barnette joked. "God knows we've done everything we could think of to make him shut up and take orders, but for some reason he just won't stop trying to tell us how to do our job."

Chris wrote, "It's a tough job but somebody has to do it."

Elizabeth shook her head and said, "He's feeling better. He using clichés."

Chris tapped his note pad in irritation. "Because it's true!!!"

Both women laughed, and Dr. Barnette left them alone.

Elizabeth kissed his brow and ran her fingers through his hair. She looked down at him and smiled. He was busy writing.

"Do you know you have to buy a video camera!" he admonished in print.

"I'll bite," Elizabeth said. "Why do I have to buy a video camera?"

"For the baby! To make memories!" was his written reply.

He looked up then to see her eyes mist over. "Yes," she said quietly and took his hand and held it to her cheek. "To make good memories."

He took his hand from hers and wrote, "This time is nothing—don't think of this time—think of the inn—think of the cabin—don't force the good back and force the bad forward! Think of our love!"

Elizabeth took the pad and tore off the sheet he'd been writing on. "You'll get writer's cramp," she said. "Now, can you see outside?" She pointed out the door of his room to the windows over the desk. He nodded.

"It's snowing," she said. "I'm going to go out when I leave here and get a snowball and put it in your bed."

He looked surprised.

"You're going to keep that fever down!" she said. "And not being medical, but being highly practical, it sounds to me like it will work as well as anything else."

Wired and tubed as he was, he couldn't laugh, but she knew she'd made him wish he could.

When her time was up, she went to the waiting room and sat. She propped her chin on her hand and watched the tops of the trees and houses get a sugary frosting of snow. She watched for half an hour and probably was daydreaming when she heard the sound of his voice. Her cheeks were flushed and her eyes bright as she watched the doctor come out of his room, and she listened to Chris say her name in a dry and cracked voice. She knew she would love him forever.

"Lissy!"

# Twenty-six

Amy came into the room, breathless and smiling. Chris sat up in bed and Elizabeth sat in the chair. "You're out of Intensive Care!" Amy cried. "I was so scared when I went up there and your bed was empty!"

Elizabeth attempted to stand but gave up; she was exhausted and it was just getting too difficult to move around. "I tried to catch you but your oldest told me you'd left. They moved him here about two hours ago."

Amy hugged Chris and Elizabeth. "You really scared us all to death," she scolded Chris.

"I'm sorry," he said. His voice was still a little raspy, but the glint of humor replaced the weary glaze of illness in his eyes. He held his hand up in a Boy Scout salute, using two fingers to cross over his heart. "I'll never do it again, cross my heart."

"I'll hold you to that," Elizabeth said, then turned to Amy. "Did you find everything?"

Amy smiled. "It's all in your room. Why don't you go back and I'll keep this joker busy."

Elizabeth reached out a hand for help, and Amy tugged to lever her out of the chair. "Thanks!" Elizabeth kissed Chris and said, "I'll be back in about an hour."

Chris looked confused. "Where are you going?"

"I'm going to my room to take a shower!" She kissed him again, nodded at Amy and left.

"You aren't very observant," Amy began. "She's been wearing those same clothes for three days now! You'd think you'd been unconscious or something." He had the grace to look shamed by her teasing.

"I've not noticed. All I see are her eyes," he admitted.

* * *

Elizabeth showered and washed her hair. She used the blow dryer. It took longer to blow-dry her hair than she had expected. She put on the clothes Amy brought. She looked at herself in the mirror in the little bathroom.

She could only see her shoulders and face. Well, she wasn't all that excited to see how big she'd grown anyway. She'd asked Amy to bring the beaded evening gown. In the light of the bathroom, the red and gold beads lit up her face and added sparkle to her eyes. She was a little pale and hadn't asked for makeup. She had a small bag out in the glove compartment of her car that had some samples she'd been given at one of the department stores. It contained blusher and eye shadow.

She put on her high heels, the first time in months. It felt very odd. Not only was her balance off, her feet hurt the moment she put them on.

She went to the parking lot and unlocked the door to the passenger's side. There was a brown paper bag just under the edge of the car, and she just missed stepping on it when she got in. She opened the glove compartment and rummaged around for the samples. She heard what she thought was the sound of a baby crying, and she looked at the cars parked around her to see if some infant had been left inside. Nothing.

She found the cosmetics and stood. Her heel caught the brown bag, and she felt something move and heard the crying sound. She jumped as much as her weight and high heels would allow. There was something moving and crying in the sack!

It was difficult for her to bend, and stooping was out of the question. She used her toe to get the sack out from under her car, and the top opened and out rolled a small black and bloody ball of fur with huge blue eyes.

It lay at her feet, weak and helpless. Its eyes were open but it was so matted and blood-covered that she didn't know if it was injured or dying or what. But it cried to her once again. Its little mouth was opened wide, and the weak baby's cry made Elizabeth go wobbly at the knees.

She took some tissues from the glove compartment and sat on the edge of the seat. Bending with difficulty, she picked up the little thing and swaddled it. The tiny razor-sharp nails dug into her arm where she held it. She used her toe again to open the sack wider. There was nothing else alive in the bag.

Elizabeth locked the car and went back to her room. She had no idea why she did what she did next. She just knew she couldn't leave things the way they were.

In the small sink in the bathroom, she bathed the kitten. The blood seemed superficial, no cuts or missing limbs. Soaking wet the poor thing looked like a black mouse. After the bath, Elizabeth saw a glint of white on the black kitten's forehead. In the center of the white spot was an oddly shaped tuft of black. She blow-dried the terrified mite. When it was warm and dry, it curled into a sleeping little ball on the white towel. Elizabeth thought it looked like an eight ball.

She looked at her watch and saw she'd been gone two hours!

She sprinkled the sample of perfume, dabbed on some blush, grabbed her key and a paper sack that Amy had brought. Then, at the last moment, she picked up the towel the kitten was sleeping so soundly on and took it with her.

Chris and Amy were talking but when she entered, her dark hair shining, the evening gown so stunning, the talk stopped.

"You look beautiful," Chris said in a throaty whisper. He sat up taller in his bed and cleared his throat. In a husky and earthy voice he said, "Damn! You are so beautiful!"

"Thank you," Elizabeth said.

"What is the occasion?" Chris asked.

"I thought a celebration was in order. But I also thought a cow suit was out of the question. So I brought you this instead." She held out the paper sack. "Fortunately you can't see below the edge of your bed." She laughed at herself and stuck her stomach out even farther. "Both of us are rather tightly in this gown, but for that reaction I'd do it all again."

Amy stood up and said, "I'm going to

have some lunch." She nodded to Elizabeth and Elizabeth nodded back as Amy left the room and quietly closed the door. Chris seemed mesmerized by the sight of Elizabeth in the beaded gown. He motioned her closer.

Elizabeth held the white towel closer but placed the sack on the bed. "Open it," she said. He did and took out a tiny stuffed cow with a cowbell and udders. "I thought it might be overkill for me to dress in the outfit, but she ought to get the point across just as well."

Chris was smiling and holding the animal in front of his face to study it closer.

"When . . . where did you get this?"

"At Babes' when you weren't looking," she said. "It's really for the baby, but you can play with it while you're here." She talked to him like a mother to a child.

He responded like anything but a child. His love for her, desire for her, was a very real thing in the room at that. They looked at each other without words for none were needed; Elizabeth standing in her high heels with the white towel in her hands, Chris in his hospital pajamas in his bed.

Somehow it was all very erotic. All Elizabeth could feel was his love for her. It was so strong it knocked all else from her mind. Elizabeth almost forgot what she had in her hands. In her mind were all the thoughts of love and desire. She wanted him. She wanted his love.

Chris was feeling how wonderful it was to be alive and aware and how much he wanted her, had always wanted her. He looked over her magnificent dress and saw the woman underneath. For a moment the thought ran through his mind, *Hey, I'm actually undressing someone with my eyes!*

The towel she held so firmly seemed to move. Chris looked again. It was definitely moving. Elizabeth looked surprised then she laughed and put the squirming towel on the bed. "I'm probably going to regret this."

She unfolded the towel. The first thing Chris saw was a tiny black tail fully extended above a black rear end. The kitten jumped as only kittens seem able, 180 degrees in place; where the black bottom and tail had once been, the black-and-white face and blue eyes now rested. The tiny thing opened its mouth in a wide yawn and made a pitiful mewing sound. It blinked twice and wobbled to Chris's outstretched hand and licked it.

"Where did you ever . . ." Chris picked it up and flipped it on its back. "I think it's a male. Where did you find this little fella?" He was grinning from ear to ear.

"In the parking lot." Elizabeth told him the details. "That's what took me so long."

Chris played with the kitten, letting it bite his finger and crawl around on his lap.

"He looks like an eight ball," Chris said.

"That's what I thought!" She noted they had thought so much alike recently.

"Do you want him? Do you want to keep him?" Chris asked full of hope.

"That's all I need, a kitten when I'm about to have a baby." Elizabeth sounded irate. Her shortness made Chris look up quickly to read her face. She looked angry.

"It's all right," he said quietly. "You don't have to get all defensive."

"I'm not!" She said. Then she reached out to rub the kitten behind its ears. The kitten rolled its head and flipped over on its back and began to bat playfully at her fingers. Elizabeth softened. He could see the anger melt.

"I couldn't leave it out there," she said. Then she played some more with the kitten, rubbing its tummy and playing with the tiny tail. She smiled.

"It was completely alone. Left for dead!" she mumbled. Chris smiled. If he kept quiet, she would talk herself into this. He did just that.

"How could anyone just abandon it that way?" she said. "They left it in a sack and maybe even ran over it! I can't bear to think of the others!" She was working up steam now. "What kind of monster leaves it like this, a helpless baby!"

She gave the kitten back to Chris and walked away. Chris played with the ball of fluff until it suddenly yawned widely and fell asleep.

Chris continued to say nothing. Elizabeth looked up at him and he looked at her, an unspoken question hung between them.

"Okay. I want the kitten," she said and picked it up. She sat on the chair with the sleeping kitten on her lap.

"Wise choice," Chris said.

"I've never had a pet, really."

"You deserve one," Chris said like a parent to a deserving child.

"You coerced me," Elizabeth said as she stroked the kitten behind its ears.

"I did not," Chris argued.

"Not you," Elizabeth said. "Eight Ball."

Amy took the kitten back to Vail with her. "I'm warning you, my kids may not let you have it back."

"We trust you," Chris said. "Blood, bullet wounds, and kittens. I trust you."

Elizabeth shook her head. "How do you work with him?" She expected no answer. Over the months she had become adept at the easy teasing and joking that went on with Chris and with the people he knew. She wasn't always positive if a lot of it was joking and teasing, but she was easier with it.

"We'll see you when you come home."

Amy kissed them both. Elizabeth went to the hallway with her, catching a last glimpse of the basket with the kitten snugly sleeping. "Just give me a call when you leave, and I'll get your cabin open," Amy offered.

"I can't tell you what all your support and friendship have meant to me. And to Chris," Elizabeth began, but Amy stopped her.

"It is what friends do, Elizabeth," she said gently. "It's just what you do."

Chris was dressed in jeans, flannel shirt, and sweater. He sat impatiently in the chair beside the bed. Now that he was officially discharged he was not about to sit in the bed. Elizabeth wore new pregnant jeans and a sweater. She had no such feelings about a hospital bed. She was happy with the head up and the knees bent and comfortably waited for the doctor to come in with the final instructions.

Chris sat with his ankle crossed over his knee. His toes keeping the impatient beat to that silent song he heard.

"I never want to be a patient in a hospital again," he said suddenly. "This is a great place. Everyone was great."

"Yes, they were," Elizabeth agreed. She waited for the rest of the statement.

"But I felt so powerless!" he finally said. He put both feet on the floor and tried to tip the chair back on two legs, but it wouldn't do it. He gave up. "It was the second most frustrating time in my life," he said with a sigh.

"I'll bite. What was the first most frustrating time?" Elizabeth said easily.

"When you were in the hospital!" he said as if he couldn't believe she wouldn't know the answer already.

"Oh!" Elizabeth blushed. He loved it when she blushed. Especially since she had looked quite pale these last few days.

"I love you, Lissy," he said.

"Thank you," she whispered.

Before he could say anything back, Dr. Barnette came in.

"Ready to go? Good. We won't have the tests back about what exactly you had for about six weeks. But whatever it was, it's gone. It is lucky—and I'm going to repeat that—it is *lucky* that you were in healthy condition to begin with. It was affecting your lungs and kidneys and your heart. I want you back in three weeks, sooner if you feel the need." She gave Chris some papers to sign and then she shook his hand.

"For a doctor, you weren't such a bad patient. For a patient, we were ready to send you to Rose Memorial Hospital." She smiled and Chris thanked her for her backhanded compliment.

Dr. Barnette turned to Elizabeth and patted the tummy and said, "Get used to it. Now that the two of you aren't in the relatively safe environs of the hospital, people are going to come up to you and pat you and say all kinds of inane things." She winked at Elizabeth. "Believe me, I know." She held up three fingers.

Elizabeth was shocked. The doctor looked so youthful and vibrant. "You've had three?"

"My oldest is nine, and my youngest is three months."

"How wonderful!" Chris said. "See, Elizabeth. You can have it all."

Elizabeth shook her head. "I'm forty-five. Dr. Barnette can't be older than thirty-five."

"I'll be forty next month. I think. It isn't easy to have this type of job and be a wife and mother and remember small details. Like how old I am. And when. I do forget dates occasionally." She laughed and wished them both well. After she left, Chris was out of his chair with bags in hand in seconds. "Come on!"

"You are going to wait to be wheeled out," Elizabeth said as she got slowly off the bed.

"The hell I am!" he insisted. "I'm going to walk out, and I'm going to walk out now."

At the huge electric doors, Chris got up from the wheelchair and sheepishly thanked the nurse's aide who brought him down while Elizabeth brought the car to the entrance.

"Every dog has his day," Elizabeth said once he was in the driver's seat.

Chris smiled. Then he laughed. "Let's go home, lady."

# Twenty-seven

Amy had the cabin ready. She even had a fire in the fireplace and the kitten, sitting in a ball on a cushion, in front of the fireplace.

"Nice touch," Chris said when he came in.

Elizabeth felt an overwhelming sense of relief when she came through the red painted door and saw her home.

She touched each and every piece. The warm vibrations she felt reminded her of how she felt about her work. Warm vibration, good company. At home she finally acknowledged the good feelings.

The fabric on her furniture was so close to the thirties fabric her grandparents had used. Deep, dark, large green leaves with dark red flowers on a cream background. All faded and worn looking, although they were really just made less than a year ago. The pine table yellow as butter in the fading sunlight, the prints and paintings on the wall and the rag rugs on the floor. She really was coming home. It really was her place on earth.

She burst into tears and for once she did not rail at herself. She felt like weeping, and she did. She deserved it.

Chris had picked up Eight Ball and he'd let the kitten climb onto his shoulder, the razor-sharp little nails digging through his flannel shirt. He was wincing when he saw Elizabeth begin to sob. "Aren't we a pair?" he said gently. "You crying, me wincing. They should do a comedy routine about us. The saddest couple in the world."

Through the tears Elizabeth began to laugh. "Thank you," she said finally. She went to his side and took the mewing kitten off his shoulder and leaned her head there while she stroked the kitten.

"You have made me happier than I have ever been," she said.

Chris held her, his arms around her at breast level; he gently stroked her and she nuzzled into his shoulder as if she hoped to meld with him. He kissed the top of her head, and they stayed that way for a long while enjoying the comfort and beauty and warmth of their home.

Chris sighed and kissed her again, then let go of her and sat heavily on the sofa. "I guess I'm still a bit tired."

Elizabeth put the kitten on the cushion. She went to the modern stove and began to make dinner. Chris turned to watch her. "You are so beautiful," he said. He loved to watch her. She moved like a woman who knew what she was doing. No hesitation; no hard, rough movement. She seemed to be in a graceful dance of dinner preparation. He felt each move was filled with love.

She made vegetable soup in beef broth and toasty muffins of white cornmeal. The thick navy blue bowls and plates set off the beautiful colors of the food and kept the warmth for a long time.

Chris had lit the old oil lamps and placed them on the pine table. In the glorious dark of the frosty autumn night, they ate their food, enjoyed their fire, and played with the kitten.

*Enjoy every moment,* Elizabeth kept repeating to herself. *Don't forget a second of this.*

And that thought caused a chill to go down her spine. The old memories. The old anger and fears. The old script of her life threatened to take this moment away. Chris felt her tense physically while sitting next to him on the couch.

"That was then, this is now," he said in his beautiful, strong voice. His golden lion's eyes mirrored the flames in the fireplace. His hair, as always just a bit too long, seemed lit by the flames. She took a deep breath and snuggled closer to him.

In a soft, teasing voice she said, "Do you always talk in clichés?"

"Day in, day out," he whispered into her ear. "I'll drive you crazy over the years," he added and gently nibbled the top of her ear.

"Too late," she answered. She struggled to get up and then tugged him to an upright position. "Put out the fire and come to bed. I'm tired."

"I see. You are tired, so I go to bed. If you are cold, must I put on a sweater?"

She nodded. He said, "And if you want to be made love to, I must oblige?"

Elizabeth raised an eyebrow in cocky agreement and said, "Sounds fair to me."

Chris bolted for the first-floor bedroom. "Last one in bed gets the top!"

Elizabeth shook her head and laughed. She followed at a slower pace. After all, she actually wanted the top.

Elizabeth woke the next morning to the aroma of freshly made coffee, and she could swear she smelled biscuits.

Chris was not in the kitchen, but he had been. He'd used what appeared to be every bowl and spoon. All the flour that wasn't in the biscuits seemed to be on the floor or countertop.

She looked for him quickly in the big room then looked out the window. He was on the front porch.

He sat on a twig chair, tilted back on two legs, one of his booted feet resting on the porch rail, the other keeping him balanced on the floor. He wore his cowboy hat and a jeans jacket and his dark sunglasses. He must have gone for a walk because he had a huge bouquet of wild grasses and the last of the golden aspen leaves bound up in a pile at his feet. He'd stripped one sprig of grass and had it in his mouth, sucking on it as she—and she thought all children—had done over the centuries.

He turned his face to her, the strong lines of his cheekbones and jaw highly defined by the sunrise, more deeply etched by his illness. He was glossed all over by the icy lemon-yellow of sunrise. He raised his hand to remove the grass from his mouth, and Elizabeth felt a rush of desire run through her at the thought of those beautiful, strong, and tender hands touching her in love. His lips parted to speak, and she actually felt their pressure on hers, as they had felt last night.

"Good morning, beautiful lady," he said.

"Good morning, dear man," she answered. Then she went to his side and pulled her robe more tightly around her, bending to kiss him. He tasted of green grass and sweet love. He smelled of soap and outdoors and pines and wood smoke. For a moment she was paralyzed by the perfection of it.

He smiled at her, a lopsided puppyish grin. she smiled back, and he let his face glow with her reflected love.

"I started breakfast," he boasted.

She nodded and said, "Ah. Yes. We need to talk about that."

He crashed the chair to all four legs and said, "I helped!" He was completely surprised at the upset tone of her voice.

"Chris, every bowl? Every spoon? What did you do? Have a flour fight with the kitten?"

"It's not that bad," he insisted and stood up. He took three steps and was inside before Elizabeth turned around. When she was inside as well, he stood with his hands on his hips, the grass back in his mouth and one foot tapping in impatience.

He hummed and he hawed and he nodded as he took the grass from his mouth.

"Yep, ma'am. It is a mess."

Just then they both seemed to sense that something was not right.

"The biscuits!" they both called. Chris made it to the big wood burning stove to remove the now black and crisp food. He dropped the pan trying to pull it too quickly from the depths of the stove. The biscuits crashed to the floor along with the pan.

Eight Ball was soon in the midst of it all, sniffing and jumping back as if bit by the aroma.

Chris looked up, took off his sunglasses. He took a deep breath and let it out slowly. "Breakfast is served," he said. With flourish, he bowed and pointed to the mess on the floor with his sunglasses.

Elizabeth began to laugh, and Chris joined her. They laughed helplessly; every time they looked at the mess, they laughed harder. Elizabeth slumped into one of the big wooden chairs at the table, and Chris began to pick up the mess.

"Let's have a big party for Thanksgiving," Chris said one day in November. "Let's invite the crew at the hospital."

Elizabeth looked at him as if he'd just turned into a goat or a bear.

"You have got to be kidding," she said.

"Well, not on Thanksgiving day, of course. Everybody does family stuff." Chris came to her side where she sat reading in the rocking chair.

"Maybe the weekend after. No turkey. Something else."

Elizabeth looked at him again as if he'd gone mad. "Why are you doing this to me?" she said.

Chris stood up. He paced the room. He stooped beside her and said, "I'll help. Really. I can cook and I can clean. I'll help!"

She sighed. "Can't we do potluck?"

"Great idea!" Chris was off again. "Church social! School picnic! I can see it all now! Great!"

He was ready for work and he picked up his jacket from the end of the bed and kissed her quickly. As he left he said over his shoulder, "Twenty people! It will be great!"

Elizabeth watched him as he drove out of the meadow. She waited until he was out of sight. Eight Ball made a mighty leap. For the first time, the feline made it into her lap without clawing halfway up.

"You're getting better," Elizabeth said to the happily purring kitten. "I don't want to do this," she said. "I don't want anyone to come here. I don't want anything to come into my house." The kitten turned around and settled again in her diminished lap. "But I'm going to do it anyway," Elizabeth said with a fateful edge to her voice. She lifted the kitten and carried him to the kitchen. Chris had done the dishes and left the fire ready to begin in both the kitchen stove and the fireplace.

She lit both fires. She had not been upstairs for months. Some nagging feeling of dust motes and spider webs taking over the beloved room made her think of navigating the steep staircase to the loft. With difficulty she laced on rubber soled shoes so she wouldn't slip on the steps. With even greater difficulty, she packed a sack with cleaning supplies and went slowly and carefully up.

The kitten beat her by several minutes. At floor level she could see dust on the scrubbed pine flooring and on the windowsills and spiders doing what they were supposed to do.

She sighed. What happened to the woman who paid for someone to clean her apartment three times a week? Whatever became of the woman who thought nothing of staying up until four A.M. to hear the Japanese market reports? The one who was found, as often as not, running up and down the stairs between the floors of the trading room and her office?

"That woman is alive and fat in Vail, Colorado," Elizabeth said aloud to the completely disinterested kitten.

She caught a glimpse of a box under the bed when she was eye level. By the time she was on the floor and reaching for the box, she was dusty, sweating, and already tired.

Eight Ball helped. He immediately proved his prowess as a jumper by overshooting the box, hitting his head on the metal frame of the bed, and sat smugly looking as if he'd meant to do that very thing. Elizabeth laughed. "I used to be married to somebody just like you," she said and lifted the kitten onto the bed for him to play.

The three-by-three-by-three box was carved wood. It had flowers, grapes, mountains, and elk carved in the wood in no discernible order. It looked as if someone were trying out a new skill.

Elizabeth remembered that the box had been at the foot of her grandmother's bed. Although she had thought on their deaths that all had been sold or given away or tossed, she found it still positioned at the foot of the bed when she came back in May.

She had pushed it under the bed and never thought of it again. The box seemed to pulse with life; it called to her. She was drawn to it. She could have no more resisted opening it than she could have stopped breathing.

The kitten was sound asleep as Elizabeth sat on the floor and went through the contents of the box. Everything she touched vibrated with a loving heat.

On top was a fine lace swath of fabric with dried flowers holding the gathers. She figured it must have been Grandmother's wedding veil.

Next, a finely wrought silver picture album. Elizabeth remembered the pattern, the same as the silver frame that held her grandmother's graduation picture. She opened it to find page after page of brown tinted photos and a few badly fading color ones.

Her grandparents on their wedding day. It must have been a large wedding. Her grandmother was stunningly beautiful, her grandfather so handsome that she could not believe the old slightly bent man she remembered could be the same man. There was a multitiered cake and several bridesmaids, all in ankle-length, non-shaped, non-waisted gowns of a sheer material. Her grandfather and his men were clad in cutaways and top hats. It was beautiful.

Her mother as a child. Her grandparents, so proud and happy, holding the child to the camera for the sweet little face to be made permanent at that point in time. Grandfather, a big man with big hands, was dressed in a fine white shirt and a suit jacket, his tie a swathe across his chest. He was holding his daughter's hand, no bigger than one of his knuckles. Her grandmother, in a sheer and frothy summer dress, looked pleased and proud of them both.

A picture in front of a university building, her grandfather with books in hand and a smile and wave for the person behind the camera. He had one foot on the stair step, going into his future.

Another picture of her grandmother behind a desk, a navy dress with white collar and cuffs, her pale golden brown hair pulled back into a perfectly coiffed French roll. She had on lipstick and nail polish. She looked sophisticated and capable, as well as lovely.

Pictures of a steam train engine with rows of men in front, an arrow drawn to a blurry face proclaiming in faded brown ink "George."

Pictures of what looked at first to be a bomb explosion, but it was described in the same brown ink as "#339 April 5, 1936, Moffatt Tunnel Explosion. Five killed–nine injured."

Page after page of photographs of the destruction. Funeral photos with banks of flowers and mourners.

Murlow! The dog that Elizabeth had heard of but never seen.

The cabin as it was being built. Page after page of happiness.

Her mother taking her first steps to the outstretched hands of her grandfather, whose body was off camera. Only his loving face and big hands were captured in the frame.

Her mother dressed in sunbonnet and ruffled dress with an Easter basket on her arm. Murlow was frozen in time tugging the basket away.

Her mother in her first-day-of-school dress. Her hair was tied in pigtails, and she clasped a pencil box in her hands. She wore thick black shoes and looked terribly uncomfortable.

Over the years her grandparents aged and seemed to become more worn and threadbare. Their daughter—her mother—became a beauty, mature at twelve; a stunning, breathtaking beauty at fourteen. And suddenly no pictures.

Her mother ran away at fifteen, and her grandparents' lives seemed to end then.

Elizabeth put the album on the floor

beside her and picked up the next item. It was a sewing basket with a hinged lid. She expected to find needle and threads but instead found a brown paper bag with an empty cookie bag and an empty pop bottle. Beneath that a small pink checked dress and a horribly scuffed pair of red leather shoes rested. It was what she had on the night she had been dumped with them.

Elizabeth held the tiny dress to her face and buried her head in the memories. She didn't feel the anger and fear and resentment that had been her usual responses to that chapter of her life. She simply felt the love. It seemed to be embedded into the thin warp and weave of the toddler's dress. She had been loved, and she had turned her back on it.

She carefully folded those items and placed them back in the basket, on top of her grade-school drawings and report cards.

Next in the box was an album designed to hold the old wax records for a vintage record player. She hadn't remembered her grandparents owning a record player.

Again, she fell into the trap of expecting to find what *should have been.*

Indeed there was a record, but a paper record of her life since the day she left the cabin in 1966.

The graduation from college listed in a newspaper from the East. The announcement of her position at Merrill Lynch. Her first newspaper article, and the years and years of magazine columns and articles. There was even a tiny scrap of a column from *TV Guide,* an announcement she'd be on a Sunday talk show. These were glued onto the brown paper pages, which were getting crispy. Elizabeth wondered if her grandmother had made the glue with flour and water. Then she noticed the handwriting. It hadn't been her grandmother at all. It had been her grandfather who had put in place each and every thing about his granddaughter.

Elizabeth closed the album and kissed the cover. "Thank you, Grandpa," she whispered.

In the bottom of the box, wrapped in white tissue paper, was a dress. White lace, now yellow with age. In many places the lace was torn. It was her grandmother's wedding dress. Lavishly tulip hemmed and draped over a satin slip that had faded unevenly into a spider web of white and yellow. It was delicate and incredibly tiny. Of course, at this stage in her pregnancy, Elizabeth thought hot air balloons were petite.

She placed everything gently into the box. She also cleaned the floor as long as she was down there. She managed to pull herself up and cleaned the rest of the room. She left the box where it was. By the time she was done, Eight Ball was awake and tearing around the room as if a ghost were chasing him.

# Twenty-eight

"The party is a go!" Chris said when he got home that evening. "Everyone thinks it's a great idea. Amy put everyone into a food category so nobody brings the same things. All we provide is a place and the dishes." He was proud of himself.

"So, what you are really saying is Amy planned it all." She aimed little arrows at his pride. One good thing about Chris was that his pride could take a few arrows and not be wounded.

He ignored her comments. "It will be held Saturday, December fourth, in the evening. Most everyone will be there. The late night staff will come in first, and the day staff will come in later when they get off."

Elizabeth stood in the kitchen area with a large ladle in her hand. She was contemplating hitting him over the head.

"How many people are you talking about here?" she said in a tightly controlled voice. "Ten? Twenty? How many?"

Chris said brightly, "Sixty or seventy. Not all at once."

She didn't hit him but she did throw the ladle. It landed about three feet from him.

"Are you out of your mind?" She was livid. "How do you expect me to do that? I have plates for four people! You think I'm going to stand here and wash dishes all night, every fifth person has to wait while I wash a plate or fork!" She was outraged. "Why are you doing this to me!"

The next second she was at his side. He flinched, thinking she might get violent, but she threw her arms around him. She begged him to forgive her; this was even more shocking than her anger before.

"I'm sorry. I'll handle it somehow. I can do it. Don't worry about a thing. I'll rent plates. I'll buy some more. No. I can't buy more. I'll think of something." She talked on and on.

Chris stood very still and held her gingerly. He was still too stunned to think of anything comforting to say. Finally he did say something when she stopped to catch her breath.

"I thought we'd use paper plates."

"PAPER PLATES!" and she was off again, pacing around the room, throwing her arms to the sky, praying for understanding from some helpless, hapless god of the kitchen. "Right! Let everybody know I have no money, no plates, nothing!"

"This is some pregnancy thing, isn't it?" Chris said under his breath when he dared to take a breath.

"I heard that!" she yelled as she went into the bedroom and then slammed the door. It was a good thing the cabin was built so well, for the reverberation alone would have tumbled a lesser structure.

Chris sat down on the sofa. He did so as if he were going to sit on newly laid eggs and didn't want to crush them.

He took three deep breaths and held

the last one, slowly letting it escape to calm him. He sat back to get more comfortable on the sofa. Just then the bedroom door flew open, and she was coming at him. Rapidly, considering her size.

"I'm so sorry!" she cried. "I don't understand this. I'm not like this! Really I'm not!"

"It's okay. I think it's the pregnancy. Really." He tried to console her, to reassure her. "I'm not going to stop loving you just because you're a little wild now and then." He wished immediately he could take those words back.

Her eyes opened wide. Her eyebrows shot up. "Oh, really! So I have to act a certain way for you to love me!" She was back in the bedroom, door slammed. Chris was truly amazed how fast she could move when she was angry.

"I'm going to go in to town for dinner," he called. He thought that might be best. He was wrong.

Out she came. "I've fixed dinner already! You are going to eat it!"

He thought about escape, then thought again. Then he thought escape *was* the right thing to do. He started for the door.

"Coward!" she called out.

He turned to face her. She had her arms folded across her chest, actually resting on the bulge. She was smiling.

He put his head down to one side, contemplating his chances. Then he smiled. "Them's fighting words, pardner," he drawled.

"This town is only big enough for the two of us," she said and patted her tummy. "But, sit down a spell and have some grub."

She was into character now. "Maybe we could come up with some . . ." she paused for emphasis, "arrangement."

He thought about it. He picked up his cowboy hat from the table where he'd dropped it when he came in and stood like a street shooter contemplating his chances with the fastest gun in the West. Then he nodded.

"Mighty grateful, ma'am." He took off his hat again, and sauntered over to the table and pulled out a chair. He swung one leg over the back and sat down. He picked up a knife in one hand and a fork in the other and held them up. "I'm ready," he said.

"Dinner, too," she said. They were no longer the playacting people they had been. They were Chris and Elizabeth, ready for dinner. But inside, each breathed a sigh of relief.

Elizabeth especially let her mind churn. *When will things get normal?* she said to herself. *And for that matter, what will I do if they do get* normal?

"It was so exciting to see those things. I can't think why I never looked in that box." As they ate dinner, Elizabeth told Chris about her afternoon.

"I must have sat up there for hours, but it only felt like minutes. Until I began to clean. Then it began to feel like hours though I really only spent minutes."

"Sounds interesting," Chris said. "Do you mind if I go up and bring it down after dinner?" She nodded.

"I haven't heard from the contractors," Elizabeth said. "Are we going to have the platform poured or not?"

Chris put down his fork and looked at her. "Elizabeth, I don't know. I am not the one who took care of that."

Elizabeth was stunned that Chris snapped at her.

Before she could reply, Chris was at her side. "I'm sorry. I guess I'm still tired and worried." He kissed her and then went upstairs. He hadn't finished eating.

When he came back down with the box, he sat on the sofa and put the box on the floor. He opened the lid and turned it upside down, taped to the top of the lid was an old, weathered legal size envelope. He looked to Elizabeth with a questioning glance.

"Go ahead," she said and slowly rose to join him.

He sliced the yellow tape and pulled the envelope from the lid then he slit the sealed paper.

"It's a marriage certificate!" he said as Elizabeth sat beside him. "And divorce papers," he added quietly.

Elizabeth took the ornate marriage certificate from him. It was embellished with doves and ribbons and flowers. In ornate scrollwork lettering it said that Alice Gorasch wed Hubert Ulysses Henderson on April 12, 1907, in Gotham City, Nebraska.

In her grandfather's unique script he'd written, *"I was eight years old, far too young or I'd have married you."*

In her grandmother's handwriting, beneath her signature on the certificate, was written, *"If I had known then."*

The divorce papers were wrapped in blue legal paper. She divorced Hubert U. Henderson in Omaha, Nebraska, in 1921. She was given back her legal name and given a settlement of one thousand dollars. They were not to go near the other. She was not to ever claim she had been married to him. No issue from the marriage could ever claim him as father.

Elizabeth must have had her mouth open. Chris told her to shut it.

"I don't believe what I'm seeing! What I'm hearing!"

"There is more," he said and quietly handed her a birth certificate.

"Baby boy Gorasch born December 1, 1922," she read aloud.

"Sisters of Mercy Hospital, Kearney,

Nebraska. Eight pounds, twenty-one inches."

"There is more," Chris said as he handed her a newspaper clipping. It was a yellowed piece with a picture of a Mr. and Mrs. Darrell Yates of Norfolk, Nebraska, holding their two-year-old son up to see the elephant at a circus parade. It was a "human interest" type of picture. Nothing really newsworthy, just a cute picture of the boy's face when he saw the elephant.

On a typewritten piece of paper, not one inch by one inch, her grandmother had typed, *"My Boy."*

"There is more here," Chris said gently. Elizabeth put down what she held and was trying to get up from the sofa. He put the papers down and helped her stand.

"I think I've seen enough right now," Elizabeth said. She put her head down and then looked up into his warm golden brown eyes. "There is too much going on, Chris I . . ."

She stopped talking and quickly hugged Chris. Then she walked to the bedroom and quietly shut the door. A few moments later Chris heard the shower begin. He went to the bedroom and opened the door, then went to the bathroom door. He put his ear to the door.

He'd expected to hear crying, but she was not. She was just taking a shower. He knocked on the door and she answered quickly.

"May I come in?" he asked.

"Sure."

The room was steamy and smelled of sweet soap and her perfume. He sat on the toilet seat and put his elbows on his knees.

"You know, this doesn't change who they are. Just what we know." He had to repeat it for her to hear when she stuck her head out of the shower.

"It changes everything." Elizabeth disagreed with him.

"Why?" he said. "They were just human beings. Not saints."

She stuck her head out again. "Chris, it isn't that. It's that I was so selfish, so self-centered. I never asked, never cared to ask."

Chris thought about it a moment before he stood up and poked his head into the shower, letting the misting water soak his hair and face.

"It wasn't your job to know these things. It wasn't what you were expected to know. You were the granddaughter, not the Grand Inquisitor. You were their granddaughter."

Elizabeth turned off the water, and he helped her from the tub. He helped dry her with a big blue towel. He helped her put on her T-shirt-gown and robe. When she bent to put on her slippers, he helped her put them on and kissed her kneecaps.

She caressed his face, looking into his eyes with great love, yet great sadness.

Chris wanted to change her expression immediately. He grinned and there was a twinkle in his eye when he said, "Besides, aren't you glad she didn't stay married to somebody whose initials were HUH!?"

Elizabeth had to laugh. He'd made a funny face when he'd said it. How could she *not* laugh at him?

"I'm not sure if you are good for me

or not. But you do make me laugh," she said gently.

"I'm definitely good for you," he said. "Haven't you heard?"

"Heard what?"

"Laughter is the best medicine."

If there had been someone around looking for a wager, she'd have bet he'd say that very thing.

That night Elizabeth dreamed of her grandparents, only they seemed to fade in and out and become she and Chris. One moment it was her grandmother walking with her grandfather, then Grandma would turn into Elizabeth and she would continue to walk with Grandpa, then Chris would be in his place and Elizabeth turned into her grandmother. It was very confusing and tiring.

Chris dreamed as well. His was more physical. He dreamed a balloon from the Macy's Thanksgiving Day Parade followed him wherever he went. In the ER, it was there. Outdoors, it followed. In the operating room, it was there, too. It followed him to the bathroom and while eating. It followed him to the racquetball court where he couldn't hit the small, hard, black ball because the giant balloon was in his way. It was so huge, though, he couldn't see what it was. His last remembered thought about the dream was Barbara saying, "Can't see the forest for the trees?"

They both awoke exhausted and looking at the other as if they were strangers. Both of their minds asking, *Who is this person, and why am I in bed with them?"*

# Twenty-nine

Elizabeth and Chris had Thanksgiving at one of the hotels. It was a major production, with costumed servers and a cabaret of performers. Chris asked several times if she was sure eating out on this most family of holidays was what she wanted.

"We will be having a big holiday party with our friends. This is exactly what I want."

He didn't seem reassured. She barely ate and she seemed not to notice the entertainment, but she kissed him and thanked him profusely when they got home that night. She, at least, did not get angry and sarcastic and fly off the handle at anything for a couple of days afterwards. A real coup, Chris felt, considering her nature these days.

The morning of the party finally dawned. It had snowed, but the roads were not impassable. The sky was pure blue with the lemon-yellow sun in the east.

Elizabeth rose, went into the kitchen to begin breakfast, then no sound at all.

Chris, grown accustomed to her wonderful noise and the aromas that soon followed, was up out of bed as if he'd been shot. There had to be something wrong.

He found her sitting on the sofa, the carved box of memorabilia at her feet, just staring at the brown envelope in her hands.

He came up behind her and wrapped her in a hug while he kissed her just below her earlobe. She smiled and ran her hand through his hair, mussing the already mussed, too long hair.

"Ready to read some more?" he said quietly

"The others are love letters, aren't they?" she said.

"Looked like a few from George to Alice and some from Alice to George."

He went back to the coffee pot and began to make some flavored decaf.

"Why not start with the earliest date." He knew that was obvious, but he wanted to nudge her from just holding the packet to actually reading them.

He heard the rustling of the tissue-thin pages and saw she was doing just that. When the coffee had brewed, he made her a cup with sugar and real cream and brought it to her.

He then sat down beside her and read the discarded pages.

*March 1, 1925*

*Dearest,*

*Please say yes. Don't keep me in suspense this way.*

*I love you and I spend my days and nights plotting ways to keep you with me for the rest of our days.*

*I want us to laugh in the sunshine for the rest of our days! I love to see you laugh! I love to make you laugh!*

*I can't sleep! I can't study!*

*All I can do is think of you!*

*Say yes before you ruin my life!*

*George*

*March 23, 1925*

*My only Darling,*

*What difference can it make? What? I don't care about it! Why must you?*

*No one here will ever know.*

*I can't think of the pain you have gone through, it makes me burn with anger and the desire to never let you be hurt again.*

*I didn't mean that you could ever ruin my life. I only meant to tell you that you are so constantly on my mind.*

*I love you. I love you. I love you.*

*That is all there is.*

*The past is over, the future isn't ours to decide, that is Fate! We only have now, my darling woman, and I want you now!*

*Chicago is not Nebraska! It is a cosmopolitan metropolis. You will be known as my wife and that is all anyone will know!*

*I can and will protect you!*

*I love you! Stop torturing me with your tears! I won't phone again if you cry the whole conversation!*

*That is not true, I will phone and*

*phone and write and phone until you agree to marry me!*

*Your only lover,*
*George*

*April 10, 1925*

*I will be there. Two weeks from today. I may be expelled, but I have my own money, I'll go back to school later.*

*I swear to you it is what I want.*

*I have planned the wedding. All my friends who loved you so when they met you last summer–all will be there. There will not be anyone in the pews for they will all be in the wedding party.*

*Do you wish the woman's choice? Do you wish to plan it? I have said you will wear white, so you will!!*

*No argument! No one knows but what we tell them!*

*Alice-Alice-Alice! I love you!*

*I know you love me as well. You protest too sweetly, you think of my reputation! (Mine!)*

*I think you crave me as I crave you.*

*I'll be there in two weeks.*

*And if you have run away, I will search for you until I find you. And I will find you. No one is as beautiful as you, as perfectly formed as you. No one's skin so white and rose.*

*I can't write anymore. My hand is shaking. How I love you!*

*Your husband (Yes!)*
*George*

Elizabeth's own hands shook as she read. Such passion! Her grandfather had been twenty-six. Her grandmother, thirty-six.

Chris put the last of George's letters down on the table.

"Wish I could say things like that," he said. He took a deep breath and let it out in a hard rush. "I feel that way. I just don't say those words."

Elizabeth looked at Chris and raised her hand to his face, her palm cupping his cheek and chin. "I know you feel that way. You can jump into a jet and be at my side in hours, not weeks, and you needn't write love letters when we see each other, have always seen each other often."

He kissed the soft swell of her palm

and said, "Don't make excuses for me, my love. Let me suffer a twinge of guilt for being a cliché-ridden child of television. I'm no wordsmith, but I do feel the same passion. Marry me, Elizabeth. As George said, marry me or ruin me."

Elizabeth playfully slapped his cheek. "He did *not* say that!"

He grabbed her hand and kissed it again. "Marry me, marry me, marry me!"

She pulled her hand away. "Let me have the others," she said and pointed to the pale pink onionskin paper with her grandmother's precise handwriting. The papers retained a waft of scent. Elizabeth held it to her nose and thought of the woman she knew as Grandmother, never smelling of anything but soap and "dime store" cologne. This scent was deeper and seemed far more expensive.

*April 24, 1925*

*This is not so much a letter, my dear George, as it is a wandering through my mind while I wait to pick you up at the train depot.*

*George, what are you doing to us?*

*Why do you insist it makes no difference? Why won't you let me go? I loved a handsome wild boy for one long and beautiful summer. He made me laugh and he made me cry and he made love to me! Now it is over!*

*I do want it over!*

*No! I do not want it over. I want it to go on until the day we die, but it is so unfair to you! I am not the one for you. How could I deserve someone as pure and decent and kind and gentle as you, my darling, laughing boy?*

*I have not told you all. I have not told you my part in my divorce.*

*I have not told you that I was a cruel and demanding woman.*

*There, I said it. I was a horrible person. A sham of a wife. I hated him and in every way I let him know. He would cause me pain, and I gave it right back. I was as horrid as he was. More so, for it was my role to take it. To put up with it and stay married to him no matter what torture he put me through.*

*You say I torture you. Oh my dear boy, you have no idea what torture is.*

*And you torture me by loving me.*

*I have just seen your beautiful face! Oh, George! How could I ever do anything but what would make you look at me in that way!*

*I love you!*

*Never stop looking at me with such love and joy and hope!*

*Alice*

*May 5, 1925*

*My one and only love.*

*How can I bear it? You have left!*

*I can't face the day without the thought of your deep devotion! Your love! That I should find your love after all these years!*

*How we laughed! I can't say I was funny, but you kept saying so. You kept laughing and in the end I laughed and said yes! YES! YES!*

*I take none of the glory of it. It is all you. You who seem to love me and life and the fight and struggle of it all. It is just more for you to love.*

*I will be there in June.*

*I will marry you.*

*We will have children and our life will be worth living.*

*I love you, George.*
*Until I die, I'm yours,*
*Alice*

Elizabeth had a smile on her face when she was through reading. A smile so big it hurt her face to keep it there, but she did.

"She was about my age when my mother was born," Elizabeth said.

"He was around my age, too," Chris said. "We seem to be fated to live their love story." He sounded pleased and happy about the whole thing.

"But they were so poor!" Elizabeth lost her smile. "So poor. And their only child left them, died! And me! Ungrateful me!"

"Hey!" Chris took her shoulders and held her, forcing her to look at him, to calm herself in his loving lion's eyes.

"We are going to relive their *love!*" He said it again, "Their love! Elizabeth! We have all this to help us with the hard times."

She shook her head. She could not see it, could not fathom the thought that love was enough.

He held her as closely as he could. He rubbed her back in small circles and soothed her as he spoke.

"We have them here. They didn't have these wonderful letters or the years we knew them. We both knew them, Elizabeth! We learned from them, the things they taught themselves. We don't have to reinvent the wheel to do this right. We just take our cues from them. They left us a legacy. It wasn't money, but it was more than any amount of money could ever buy. They are showing us the way."

He held her away from him and looked into her eyes, giving her all the strength he had, all the love his parents had for him, and the care that George had given him when Chris was a lonely and orphaned youth.

He gave her all his strength and the promise that there was more in store. It would not dry up, die, or go away angry.

Eight Ball chose that moment to leap onto Elizabeth's lap, hit her square on the belly, and flew like a furry black ball onto the heap of papers, scattering them all over the floor. He then sat up and licked a paw to wipe his brow and slowly came back. Poised to leap once again, Chris bent down to scoop him up and save the poor kitten the humiliation. Elizabeth was laughing, and the baby was visibly kicking, and Eight Ball was purring.

The aroma of coffee filled the now sun-filled room.

All was right in Elizabeth's paradise.

# Thirty

She had caved in to paper plates, surrendered to paper napkins and cups. She hated it, but they also had plastic knives, forks, and spoons. She felt as if she and she alone were desecrating the landfills of the earth and deforesting the rain-forest.

Chris ignored a great number of the sighs and huffs and puffs of discontent. He was going to work his shift, and he would be back just before the first group came.

It was a typical day in the ER. Broken ankles, broken arms, head cold, chest cold, flu, earaches, altitude sickness, frostbite, overeating, overdrinking, heart attacks, insulin overdose, lack-of-insulin coma.

Just a typical day.

In between, he peeked inside foil-wrapped packages of food for the party, was teased and teased others. He grabbed a nap for a half hour. He called Elizabeth and reminded her to put the kitten upstairs and close the trapdoor.

Elizabeth thanked him for reminding her. Silently she raved, *Good God! I'm just pregnant! Not going senile!* She then promptly forgot to put Eight Ball upstairs.

Angeline called from Los Angeles. "Are you ready?" she asked, hopeful of a positive reply.

"For dinner for sixty, yes. For a newsletter, no." Elizabeth dashed her hopes. "The cement isn't poured, the electrician hasn't been able to come to install more lines. I haven't been able to concentrate on anything longer than a few minutes!" She threw up the hand not holding the phone and then slammed it on the kitchen table. "How on earth do women work at full-time jobs and raise families and be pregnant!"

"Well, I can't speak for everybody, but I found it quite hard to do," Angeline said. "I had four. My idiot husband seemed to think it kept me out of trouble. I showed him!"

"All I can think of is the baby," Elizabeth said. "I'll be doing the dishes, and I'll think of what my child will say when I tell her to do the dishes. I'll actually argue with this prepubescent imaginary child. The next thing I know, I'm in the bedroom lying down with rubber gloves dripping bubbles and grease down my arms, and I'll look around and say, 'How did I get here!' I'm going senile!"

"You are creating, dear. Just accept it. I know my husband was very jealous of me," Angeline paused.

Elizabeth thought for a moment how could anyone think of being jealous of her blimp-like body, swollen veins, and heartburn. How could anyone want the lack of concentration or the nagging backache that never went away?

"One of the only really good things he ever said to me was that he envied me my ability to create. A baby, the only truly creative thing on earth." Angeline was quiet a moment. Then she said, "Don't worry about it, now. When you are ready, give me a call. I will wait. You are the best, and you are worth waiting for."

"Thank you," Elizabeth said. It was a phrase she had said more in the last few months than she had ever said in her entire life.

Chris came home to find her on her hands and knees cleaning up some puddle of water. His first thought was that her water broke.

"Nothing so good." She quickly squashed that idea. "I was trying to get a drink, and I dropped the glass. I think I need plastic. I can't seem to keep anything in my hands."

He finished cleaning it up, and helped her to change into a pretty jumper and turtleneck. She could not bend to put on her shoes. This time he assisted her because she couldn't, not because he got a chance to kiss her. He did that, too.

She sighed. She sighed again. She held her hands out to be helped up from the chair. "Any time now, kid," she said to her mound. She patted it and rubbed both her hands in circles around the bulge.

"Now I know why you are supposed to be young to have kids. I'm exhausted."

Chris put his arm around her shoulders and walked with her to the big main room. "Honey, if you were nineteen you'd be tired at this point." He tried to assure her; she just scowled.

A couple Elizabeth hadn't met were the first to arrive. They brought three types of homemade bread and a child about three years old. No matter how she tried, Elizabeth could not tell if this straggly-haired corduroy-clad child were a girl or a boy. Elizabeth asked the mother the child's name. "Jerry," the mother said. No help.

Elizabeth bent as much as was possible to get to the child's height. *The hell with tact, what did children know of tact?* she told herself. "Are you a little girl or a little boy?" Elizabeth asked. The child respond by making a rude spitting noise and ran to its mother screaming to go to the "potty."

Chris led the way. Elizabeth wondered if she wanted the child inside her to be here so quickly after all.

Next arrival was a nurse and her husband. Elizabeth had talked to her before, and she felt less uneasy. They brought a dessert and did not bring a child.

Amy was next with her husband and six children ranging in age from mid teens to just beginning to walk.

They brought every conceivable kind of dip and chip and vegetables and fruit.

By the time the introductions were done, three more couples with children had arrived. Elizabeth's huge main room, once seemingly so vast, was now cramped, and the din from the adults' voices and the children's squeals was almost deafening.

Elizabeth could not find Chris. Food and drinks were handed out and no matter where you stepped or stood you found someone there with plate and cup and plastic.

Elizabeth began to work the room trying to find Chris. She caught fragments of conversation as she went by pools of people.

"It can't happen! I've told her, she takes the car, she takes me! I am not giving up the car just to get divorced! I'll stay with her before my Beemer goes!"

"I hate it! I can't have a moment to myself! I tried to take a bath last night and three of them came pounding on the door. One wasn't even mine!"

"MOM! Davey has his hands in the dip! MOM!"

"MOMMY! Make him stop it ! He's looking at me! MOMMY! MAKE HIM STOP!"

"MA! That boy wiped his hands on me, and look!"

"So I went to the grocery store without them and damned if they didn't call me there . . . did you hear my kid! No that's not mine. Thank God."

"MOMMY!"

Food was on the floor, the paper plates were everywhere. She still hadn't found Chris. Although she could have sworn that some people had left, the children had multiplied.

"I WON'T! NO! NO! MOM!"

"MOM! Davey has his hands in the pie!"

"She comes downstairs, see, in this dark green thing with yellow stripes. I don't know why they put stripes on it, supposed to make the pregnant woman look thinner. Doesn't. Anyway the oldest screams out, 'LOOK OUT IT'S THE WATERMELON FROM HELL!' And all the others join in. I'm telling you. It was not a pretty sight. She grounded them all for three months.

"So I say, 'Amy, honey, if you ground them all here, they will all be underfoot.' So she let up. I'm telling you. This is the last one!"

Elizabeth looked to see who Amy's husband was talking to and found Chris huddled in a far corner with a plate heaped with food,

Just then, the child who could only have been Davey, judging from the amount of food on his face, clothes, and hands, ran up to grab onto his father's blue jeans. "DAD!" he screamed.

From the volume and urgency of the scream, Elizabeth was certain she would find he had broken an arm or one of his siblings had cut off a hand. Her mouth formed a perfect "O."

No such luck. He just wanted help with the bathroom, the food wouldn't go down he told his father.

Chris told Elizabeth to close her mouth. "It's okay. Dave can handle it," he assured her. She wasn't assured.

More people came and went, somehow the number of children seemed to grow and grow. They were like a cloning experiment gone haywire.

There seemed to be no intelligent conversation going on in the room. It all centered on how awful life with the spouse was becoming, how horrible the last birth had been, how expensive the doctors' bills were getting, could anybody recommend a good orthodontist, and aren't those other people's children just the worst little brats you ever saw.

* * *

At ten o'clock, they said goodbye to the last couple and ran a room check to make sure no one had left behind, accidentally or on purpose, some little reminder of the creativity of life. Elizabeth sat on the only clean spot she could find, a step three up from the bottom, put her head in her hands, and shook with dry sobs.

Chris was cleaning up the disaster. Big black plastic bags of paper and plastic and overflowing food loomed around the room like cancers about ready to spread. When he noticed her posture, he dropped what he was doing and went to her.

"Tired?" he said.

She shook her head, indeed her whole body shook.

Chris sat down on the step beneath her and rubbed her swollen ankles. "It's okay to be tired!" He tried to reassure her, but he just did not understand. He'd had a wonderful time. *Thank God the floors were not carpeted. Thank God a couple of the other men knew how to unstop a toilet.*

"Want to tell me about it?" he dared to ask.

*Big mistake!*

Her head shot up and out of her arms, and she began to rant and rave.

"I can't do this! I can't raise a child! I'll kill it before it gets to kindergarten!"

"Now, Elizabeth." He tried to sound calm, but even he knew she was on the edge.

"Don't 'Now, Elizabeth' me!" she screamed. "Did you ever in your life see such hideous things? All in one place! I'm surprised I'm not deaf!" She hit her head against her hands. "I'm surprised I'm not maimed!"

"Lissy—" he began, but he knew he had no chance.

"Don't you 'Lissy' me! I'm telling you I don't want this baby! I don't want to put myself in that kind of situation! Did you see the one who stood—STOOD!—on the table with the food on it and put his tennis shoes in the punch!" She waited a half a second then said, "Well? Did you?"

"His father got him down, he didn't get hurt." Chris was thinking she might be upset because the child could have fallen and hurt himself.

"HE DIDN'T GET HURT!" Elizabeth nearly lost her voice on that one. "I'm going to die from athlete's foot of the mouth, and you worry about the kid!"

Chris finally came out of the fog of having had a really great time. He finally saw what Elizabeth was really so hysterical about.

He got her a cup of the leftover punch, thought better about that, and got her a glass of ice water. He came back to her side where she sat with her head in her hand, shaking her head back and forth, saying, "I can't do it. I just can't do it."

"Drink this," he said in his most doctorly voice. She did take a sip, then another. Now she held the glass instead of her head.

"Once upon a time," Chris started, ignoring the look of shock on her face at the beginning of what had to be a fairy tale, "at a church program, a group of kids from the ages of sixteen to about three put on a show for their parents." Chris stopped to see if she would follow what he was saying.

"The oldest child there was sixteen.

She took herself pretty damn seriously. She was supposed to see that each and every one of her younger charges got where they were supposed to be, wore what they were supposed to be wearing, and did what they were supposed to be doing."

Chris took the glass from her hand and took a sip. "Her biggest problem wasn't the kids. Her biggest problem was that she had to be absolutely perfect and every one of those kids had to be, too, or else."

Elizabeth sighed. "All right, Chris."

"I'm not through yet!" he insisted. "She ran here and there and everywhere. Pretty soon everything was going along just fine when one of the younger ones, ten years younger to be exact, lost his prop. He was supposed to have a stuffed lamb and he'd lost it. He looked everywhere for it. He started crying and the girl just threw up her hands and said, 'I can't do it! Find it yourself!' "

Elizabeth tried to get up from the stair step, but Chris held her there with his gaze.

"She ignored his crying for her to help

him, and finally he got so mad he bit her. Hard."

Elizabeth blushed so deeply and vividly that she looked like a cherry.

"The first thing she did—she swatted his rear end with a big flat whack of her palm. And when she did, the little lamb fell out from under her arm. She'd forgotten she had it there. She was so concerned with doing her perfect job that she had forgotten it."

Chris paused, and then he decided he'd said enough.

He waited.

"I had forgotten it," Elizabeth said quietly. "I had no idea it was there. I don't think I even remembered how it got there."

"I do," Chris said tauntingly. "I was hitting Joanie Buck over the head with it to make her pay attention to me." He seemed proud of it.

"Chris, what is the point? I couldn't handle children then and I am even less capable now."

Chris held up his hand and ran his fingers along her hairline at her cheek. He pulled strands of her hair from the ponytail and kissed them. He leaned over and kissed Elizabeth softly on the lips. Then he pulled back to look at her face with a tenderness she didn't believe was possible in a man.

"I survived," he said. "And you survived, and Joanie has four kids and is surviving."

"Not good enough," Elizabeth said.

Chris kissed her again. "But it is. You have to trust me on this."

She pushed her head into his chest and closed her eyes tightly. When she spoke, she sounded so lost.

"I'm afraid."

"And I'm right here with you telling you that you will be fine and the baby will be fine."

He helped her from the step, took her into the bedroom, and helped her with her shower and dressing for bed.

After he changed the sheets—they found apple pie smeared between the linen—he tucked her in and kissed her lightly on the brow.

Before he left the room, Elizabeth called out to him.

"If I have ever done anything so good

as to deserve you, what on earth did you do so bad to deserve me?"

"I loved you. From the moment I saw into your soul," he confided as he left the room. While she listened to him cleaning up the remnants of the party, she dreamed, wide-awake, of their life together. He would make her laugh and make the baby laugh. He would love her and love the baby. Little scenes made themselves clear. She fell asleep long before he came into the bedroom. She slept well and solidly.

# Thirty-one

"Weeks in bed, weeks of SEC interrogations, you in the hospital, almost two more weeks until the baby is born." Elizabeth sat up in bed with great difficulty as she spoke. "When are things going to get *normal,* Chris?"

"Today. This instant. Look!" He pointed out the huge bay window in the bedroom as he pulled open the room-darkening drapes. Giant white flakes fell, flakes like hand cut paper lace. "December fifth, in the Rocky Mountains, snow falling. Normal!"

Elizabeth was not reacting the way he wanted her to. Chris wanted her to be happy and laugh, instead she was more miserable than ever, complaining about everything. Even though he considered himself a sensitive man, he was definitely ready for her to have the baby. The sooner, the better. He said, "What could be more normal than that?"

"Oh, *that's* normal. I want to get a Christmas tree, and it's snowing. That's normal all right."

"I wasn't going to let you go anyway," Chris said. He held out her slippers, but the look she gave him made him come to the bedside and kneel down. He slipped them on her feet and kissed her kneecaps. He felt a twinge of guilt. She couldn't even put on her own shoes because of the baby. He kissed her knees again.

She made a wry face. "I'm going to make breakfast," he said. She tried to stand as quickly as possible, but it wasn't easy.

"Oh, no, you're not," she insisted. "I'll cook. I have to do something or I'll go crazy."

"Too late," Chris said matter-of-factly, then he smiled. Elizabeth thought about it for a moment, and finally saw the humor or the effort at humor.

"I'll make breakfast, you get the tree.

I'll make lunch, you make the tree holder. I'll make dinner, and *I'll* decorate the tree," she said adamantly.

"We'll see about that. But as long as you are making breakfast, I'd like buttermilk pancakes."

Elizabeth laughed and threw a pillow at him. "Demanding male."

"Controlling female," he countercharged.

The rest of the morning went at a slow and delightful pace. Chris cut a beautiful, full tree and placed it in a holder outside on the covered porch for the snow to melt. Elizabeth felt an urge to clean the closets and rewash the baby clothes. After lunch she washed windows and Chris waxed the floors.

When the cabin sparkled and Elizabeth could find no more cleaning to do, Chris brought in the tree and some extra pine boughs. He set the tree in a corner near the fireplace and draped the pine bough on the fireplace. As they warmed the aroma of cedar and pine filled the cabin.

Elizabeth began to make an apple pie. Chris watched her from his place on the sofa. "Why don't you sit down?" he said.

He repeated it with more emphasis. "Sit down!"

"I will." But she continued to cook, cutting up vegetables and putting together a vegetable stew for dinner. She occasionally stopped to rub her back. In spite of her good feelings, a sigh would escape every now and then.

Chris fell asleep on the sofa. Elizabeth sat on the straight backed chair at the table and watched him as he slept. "He is so dear," she whispered to the room, thinking he would not hear.

"I'm not a deer, I'm a doctor," Chris whispered back.

"You are awake," she said.

"Sort of awake," he said. "Come sit by me."

Elizabeth slowly rose, and he made room for her. Then he tried to put his head in her lap, but they had to laugh because it just would not work. "Two more weeks," she said, "And then you won't be able to put your head in my lap because the baby will be there."

Chris was about to speak when the phone rang. He sat up and went to the phone, noting on the way that the snow had stopped.

Elizabeth rose from the sofa with difficulty. She was going to look out the window, and no mere physical thing like a belly the size of a sixty-pound bowling ball was going to stop her. She still had control of standing and sitting and . . . controlling her life. She was only trying to control her life which had gotten so wildly away from all her plans.

Elizabeth stood at the multipaned window looking out on the sparkle of fresh snow. It was like looking out onto a field of diamond powder. The lake was frozen to blue-white and the stream, a delicate lacy fringe of ice on the edges, sparkled as it continued to flow in a thin, assertive path past the cabin. Each cedar and pine tree was frosted with six-inch-deep piles of snow weighing down each limb, and the stand of leafless aspens made beautiful blue shadows in the snow. Usual sunsets in the high country involved the sun being there one moment and gone the next. This afternoon a few puffy clouds helped give background to a pink, orange, purple, and sapphire sky.

The fire in the fireplace crackled and spit, the fresh clean smell of their Christmas tree in the corner, the aroma of the stew on the old wood burning stove and apple pie cooling on the pine table added to Elizabeth's sense of peace. She felt as if she had stepped back in time, slowed down its progress, taken control. She was back in control of her life.

She leaned her forehead against the sill and blew on the windowpane to frost it over. Then she took her fingertip for a paintbrush and drew a heart with an arrow through it.

"I've got to go in. Avalanche." Chris said when he hung up the phone.

"That's okay." Elizabeth smiled. "I'll be fine. I'm going to decorate the Christmas tree."

"Save the star for me," Chris said. He quickly kissed her, walked to the door and stopped as if he'd forgotten something. "Are you sure you'll be all right?"

"Of course." She smiled at him. Nothing could happen.

"I'll be gone four hours, tops."

"Go!" she said and slowly walked to

his side and gave him another kiss, getting as close as her size would allow.

He left then. She stood at the door, inhaling the clean cold air and the breathless beauty of her home. She was home, and everything would be fine.

An avalanche had claimed one victim, a back country skier, ignoring the signs and warnings, all ready to believe that bad happens only to others. One of his companions was hanging on to life by sheer luck, although two broken legs and arms, his face crushed when he was forced against a tree, could only just qualify as *luck*. The tree had saved his life because his skis caught in such a way that the force of the snow shoved him high into the tree. The other members of the skiing party saw his ski pole sticking out of the treetop and dug for him first. The other skier wasn't found for hours, buried under twenty-five feet of hard packed snow.

Chris was with this patient longer than he anticipated. After six hours he happened to look out the double doors to see in the dusky dark that a hard blizzard had been raging all of the time he'd been there. He went out the doors quickly and realized he couldn't even see his own car in the parking lot, not fifteen feet from the door. The snow was dramatically thick, and the howling wind was blowing it almost horizontally straight.

He ran back inside and called Lissy. The phone crackled and popped, he heard shadows of conversations, but no connection with the cabin. He tried three more times. No luck.

The state patrol came in with the report that another avalanche had trapped four cars on Interstate 70 and to be prepared for the worst. Chris asked about the phone lines.

"They've been down for about three hours up north and the water supply is shut off as well, a semi turned over and cracked the water lines, we have a flood and snow and ice."

Chris was concerned, but not worried. Elizabeth was not due for nearly two weeks. Just then the first victims of the interstate avalanche were being brought in, and the driver of the semi had finally been freed from the roll-over. Chris was back in the thick of it before he could think of Elizabeth and the uneasy qualms he felt in his stomach. *No,* he thought, *it can't be time.*

At that moment Elizabeth slid from a seated position on the couch to a semi-prone one, her moans and gasps unheard by anyone but Eight Ball, who sat curled under the table ignoring everything.

*It can't be time,* Elizabeth thought frantically. *It just can't.* She had just done too much in trying to decorate the tree. When the first spasm had passed, she sat up and caught her breath. She had felt small nagging pains all day. When she bent over to pick up the decorations, a stab of pain hit her in the small of her back, so she had just left everything on the floor for the kitten to bat around and play with. When she cleaned out the kitchen cupboards and she stretched too far, she left out everything she had taken down. She had felt such a need to clean and organize, but everything was a complete disaster now. She looked around. The place looked as if a tornado had hit it. Laundry folding begun but not finished, dinner begun but not finished. Dishes begun but. . . .

She looked at the mantel clock and saw it was after ten. Chris would be back soon. *Better get it cleaned up,* she thought. She struggled to the edge of the sofa, balanced her belly and stood up in one slow-motion swoop. Immediately water gushed from her, soaking her legs and socks and shoes, leaving a puddle on the rag rug.

Another pain began, taking the breath from her. She fell to the couch again. When her mind could think and her body didn't arch with pain, she struggled to the phone and called the hospital. Nothing. She pushed the numbers again and again. The sound of her button pushing was all she heard. She doubled up her fist and pounded on the phone, and threw the handset against it. "Damn!" Another pain began, this one from a spot somewhere this side of hell. She cried out, "CHRIS!" Eight Ball woke, stretched himself, and mewed in irritation at being disturbed from his nap.

Sweat broke out on Elizabeth's forehead, her heart beat madly. This baby was coming, coming now! "CHRIS!"

Sweat broke out on Christian's forehead, Amy dabbed it off with a surgical sponge. They were not in surgery, but in the hallway doing triage on the three-car accident that happened on the ice slick interstate because impatient skiers ignored the driving conditions and were going sixty-five when they hit the ice from the broken water line.

"This one first. Hey, Joe!" he called to the only other doctor in the hospital. "This one!" Chris indicated the ghost-white patient who was unresponsive except for deep moans when his abdomen was touched. "The breaks and the possible concussion go to radiology, and the two teenagers in C can be sewn up, nothing on their faces, so I'll do a few quick stitches." Chris looked confused a moment, turned as if someone had called his name. "Did you hear that?" he asked Amy.

"What?" She obviously didn't hear anything but rolling gurneys, moans and cries, state patrol and ambulance people conversing, and the phone ringing off the hook.

"We've got a helicopter coming in with two more avalanche victims. Hypothermia, shock, no visible bleeding," the nurse at the desk announced. "ETA fifteen minutes. Doing CPR on both." She suddenly looked down at the phone bank. No phones were ringing. She picked up one line after another. "Phones are out," she said as if it were just another event, nothing drastic. Then she surprised everyone by saying, "Shit!"

Chris and Amy looked out the double door. If anything, the visibility was worse. They looked at each other and shook their heads. Chris went into room C.

Elizabeth managed to get to the bedroom before another contraction hit. *Contraction, hell!* she thought. *This is sheer pain!* She put towels on the bed. After another contraction she got water in a pitcher with ice and turned on the radio beside the bed. There was no music, only the weather reports and all the closings. The announcer cautioning motorists to stay home. She picked up the phone again, just to check, but there was no welcoming buzz. Nothing.

She lay there for a half hour and counted the contractions and how long they lasted. Three—lasting from three to five minutes from beginning to end. The wind howled a symphony like a bassoon outside the cozy cabin. She could see nothing at all but the blue-white snow blowing straight across her picture window. Chris would be home soon, she reminded herself. He had left the hospital before the roads were closed. He would be here in moments. *I am warm, I am in control,* she constantly reminded herself. *What else can I do? What else could happen?*

Chris couldn't believe this night. Three more car accidents, another stranded skier brought in with hypothermia. The helicopter that had brought in the injured parties had taken a spin, and the pilot, who ought to get a medal for not killing everyone, had broken his arm and leg in the landing. No other doctors could get in, no other nurses. What else could happen?

Chris grabbed a quick sandwich, drank coffee until he felt like he had it running through his veins, not blood. He could not get rid of the nagging feeling that tugged at him in his guts that something was wrong with Lissy. He tried to shake it off, tried to talk himself out of it. It was just the general atmosphere of the night, the weather, and not being able to talk to her. He was tired. None of this self-talk worked. He told Amy. Amy, herself, was just one month behind Elizabeth, her baby due in six weeks. She was exhausted and her baby, usually quiet, was punching and kicking in anger that Mom wasn't calm herself.

Every wince, every groan, everytime she reached for her abdomen to soothe the one growing in her, Chris became doubly worried for Elizabeth. Amy tried to comfort him, but they barely had time to concentrate on anything but the many injured and the next X ray or frostbite victim.

He checked the phones every time he went by one. Any quiet second he had, he tried to focus on Lissy being okay. Nothing worked. After the last emergency—three snowmobilers who had gone too far in the bad weather and were finally found by friends and brought back to the hospital for frostbite—Chris sat down in the only quiet place in the hospital. The delivery room.

He looked at the clock on the wall. The one used to place the time of birth. He'd been gone from the cabin for sixteen hours.

He sat on a high stool. He precariously leaned on two metal legs against the tiled walls, so cold that they made him shiver. Was it the tile or exhaustion?

He closed his eyes tightly, squeezed them as hard as he could and ground his teeth together. His lips quivered and, in spite of his effort not to let it happen, it did. He cried. He put his head into his hands and cried out. "Help Lissy!" He sobbed again, "Somebody! Help Lissy!"

The tears and despair were over as

quickly as they began. He sat the stool up straight on all four legs, wiped his eyes and nose with a sterile wipe, turned to go through the giant double doors when he saw an elderly man in clean but worn coveralls and a denim jacket standing in the room in front of the doors.

Elizabeth had long ago given up looking at the clock in the radio to time the contractions. She was unaware of much of anything except the relentless, ongoing force of the muscles and the insistence of the baby to get out, to be born. Elizabeth didn't realize that the electricity had gone out hours ago. She was shivering and sweating and nothing kept her from screaming. Eight Ball had set up post on the dresser which sat directly behind the big wood burning stove and thus was warm. He would look up and yawn huge gaping yawns when Elizabeth would begin to yell. Elizabeth broke into laughter after one of these. She spoke to the cat in gasps, "You think you're bored!" But she was soon in another spasm of pain.

She had no idea how long she'd been this way. She had checked whenever she could to see that she was not bleeding. For some reason it stuck in her mind over and over, *don't bleed.* That and the words to an old Everly Brothers' song she sang to herself over and over and over again. Over and over and over again those same words. Not the next phrase or even other Everly Brothers' songs, just that one.

She knew that something was very wrong. The same force, same pressure and same space and length of time seemed to be happening. No progress, no more or less power of duration. Just the constant, urgent, insistent pain.

She didn't know it had been sixteen hours, or that it was dawn. She knew she was cold in between contractions. When her mind finally put the whole thing together, she realized she had no heat. She thought if she could just get out of bed she would put logs in the big wood burning stove. It would warm the room somewhat. She began to pull her legs to the side of the bed when she saw her rocking chair begin to rock. She thought the cat had jumped into the seat, but he was still on the dresser. She slowly pulled herself to a sitting position, another contraction drove her back. She sat up again. The rocker rocked harder, and she turned to it to see why.

The room was suddenly suffused with heat and light. She felt so warm that she smiled in relief. She looked at the room, in every corner, and then looked outside. The snow had stopped. She sat there wiping her dripping face with the corner of the sheet, a big smile on her lips. She thought, *It's over.*

"It's not over," a woman's voice said to her. She recognized it. She turned to the rocking chair, and there was her grandfather and behind him her grandmother. They looked immaculate, scrubbed and shining clean. Familiar clothes. She had to shake her head and chuckle.

"Grandma, you wore your best dress," she said.

"Why, yes, dear. I did." She looked so pleased Elizabeth had noticed. "Don't worry about the stove, Grandpa put a log or two in."

"Grandpa. Your jacket doesn't have

that old tear in it." She pointed to the sleeve.

"No. Everything has been fixed," he said and nodded to her and gestured. "Get back under those covers, you know it's cold. Never could get you to stay in bed when you needed to."

She did as she was told.

"Now, you just lay there a bit while we watch over you," he said and began to rock. Grandma picked invisible lint from his shoulder each time he came within reach.

"Okay," Elizabeth said. She looked around the room again, it seemed to be bathed in opalescent light. Not gold and not white, more like the inside of a seashell. She felt warm; she felt no pain.

"And by the way," Grandpa said. "If you have to sing a silly song, make it one your grandmother and I know."

Elizabeth smiled. "I'm singing about my clown, did you know he was a clown?" She looked at them, and they both smiled and nodded. "How about 'There'll Be a Hot Time In The Old Town Tonight.' Oh, never mind. I don't know the words."

"You don't know the words to the one you're singing!" Grandpa said.

"I'm sorry," Elizabeth answered.

"Don't need to be sorry, just quit singing it," he said.

"I mean I'm sorry for everything I've done to you two."

"Don't give it a thought, dear," Grandma said.

"She can give it a thought if she quits singing that damn tune," Grandpa said. Then he stopped rocking. He looked at her for a long moment and Elizabeth felt a great rush of strength envelop her. "You can love that baby and that man," he said. "That would be the best thing of all."

"I don't know how to love anyone," Elizabeth said.

"Well, just what in the hell do you think you have been doing for nine months? You have been loving that baby!" Grandpa insisted. "And you have been learning what love is from a man who loves you, and you love him."

"I do love him."

"Lissy." He leaned forward in the rocker and spoke intensely. "You only have right now, this very moment. Not yesterday, not the future, just right now."

Grandmother nodded agreement. "Love is wonderful, but only for the moment you have it. It doesn't matter what happened in the past, and the future isn't here yet. Just know that you love and are loved right now."

"Thank you," Elizabeth said. She thought she said it again, but maybe not. She saw the snow outside turn from sapphire to rose quartz to topaz to pure white blazing diamonds. It was daylight. She had made it through the night. Grandma and Grandpa were here. Chris would be here soon. She closed her eyes.

# Thirty-two

Chris saw the magnificent sunrise, the snow glowing with a pink-gold beauty. It was hard to believe when looking at the dawn that the blizzard before had caused so much pain and death and suffering. But it was over. Now he had to get to Lissy. Roads weren't open. The State Patrol said it would be four hours.

Chris stood at the doors to the emergency room, panic evidencing itself in cold sweat and rapid heartbeat. He stopped himself from his own check list. He had to get to Lissy.

The road graders and sand trucks went by. Chris noted the cars in the parking lot: the patrol cars, trucks, the trailer with the snowmobiles in the back.

Chris jumped into gear. He dressed,

found one of the uninjured stranded snowmobilers, and grabbed him. In minutes they were taking off. Chris sat behind the drive and told him directions. They would go cross-country. Avalanche danger was the big problem. None of the routes was safe. Chris explained it to the driver, and he explained it to Amy.

"I have to try. I have to get to her."

Amy argued. The State Patrol told him he'd be the next one they would be out searching for. The owner of the snowmobile was excited. "Far-out, man! Rad! Let's go, dude!"

Chris was excited, but he was also frightened, not for himself, but for Lissy and the baby.

He seemed to feel every contraction. He felt Lissy's back twist and arch in pain, he could her moans and the baby's heartbeat get slower and slower. He knew. He just knew.

Chris was not dressed for flying across the snow at speeds up to sixty miles per hour with snow flying up to sting him in the face like icy pins. He'd worn what he was wearing for a quick trip from the house to the hospital and back in a comfortable warm car. He was dressed in a ski jacket and gloves and his cowboy boots. His feet were cold. His hands were fine. His face was soon white, his ears went numb, and his breathing became labored from the air chill index: The more wind, the colder the temperature. He bent his head down behind the body of Joe, the driver, but the wind and snow still found a way to whip around and slap him. His ears were especially brutalized.

By car, the trip took one hour. He hoped, cutting cross-country, it would take half that time.

Or that an avalanche would not stop them. Permanently.

The trip took forty-five minutes and they caused, but missed narrowly, two avalanches because of the roar of the snowmobile engine echoing on the precariously balanced snow cliffs.

Elizabeth felt luxuriously warm, the room was filled with white light. She thought it must be the sun glaring off the snow. She could barely discern the outlines of her furniture, but it was all washed with white. She saw her grandmother, still standing behind her grandfather. He rocked peacefully, Grandmother knitted.

Eight Ball stretched and yawned, circled and wrapped himself into a ball again and went back to napping.

Elizabeth tried to cry out to her grandparents, but although she made every effort, no sound came out. Just a gasp for breath afterwards. She tried to move but could not lift even a finger.

The room became more washed in white, only the warmth of the faces and the black of the cat were now visible to her.

A woman came to her bed. She was small, dark-haired. Small hands wiped Elizabeth's brow and a sweet voice said, "Shh."

"You don't want to do this," the woman said.

Elizabeth couldn't answer.

"Look," she said and waved her hand to the broad window.

Elizabeth looked where she pointed and saw the woman beside her with a baby girl. Elizabeth knew the baby girl was herself as an infant.

The woman and the baby Elizabeth were cooing and talking to one another as mother and child do in those intimate moments between a mother and her child. Elizabeth's star-shaped infant hand reached up and touched the mother's face, and the mother kissed her tiny palm.

"You will miss that if you do this," the woman said. The vision was gone. The room was black.

"Lissy!" She heard her name called. "Lissy!" Again she heard the name but she still could not respond. She saw her grandfather get up from the rocker and her grandmother put away her knitting. She saw the woman walk to them and hug and kiss each one. Then they walked from the room, they faded from sight slowly as they walked from the room.

She saw Christian running outside and forcing open the front door. She was absolutely powerless to halt either the passing of the three . . . or the coming of the one.

* * *

Chris told Joe to get the wood stove fired up. "Make it red-hot, it has to heat the whole place, and I need boiling water. You may have to melt snow. And start up the fireplace as well." When Joe didn't move, Chris yelled the instructions again. When he still stood where he was, Chris took a closer look.

He thought the driver was a man, maybe in his panic he hadn't really noticed or blanked it from his mind. But now he could see. "How old are you Joe?" he asked quietly.

"Uh, I'm, uh, fifteen."

Chris took in a quick breath. God, he'd risked a child's life! A big, well-developed child, but a child nonetheless.

"You've done a hell of a job, Joe. I'm real proud of you. But now we have the really important part. We have to save two lives here, Joe, and I need you to help. Can you do that?" Chris talked quietly but with urgency.

"I think so." Joe had lost some of his earlier bravado. It had been an exciting adventure, but this was scary.

Chris said the instructions again, and this time Joe began to do them.

Chris ran up the stairs to the brass bed and grabbed the quilts and blankets from it. He leaped down, missing most of the stairs, risking a broken leg. The cabin was an icebox. They could see their breaths in the air in front of them.

Elizabeth was just conscious, but the baby had no heartbeat that Chris could hear.

He'd brought instruments and medications. After giving Elizabeth a local anesthetic, he took the baby by forceps. She was turned in the wrong direction, her forehead presenting first. All Elizabeth's labor had done was to press the tiny head back, not forward and out. Hours of intense labor with no results.

Chris could feel the life draining from Elizabeth as the birth progressed. He could tell she was on the verge of giving up. "Lissy, fight! Fight, damn it! I'm here! Now don't give up! I love you! I want you!" He spoke to her constantly and pleaded with her to stay alive.

Elizabeth heard him calling to her, she wanted to follow the three people who had been with her earlier, but then she heard Chris calling to her. She wanted to tell him how much she loved him, how much he had given her in his love of her, how much she wanted to make his life as good as he had made hers. She felt herself pulled toward the fading light and tugged to the bed, pulled to the sky and the sunshine, then yanked back to the dark. She was torn apart in every sense. She had no idea what to do next. Finally, in silence, she decided which way to go.

Elizabeth came fully conscious just as Chris laid the blue baby on her chest and wrapped them both immediately in his own coat, which was still warm from his body.

At that moment, Elizabeth saw a miracle. For an instant—brief as a flash of lightning—some strong emotion, helped perhaps by the trick of light, showed her the face of her baby twenty years in the future.

Startled, Elizabeth said, "Oh, Chris! She looks like my mother." And she then pulled the baby closer to her chest, cradled and kissed her head, held her to her chest and wrapped her once again in the coat. At the moment she bent her lips to kiss the child on her blue ones, the baby gasped, took a deep breath, and screamed to high heaven.

Chris took the baby from Elizabeth, ran to the kitchen and the petrified Joe, told him to pour hot water on the towels from the bathroom, took towels and begun to bathe the now screaming child on the big pine table.

As he rubbed her vigorously, she began to turn violet, then rose, then healthy pink. Her forehead was badly misshapen, her ears red and bruised from the forceps. Her tiny hands were curled into angry fists, and her eyes screwed up into thin lines of rage. Chris felt like he never had felt before. He had delivered a few babies in his lifetime as a doctor, all of them miraculous and wonderful in every way. But he'd never felt like this.

He held the baby up and looked at her, calling to her to open her eyes. She did. Large milk-blue eyes, fringed by thick black lashes. She stopped crying and looked directly into his own eyes as if to say, "All right, I'm here. Now what are you going to do about it?"

Chris laughed and held her closer to his body while Joe brought dry oven-heated towels to wrap her. Joe was speechless. Smiling and awestruck, but speechless. Chris took her back to Elizabeth.

Elizabeth held her closely, singing and saying soothing words to her. "It's all right now, darling. Shhh! It's all right! You're safe now." Chris finished the rest of the delivery. If Elizabeth felt any discomfort, she did not let on. So enthralled with the baby in her arms, she seemed not to be aware of anything else.

Joe came in and peeked around the door.

"Hey! Awesome!"

Elizabeth looked at Chris and he at her. They both smiled and then looked at the still screaming infant.

"Isn't she beautiful?" Elizabeth asked.

"As beautiful as her mother," Chris said. He was amazed to find tears forming, and he let them fall.

Elizabeth was too happy to cry. Too happy to worry about what nearly happened. Her beautiful child was in her arms. Christian was here, and she was happy.

Chris lifted her, the child, and several

blankets up and put her on the sofa in the big living room near the now roaring fireplace and the big black wood burning stove.

The phone rang, surprising them all. "Hello?" Chris answered.

"Well?" It was Amy.

"Baby girl. Mother and baby doing fine," Chris said.

"Thank God," Amy said. "Shall we send a rescue unit?"

"At this point, it isn't dire. I do want them both in the hospital soon, but nothing emergency."

"Okay, looks like it will be about three hours then." Amy hung up, and Chris went back to Elizabeth.

"We're both hungry!" she said. The baby was nuzzling close to Elizabeth's breast. Chris laughed and Joe said he could do with some food as well. The two men prepared heaping bowls of stew, big chunks of bread with golden globs of butter. Between the three they polished off a pan of gingerbread. The baby nuzzled at Elizabeth's breast, contented and warm. Her eyes opening occasionally to look up into her mother's own eyes.

The lights suddenly came on. The Christmas tree blazed in the beauty of its thousands of tiny lights. The wall heaters came on warming every room. Elizabeth heard the water pump begin. The radio came on playing jazz. Life was back to normal. Yet it would never be the same.

Joe went upstairs to take a quick nap before he attempted to drive back. It had been a long two days for the teenager.

It was just noon by the announcer on the radio. The baby slept deeply cradled in Elizabeth's arms. Chris sat beside Elizabeth on the sofa, moving only to put a log on the fire, or to kiss and hold Elizabeth.

Elizabeth leaned toward Chris and kissed him on the cheek.

"Thank you," she said.

"I'm going to have to keep working on you, I can see. You don't say *thank you,* you say *I love you.* Now repeat after me, 'I LOVE YOU.' "

"I love you," Elizabeth said. "But thank you for my baby."

Chris nodded and looked down, then he said, "It was quite a battle there for a minute. I wondered who would win. And then I knew."

Elizabeth looked into his beautiful eyes and said, "I wondered at times why you fought so hard."

"Doctors are just naturally fighters!" Chris said. "I wouldn't usually admit that I need any further incentive to put up a good fight than the presence of death. But in your case there was something else. My love for you." He kissed her gently on the lips, then leaned down to kiss the now feathery black-haired head of the baby. "You put up a good fight yourself. Why?"

"Why?" Elizabeth was shocked by his blunt question.

"You have seemed to hate nearly every moment of your life. Why did you fight now?"

"The same reason as you. I love you. And one more reason," Elizabeth said. "The need to see her." Elizabeth looked down at her sleeping daughter. "That was enough on its own. And now I know I am not to leave this life until I have . . ." She stopped.

"What? Until you have what?" Chris prompted.

"Actually, I still don't know. Before you came, I thought I knew just what to do. Now, I just know that the trip isn't over yet."

"And you won't be alone." Chris kissed her again.

"I've never been alone," Elizabeth said.

The rescue team arrived. They had a bubble-gum cigar for Chris, a bouquet of roses for Elizabeth, and a pediatrician for the baby. Two hours later the baby was official:

Ellen Alice Avery
Born 12/6/93
10:25 A.M.
7 pounds, 10 ounces
22 inches long

In the safety and quiet of the hospital, Elizabeth held her child closely and said, "Someday I'll tell you all about the day you were born. I'll tell you all about the many people who helped you be born, and you will ask me questions, won't you?"

The baby opened her mouth and kissed the sweet air. She yawned and sneezed and Elizabeth laughed.

"You are loved," she told the baby. "You will always know you are loved."

# Thirty-three

Valentine's Day began with light snow on top of the eighty-six inches Vail had already endured. By ten A.M. it had stopped, and the sun was brightly shining on the diamond flakes. The sky was pure crystal blue.

Elizabeth fed and bathed the baby. Dressed her in her linen and lace gown, put a sweet ruffled cap on her black baby-curled hair, and put her back in her crib while she bathed and dressed.

Chris had left while it was still snowing. He had to pick up so many people and then lead them all back to the house.

By noon, everyone was there. Barbara, DeDe, and Harry from New York. Angeline from California. Amy and her husband and seven children, several other friends from the hospital, Harriet, and other Vail acquaintances. The judge and even Joe, now feeling far more adult at sixteen, were there.

The little cabin was decorated in pine bough and red roses with white carnations and small purple orchids for color. It smelled of those flowers and the aroma of freshly made cake and brewed coffee. On the huge dining-room table were small sandwiches, trays of vegetables and fruit, and red punch.

The furniture had been moved to accommodate folding chairs covered in white fabric and draped in ribbons, pine, and roses.

At twelve-thirty Elizabeth came down the staircase from the loft bedroom. She was dressed in an antique ivory lace dress over a silk slip. She carried white roses with one red rose in the center. Her hair was in the softly draped ponytail Chris liked so much, but with the roses and baby's breath was a crown. Chris waited for her beside the judge by the fireplace. Chris held Ellen who was sound asleep.

A tape played a selection of classical music as Elizabeth walked to the side of the two people she loved.

Chris beamed with pride. He was so happy that for a moment he thought he might cry, but instead he looked at the child in his arms and whispered, "Look at your mommy! She is so beautiful!" Ellen opened her eyes, for she always responded to Chris when he spoke, but closed them again.

Chris had asked one of his friends from the hospital to be his Best Man and Elizabeth had De as her Matron of Honor. De took the bouquet from Elizabeth, Chris gave Ellen to Elizabeth, and the three of them stood in front of the judge.

While their friends looked on, they vowed to love and honor the other, to stay with the other through all the joy and wonder and possible tears and pain that life gives to us. They also vowed to love and teach only love to Ellen.

Chris held Elizabeth and the baby in his arms at the end of the ceremony. He kissed Elizabeth with passion, then with tenderness. He kissed the baby's head, and she opened her eyes and made one sweet sound, then put her small fist in her mouth to suck and fell asleep.

Elizabeth looked around at all her friends, at her home, at her husband and baby. She had never thought to have all this. A year ago, if she *had* thought it, she would have dismissed it as ridiculous. The Wicked Witch of Wall Street would never have seen herself in this cabin, with this man and this child. *That* woman would never have been this happy. Would never have allowed herself to feel this depth of love. She turned back to Chris.

A year ago she was putting her hands on pieces of paper, hoping they would give her the answers she had been searching for. This whole room vibrated with the heat she had looked for in the past. In the past that heat had meant money, and the money meant security. In this room, with these people, the vibration meant love and kindness, generosity of spirit and great trust. She had found what she had been looking for, searching for, feeling for, at last.

Amid the cheers of their friends and

the laughter and cries of the children, she said to Chris, "I love you."

After all the storms and pain and confusion, they knew they would, as the old fairy tale said, live happily ever after.

They weren't going to have a true honeymoon with a trip and weeks to be alone. Chris had to be back at the hospital, and Elizabeth had a deadline. They went for one night to the Bed and Breakfast inn where they had stayed before. Chris had arranged to get the same room. Ellen stayed with Amy.

The room was beautiful. Elizabeth did remember that it had a canopied bed, but she had forgotten the details of the room. Tonight while Chris got ready for bed, she memorized the room, storing it for the good memories.

It was burgundy red and cream in color. Huge cabbage roses on the wallpaper, matching draperies. The bed had a burgundy satin spread with a cream crochet blanket cover, cream sheets with crochet trim and many pillows in multicolored fabrics and tapestries. A small writing table with a Chippendale chair sat next to the fireplace, and on the other side were two velvet wingback chairs in bottle green. The wood in the room was aged cherry, and a lovely picture of a Victorian couple walking in an autumn setting hung over the bed. A heart-shaped wreath of dried flowers and roses hung over the fireplace. Candles in brass and silver candle holders were placed about the room. She had lit these as she waited for Chris.

He came out of their private bathroom dressed in the bottoms only of striped silk pajamas that Harry and DeDe gave him for a wedding present. Elizabeth wore the top.

She sat on the bed, her legs crossed Indian-style. she had taken down her hair from the ponytail he loved, and it hung to her shoulder blades in a glossy drape. She had no makeup on and wore only a drop or two of the perfume he gave her for Christmas.

Chris was sun- and windburned on his face. He'd finally gone skiing. He grinned and lifted his eyebrows at her when he had given her a long look. "You look mighty inviting sitting there, Lissy," he said and then he sat down in the same fashion on the bed.

"I'm glad you think so." Lissy smiled and kissed him softly, her long hair falling down to cover their faces as she did. He straightened out his legs and pulled her down to lie beside him. They quietly held each other and looked about the romantic room.

"Do you remember the last we were here?" Chris asked.

Elizabeth smiled and said, "I remember certain very important moments, but, I have to admit, I don't remember the room being this beautiful."

"You were this beautiful. You were pregnant and beautiful."

"You liked me pregnant." Elizabeth said it as a statement of fact, not a question.

"I loved you pregnant," he said and hugged her tightly, kissing her hair and drawing the strands through his hands like falling ribbons.

"Well, that's good," Elizabeth said.

Chris nodded. Thought about it a moment and said, "What do you mean that's good?"

Elizabeth sat up on one arm and leaned over his body. "I mean that I think I'm going to have another baby."

"So soon?"

"Seems to be," Elizabeth said. "It may be a little early, another two weeks to be absolutely sure, but it looks like Ellen will have a brother or sister about eleven months younger than she is."

Chris lay still. For a moment a look of worry passed over Elizabeth's face. He saw that worry and reached out to pull her down to him and hold her tightly.

"Does it make you happy?" Elizabeth asked.

"I'm happy," he said in a very gentle voice. "I'm worried for you. Is it going to be okay? Have you talked to Harriet?"

"I've talked to Harriet."

Chris sat up and walked around the room.

"Are you sure *you're* happy about this?" he finally asked.

She got up and came to him and wrapped her arms around his waist. "I'm so happy I can't describe it. And furthermore, if I'm not pregnant, I think we ought to get right to work on it."

"I love you," Chris said.

"Thank–"

He interrupted her. "Lady! What do I have to do? You don't say thank you! You say–"

Elizabeth interrupted him. "I love you."

## WATCH AS THESE WOMEN LEARN TO LOVE AGAIN

HELLO LOVE (4094, $4.50/$5.50)
by Joan Shapiro
Family tragedy leaves Barbara Sinclair alone with her success. The fight to gain custody of her young granddaughter brings a confrontation with the determined rancher Sam Douglass. Also widowed, Sam has been caring for Emily alone, guided by his own ideas of childrearing. Barbara challenges his ideas. And that's not all she challenges . . . Long-buried desires surface, then gentle affection. Sam and Barbara cannot ignore the chance to love again.

THE BEST MEDICINE (4220, $4.50/$5.50)
by Janet Lane Walters
Her late husband's expenses push Maggie Carr back to nursing, the career she left almost thirty years ago. The night shift is difficult, but it's harder still to ignore the way handsome Dr. Jason Knight soothes his patients. When she lends a hand to help his daughter, Jason and Maggie grow closer than simply doctor and nurse. Obstacles to romance seem insurmountable, but Maggie knows that love is always the best medicine.

AND BE MY LOVE (4291, $4.50/$5.50)
by Joyce C. Ware
Selflessly catering first to husband, then children, grandchildren, and her aging, though imperious mother, leaves Beth Volmar little time for her own adventures or passions. Then, the handsome archaeologist Karim Donovan arrives and campaigns to widen the boundaries of her narrow life. Beth finds new freedom when Karim insists that she accompany him to Turkey on an archaeological dig . . . and a journey towards loving again.

OVER THE RAINBOW (4032, $4.50/$5.50)
by Marjorie Eatock
Fifty-something, divorced for years, courted by more than one attractive man, and thoroughly enjoying her job with a large insurance company, Marian's sudden restlessness confuses her. She welcomes the chance to travel on business to a small Mississippi town. Full of good humor and words of love, Don Worth makes her feel needed, and not just to assess property damage. Marian takes the risk.

A KISS AT SUNRISE (4260, $4.50/$5.50)
by Charlotte Sherman
Beginning widowhood and retirement, Ruth Nichols has her first taste of freedom. Against the advice of her mother and daughter, Ruth heads for an adventure in the motor home that has sat unused since her husband's death. Long days and lonely campgrounds start to dampen the excitement of traveling alone. That is, until a dapper widower named Jack parks next door and invites her for dinner. On the road, Ruth and Jack find the chance to love again.